Books by Jonathan Kellerman

FICTION

ALEX DELAWARE NOVELS

Victims (2012)
Mystery (2011)
Deception (2010)
Evidence (2009)
Bones (2008)
Compulsion (2008)
Obsession (2007)
Gone (2006)
Rage (2005)
Therapy (2004)
A Cold Heart (2003)
The Murder Book (2002)
Flesh and Blood (2001)
Dr. Death (2000)

Monster (1999)
Survival of the Fittest (1997)
The Clinic (1997)
The Web (1996)
Self-Defense (1995)
Bad Love (1994)
Devil's Waltz (1993)
Private Eyes (1992)
Time Bomb (1990)
Silent Partner (1989)
Over the Edge (1987)
Blood Test (1986)
When the Bough Breaks (1985)

OTHER NOVELS

True Detectives (2009)
Capital Crimes (with Faye Kellerman, 2006)
Twisted (2004)
Double Homicide (with Faye Kellerman, 2004)
The Conspiracy Club (2003)
Billy Straight (1998)
The Butcher's Theater (1988)

NONFICTION

With Strings Attached: The Art and Beauty of Vintage Guitars (2008)
Savage Spawn: Reflections on Violent Children (1999)
Helping the Fearful Child (1981)
Psychological Aspects of Childhood Cancer (1980)

FOR CHILDREN, WRITTEN AND ILLUSTRATED

Jonathan Kellerman's ABC of Weird Creatures (1995)
Daddy, Daddy, Can You Touch the Sky? (1994)

SILENT
PARTNER

SILENT PARTNER

THE GRAPHIC NOVEL

JONATHAN KELLERMAN

ADAPTED BY **ANDE PARKS**

ART BY **MICHAEL GAYDOS**

VILLARD BOOKS • **NEW YORK**

Copyright © 2012 by Jonathan Kellerman
Excerpt from *Victims* by Jonathan Kellerman copyright © 2012
by Jonathan Kellerman

Published in the United States by Villard Books, an imprint of
The Random House Publishing Group, a division of Random House,
Inc., New York.

Villard Books and Villard & "V" Circled Design are registered
trademarks of Random House, Inc.

Library of Congress Cataloging-in-Publication Data

Kellerman, Jonathan.
   Silent partner : the graphic novel / Jonathan Kellerman ; adapted
by Ande Parks ; art by Michael Gaydos.
     p. cm.
   ISBN 978-0-440-42363-8 (hardcover : acid-free paper) —
   ISBN 978-0-345-53545-0 (ebook)
   1. Graphic novels. I. Parks, Ande. II. Gaydos, Michael. III. Title.
PN6727.K386S55 2012
741.5'973—dc23   2011048293

Printed in the United States of America on acid-free paper

www.villard.com

9 8 7 6 5 4 3 2 1

First Edition

Text design by Dana Hayward

SILENT
PARTNER

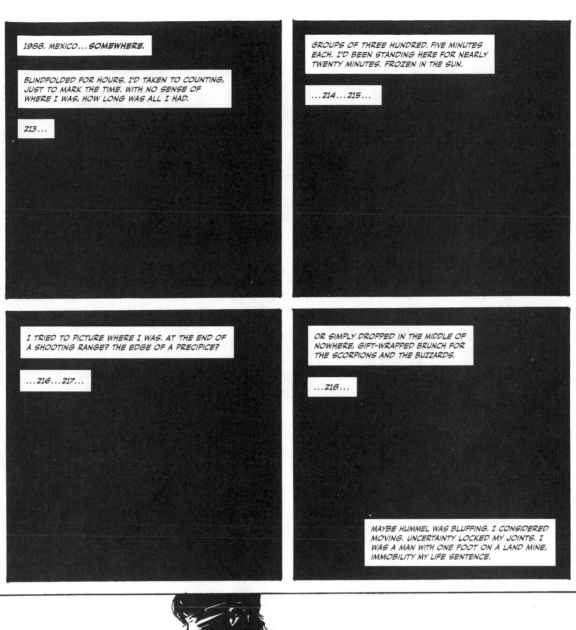

1988. MEXICO...SOMEWHERE.

BLINDFOLDED FOR HOURS. I'D TAKEN TO COUNTING, JUST TO MARK THE TIME. WITH NO SENSE OF WHERE I WAS, HOW LONG WAS ALL I HAD.

213...

GROUPS OF THREE HUNDRED. FIVE MINUTES EACH. I'D BEEN STANDING HERE FOR NEARLY TWENTY MINUTES. FROZEN IN THE SUN.

...214...215...

I TRIED TO PICTURE WHERE I WAS. AT THE END OF A SHOOTING RANGE? THE EDGE OF A PRECIPICE?

...216...217...

OR SIMPLY DROPPED IN THE MIDDLE OF NOWHERE, GIFT-WRAPPED BRUNCH FOR THE SCORPIONS AND THE BUZZARDS.

...218...

MAYBE HUMMEL WAS BLUFFING. I CONSIDERED MOVING. UNCERTAINTY LOCKED MY JOINTS. I WAS A MAN WITH ONE FOOT ON A LAND MINE, IMMOBILITY MY LIFE SENTENCE.

I STOOD THERE, COUNTING, SWEATING, TRYING TO MAINTAIN. ENDURING THE MOLASSES DRIP OF TIME SLOWED BY FEAR.

...219...220...

TWO WEEKS EARLIER. LOS ANGELES.

THURSDAY MORNING. FIVE WEEKS SINCE ROBIN LEFT. I FOCUSED ON MY PATIENTS.

Darren Burkhalter. Twenty-six months old.

Eighteen months at the time of the accident.

In six sessions, the car sounds are the closest Darren has come to speaking.

The pattern is constant: First, the cars alone, then the dolls...

...the reenactment of his father's injury...

...and its aftermath.

The pattern continues after the doll's decapitation. A burst of hyperactivity...

ANY QUESTIONS YOU WANT TO ASK ME, DENISE?

NOPE.

...followed by complete physical and emotional exhaustion.

HOW'D HE SLEEP THIS WEEK? STILL HAVING SIX OR SEVEN NIGHT-MARES?

ABOUT THE SAME. I DIDN'T COUNT. DO I STILL HAVE TO?

IT WOULD HELP TO KNOW WHAT'S GOING ON.

HE'S COME A LONG WAY, BUT THERE'S STILL ANGER AND FEAR THAT HE'S NOT EXPRESSING. I'D LIKE TO SEE HIM MORE.

IT'S FAR, COMING UP HERE. TOOK US NEAR TWO HOURS. WHY DO YOU MAKE YOURSELF SO HARD TO GET TO, LIVING UP HERE?!

I KNOW IT'S BEEN ROUGH, DENISE. IF YOU'D RATHER MEET IN—

OH, FORGET IT!

I TAGGED THE VIDEOCASSETTE AND BEGAN MY REPORT, WORKING SLOWLY, WITH EVEN GREATER PRECISION THAN USUAL.

TRYING TO FORESTALL THE INEVITABLE.

SEVERAL HOURS LATER THE DAMNED THING WAS FINISHED; EVICTED FROM THE HELPER ROLE, I WAS, ONCE AGAIN, SOMEONE WHO NEEDED HELP.

NUMBNESS ROLLED OVER ME, AS INEVITABLE AS THE TIDE.

I CONSIDERED CALLING ROBIN, DECIDED AGAINST IT.

OUR LAST CONVERSATION HAD BEEN ANYTHING BUT TRIUMPHANT.

A WEEK'S WORTH OF MAIL THAT I'D BEEN AVOIDING, NOT UP TO FACING THE SUPERFICIAL CARESSES OF COME-ONS, COUPONS, AND GET-HAPPY-QUICK SCHEMES.

WHAT THE HELL. KEEPING MY MIND TETHERED TO MINUTIAE MIGHT FREE ME FROM THE PERILS OF INTROSPECTION.

Skylark
La Mar Road
Los Angeles, CA 90077

HEAVY LINEN STOCK, A HOLMBY HILLS ADDRESS. AS A SALES PITCH, A LITTLE RICH FOR MY BLOOD.

A PARTY TO HONOR THE NEW PSYCHOLOGY DEPARTMENT CHAIR, DOCTOR PAUL KRUSE.

AN **ENDOWED** CHAIR, THE ULTIMATE REWARD FOR EXCEPTIONAL SCHOLARSHIP.

IT MADE NO SENSE. KRUSE WAS ANYTHING BUT A SCHOLAR. ADVICE COLUMNIST AND TALK SHOW DARLING, WRITER OF "WOMEN'S" MAGAZINE ARTICLES THAT OFFERED SEXUAL IQ TESTS DESIGNED TO MAKE ANYONE FEEL INADEQUATE.

THE SLIMMEST PRETENSE OF CONDUCTING ANY REAL RESEARCH—SOMETHING TO DO WITH HUMAN SEXUALITY THAT NEVER PRODUCED A SHRED OF DATA.

FROM THAT TO BLALOCK ENDOWED PROFESSOR. INCREDIBLE.

THE PARTY WAS IN JUST TWO DAYS. FAST CARS, WEAK DRINKS, AND NUMBING BANTER WAFTING ACROSS MONEY-GREEN LAWNS. NOT MY IDEA OF FUN.

SORTING THE JUNK MAIL PROVIDED LITTLE DISTRACTION.

HALF A SIX-PACK DIDN'T HELP SLEEP COME. I TOSSED AND TURNED IN THE BED THAT WAS SUDDENLY TOO LARGE.

THE SHOEMAKER'S CHILDREN...

SHE CRAFTED AND REPAIRED GUITARS AND MANDOLINS, SURROUNDED BY HER CLIENTS, SAD-EYED MUSICIANS CRADLING MANGLED INSTRUMENTS, SINGING ONE FORM OF BLUES OR THE OTHER.

MORNING, BABE. WHAT'S THE RUSH?

LOTS OF THINGS TO DO.

ROBIN AND I WERE LOVERS FOR TWO YEARS BEFORE SHE AGREED TO LIVE WITH ME. EVEN THEN SHE HELD ON TO HER VENICE STUDIO.

OVER TIME, SHE ESCAPED THERE MORE AND MORE. I GRITTED MY TEETH, BACKED OFF, TOLD MYSELF TO BE PATIENT.

ON A SUNDAY?

SUNDAY, MONDAY, IT DOESN'T MATTER.

I MADE JUICE—THERE'S A PITCHER IN THE FRIDGE.

STAY JUST A LITTLE LONGER. LET'S TALK.

SHE'D COME HOME AT RANDOM INTERVALS TO RETRIEVE SOMETHING. SHE'D MAKE LOVE TO ME WITH A WORKMANLIKE DETERMINATION THAT SCARED ME BUT WAS BETTER THAN NOTHING.

SOMETHING HAD TO GIVE.

TALK ABOUT WHAT?

EARLY IN MAY, IT DID.

"ABOUT US, ROBIN."

I DON'T KNOW HOW TO PUT THIS WITHOUT BEING HURTFUL.

DON'T WORRY ABOUT THAT. JUST LET IT OUT.

YEAH...WHATEVER YOU SAY, DOCTOR.

ALEX, I'VE BEEN LIVING A LIE HERE—VIEWING MYSELF AS STRONG AND SELF-SUFFICIENT.

YOU ARE STRONG.

THAT WAS DADDY'S LINE. HE'D GET MAD AT ME WHEN MY CONFIDENCE LAGGED, YELL AT ME OVER AND OVER THAT I WAS DIFFERENT FROM THE OTHER GIRLS. STRONGER THAN THEM.

FOR YEARS I BOUGHT INTO IT. NOW, HERE I AM, TAKING A GOOD LOOK IN THE MIRROR, AND ALL I SEE IS ANOTHER WEAK WOMAN LIVING OFF A MAN.

BABE, I NEVER MEANT TO HEM YOU IN.

THAT'S THE PROBLEM! I'M A BABE—A DAMN BABY! HELPLESS AND READY TO BE FIXED BY DOCTOR ALEX!

I DON'T VIEW YOU AS A PATIENT. I LOVE YOU, FOR GOD'S SAKE.

LOVE... WHATEVER THE HELL THAT MEANS.

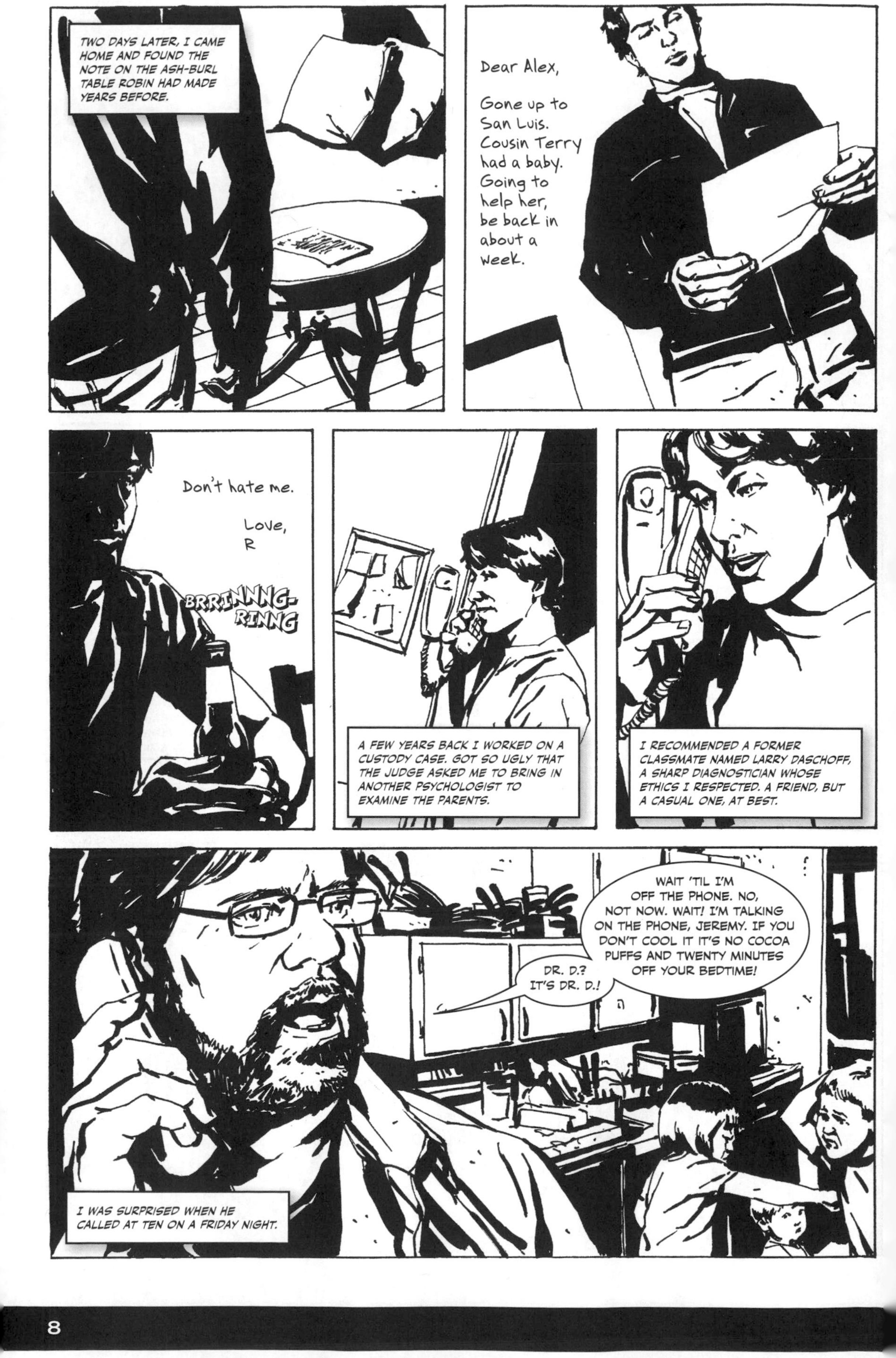
TWO DAYS LATER, I CAME HOME AND FOUND THE NOTE ON THE ASH-BURL TABLE ROBIN HAD MADE YEARS BEFORE.
Dear Alex,
Gone up to San Luis. Cousin Terry had a baby. Going to help her, be back in about a week.
Don't hate me.
Love, R
BRRINNNG-RINNG
A FEW YEARS BACK I WORKED ON A CUSTODY CASE. GOT SO UGLY THAT THE JUDGE ASKED ME TO BRING IN ANOTHER PSYCHOLOGIST TO EXAMINE THE PARENTS.
I RECOMMENDED A FORMER CLASSMATE NAMED LARRY DASCHOFF, A SHARP DIAGNOSTICIAN WHOSE ETHICS I RESPECTED. A FRIEND, BUT A CASUAL ONE, AT BEST.
I WAS SURPRISED WHEN HE CALLED AT TEN ON A FRIDAY NIGHT.
DR. D.? IT'S DR. D.!
WAIT 'TIL I'M OFF THE PHONE. NO, NOT NOW. WAIT! I'M TALKING ON THE PHONE, JEREMY. IF YOU DON'T COOL IT IT'S NO COCOA PUFFS AND TWENTY MINUTES OFF YOUR BEDTIME!

WHAT'S UP IS BRENDA IS CRAMMING AT THE LAW LIBRARY AND I'VE GOT ALL FIVE MON-STERS TO MYSELF.

MONDAY I'M SENDING AWAY FOR HALF A DOZEN CATTLE PRODS. ONE FOR EACH OF THEM AND ONE TO SHOVE UP MY OWN ASS FOR ENCOURAGING BRENDA TO GO BACK TO SCHOOL. IF ROBIN EVER COMES UP WITH AN IDEA LIKE THAT, CHANGE THE SUBJECT...*FAST.*

I'LL BE SURE TO DO THAT, LARRY.

YEAH, I GOT THE INVITATION. IT'S GRACING THE BOTTOM OF MY WASTE-BASKET. ROBIN COULDN'T MAKE IT, ANYWAY. OUT OF TOWN. YEAH...*SOMETHING* LIKE THAT.

NO...I'M FINE. JUST TIRED.

LARRY SOUNDED GENUINELY DISAPPOINTED. I THOUGHT ABOUT IT FOR A MOMENT, CONSIDERED ANOTHER LONELY DAY AT HOME AND SAID...

"NO...ACTUALLY, LARRY, I'M FREE."

KEYS?

NO KEYS. I WALKED.

WE PARK.

HOLMBY HILLS, WHERE THE RICH GIVE THEIR HOMES NAMES. NAMES LIKE "SKYLARK."

IS A CAR NECESSARY FOR COLLATERAL?

NEIGHBOR?

INVITED GUEST. MY NAME IS ALEX DELAWARE. DR. DELAWARE.

ONE MINUTE.

HEY... SEE THAT BROWN STATION WAGON OVER THERE? LET ME TELL YOU SOMETHING ABOUT IT.

YES? WHAT?

THAT CAR IS OWNED BY THE RICHEST GUY AT THIS PARTY. TREAT IT WELL...

"...HE'S BEEN KNOWN TO GIVE HUGE TIPS."

HEY, LET'S GET THAT WAGON OUT OF HERE!

I COULD HEAR THE PARTY BEFORE I SAW IT. FROM OVER THE CREST, A STRING SECTION PLAYING SOMETHING BAROQUE.

THE SOUND COORDINATED WELL WITH JEEVES, RIGHT OUT OF CENTRAL CASTING.

DR. DELAWARE, SIR?

YES?

I'M RAMEY, DR. DELAWARE, JUST COMING TO GET YOU, SIR.

PLEASE FORGIVE THE INCONVENIENCE, SIR.

NO PROBLEM. I GUESS THE VALETS AREN'T EQUIPPED TO DEAL WITH PEDESTRIANS.

I MADE A NOTE TO THANK LARRY FOR GETTING ME OUT TO WITNESS THIS AFFAIR FIRSTHAND.

LIMESTONE FOUNTAINS, A PHILHARMONIC, GRAVEL PATHS, A MAZE OF BOXWOOD HEDGES, REFLECTING POOL, HUNDREDS OF BEDS OF ROSES SO BRIGHT THEY SEEMED FLUORESCENT, AND HUNDREDS OF PARTYGOERS CLUTCHING LONG-STEMMED GLASSES AND ADMIRING THEMSELVES IN THE MIRRORED WATER OF THE POOLS.

IT CERTAINLY WASN'T JUST ANOTHER NIGHT AT THE DELAWARE HOME.

RAMEY BROUGHT ME A SODA WATER AND I SOAKED IN THE OTHER ATTENDEES.

THE CROWD, IT SOON BECAME OBVIOUS, WAS DIVIDED INTO TWO DISCRETE GROUPS, A SOCIOLOGIC SPLIT THAT ECHOED THE LINES OF DOUBLE-FILED CARS OUT FRONT.

CENTER STAGE WAS DOMINATED BY THE BIG RICH, AN ASSEMBLAGE OF **SWANS**. DEEPLY TAN AND LOOSE-LIMBED IN CONSERVATIVE HAUTE COUTURE...

...THEY GREETED ONE ANOTHER WITH CHEEK-PECKS, LAUGHED SOFTLY AND DISCREETLY, DRANK STEADILY AND NOT SO DISCREETLY, AND TOOK NO NOTICE OF THE ETHNICALLY DIVERSE BUNCH SITTING OFF TO THE SIDE.

THE UNIVERSITY PEOPLE WERE THE **MAGPIES**, INTENSE, WATCHFUL, BRIMMING WITH NERVOUS CHATTER. SOME WERE CONSPICUOUSLY SLEEK IN OFF-THE-RACK SUITS AND SPECIAL-OCCASION PARTY DRESSES; OTHERS HAD MADE A POINT OF DRESSING DOWN.

A FEW STILL GAPED AT THEIR SURROUNDINGS, BUT MOST WERE CONTENT TO OBSERVE THE RITUALS OF THE SWANS WITH A MIXTURE OF RAW HUNGER AND ANALYTIC CONTEMPT.

A RIPPLE SPREAD THROUGH THE PATIO— THROUGH BOTH CAMPS. PAUL KRUSE, THE MAN OF THE HOUR, APPEARED IN ITS WAKE, WEAVING HIS WAY THROUGH TOWN AND GOWN.

THE NEW DEPARTMENT CHAIR HAD TO BE CLOSE TO SIXTY BY NOW, FIGHTING ENTROPY WITH CHEMISTRY AND GOOD POSTURE. HE FLASHED A MOUTHFUL OF WHITE CAPS, SHOOK HANDS, AND OFFERED KISSES, AND THEN MOVED ON TO THE NEXT SET OF WELL-WISHERS.

SMOOTH, HUH?

HELLO, LARRY.

I WAS OVER BY THE ROSES, TRYING TO FIGURE OUT HOW THEY GET THEM TO FLOWER LIKE THAT. PROBABLY FERTILIZE THEM WITH OLD DOLLAR BILLS.

NICE LITTLE COTTAGE, HUH?

COZY.

YOUR MENTOR KRUSE IS IN FINE FORM.

UGH. I TOLD YOU I WAS DEAD BUSTED, D. WOULD HAVE WORKED FOR THE DEVIL **HIMSELF**— A BARGAIN-BASEMENT FAUST.

WHOLE SEMESTER WITH HIM WAS A WASTE. KRUSE AND I HAD NOTHING TO DO WITH EACH OTHER.

I DIDN'T LIKE HIM BECAUSE HE WAS A SHALLOW PHONY. HE RESENTED ME 'CAUSE I WAS MALE. ALL HIS OTHER ASSISTANTS WERE WOMEN.

HE ONLY HIRED ME BECAUSE HIS SO-CALLED RESEARCH SUBJECTS WERE MALES AND THEY WEREN'T LIKELY TO RELAX WATCHING DIRTY MOVIES WITH A WOMAN TAKING NOTES AND ASKING QUESTIONS.

"HOW OFTEN DO YOU JERK OFF? HOW OFTEN AND WHO DO YOU FUCK? HOW LONG DOES IT TAKE YOU TO COME? WHAT WAS THEIR DEEP-SEATED PRIMAL ATTITUDE TOWARD LIVER IN A CAN?"

SAD THING IS, IT COULD HAVE BEEN VALUABLE, BUT KRUSE WASN'T SERIOUS ABOUT COLLECTING DATA. HE WAS JUST GOING THROUGH THE MOTIONS. THE MONEY FOR THE STUDY CAME FROM PRIVATE SOURCES—RICH PORN FREAKS.

KRUSE PROMISED TO MAKE THEM RESPECTABLE. PUT THE ACADEMIC IMPRIMATUR ON THEIR HOBBY.

"SO, YOU REMEMBER MRS. KRUSE? SUZY STRADDLE, THE TALK OF THE DEPARTMENT?"

"CAMPUS CELEBRITY. FORMER PORN ACTRESS, GOT HER NICKNAME FOR BEING...LIMBER. KRUSE MET HER AT SOME HOLLYWOOD PARTY, DOING 'RESEARCH!' LEFT HIS SECOND WIFE FOR HER."

MUST BE TRUE LOVE. HE STUCK WITH HER ALL THESE YEARS.

DON'T BET THAT IT'S WHOLESOME MONOGAMY. KRUSE'S GOT A REP AS A MAJOR-LEAGUE PUSSY HOUND AND SUZY'S KNOWN TO BE TOLERANT... "SUBMISSIVE."

LITERALLY?

HEH. YOU WERE OUT OF THERE BY '75, WEREN'T YOU? YOU MISSED THE PARTIES. I MADE IT TO THE DOOR OF ONE ONCE.

BRENDA TOOK ONE LOOK AT THEM COATING THE FLOOR WITH WESSON OIL AND HAULED MY ASS OUT OF THERE.

SUZY STRADDLE WAS ONE OF THE MAIN ATTRACTIONS—TIED UP, HARNESSED, MUZZLED, AND FLOGGED. KRUSE DID THE FLOGGING. HELL, **EVERYONE** DID.

THERE, LOOK AT HER, HOW SHE'S HOLDING ON TO HIM FOR DEAR LIFE. DOESN'T SHE SEEM SUBMISSIVE?

PROBABLY A PASSIVE-DEPENDENT PERSONALITY, PERFECT SYMBIOTIC FIT FOR A POWER JUNKIE LIKE KRUSE.

LOW SELF-ESTEEM. YOU'D HAVE TO BE DOWN ON YOURSELF TO FUCK ON FILM.

I GUESS SO.

BUT ENOUGH OF THEIR BULLSHIT. WE'RE BOTH DOING GREAT. THAT'S WHY WE'RE HERE AT A PARTY WITHOUT OUR WOMEN, RIGHT?

SO, HOW IS ROBIN, ANYWAY?

LARRY, ROBIN AND I ARE SEPARATED.

YOU KNOW WHAT? THINK I WILL GO GET SOMETHING STRONGER.

I ELBOWED MY WAY THROUGH THE CRUSH AT THE BAR AND ORDERED A DOUBLE GIN AND TONIC THAT FELL JUST SHORT OF SINGLE STRENGTH. ON THE WAY BACK TO THE TABLE I CAME FACE-TO-FACE WITH KRUSE.

SO NICE OF YOU TO COME!

BEFORE I HAD A CHANCE TO REPLY, HE'D USED THE HANDSHAKE AS LEVERAGE TO PROPEL HIMSELF PAST ME. POLITICIAN'S HUSTLE. I'D BEEN EXPERTLY MANIPULATED.

AGAIN.

KRUSE MOVED ON TO SOMEONE FAR MORE IMPORTANT—OUR HOSTESS HERE AT SKYLARK, HOPE BLALOCK.

SO WELL PUT TOGETHER SHE COULD HAVE BEEN ANY PRESIDENT'S FIRST LADY. A FINISHING SCHOOL SMILE. GENETIC POISE.

WHAT DID THIS VENERABLE LADY SEE IN SOMEONE LIKE KRUSE? HARDLY FROM THE SAME SOCIAL—

OVER THE NOISE OF THE CROWD, FAMILIAR TONES. A VOICE FROM THE PAST.

I TOLD MYSELF IT WAS MY IMAGINATION. THE VOICE PERSISTED. I TURNED TO SCAN THE CROWD.

I SPOTTED HER IN SECONDS. A TIME MACHINE JOLT. I TRIED TO LOOK AWAY, COULDN'T.

SHARON EXQUISITE AS EVER. I KNEW HER AGE WITHOUT CALCULATING. THIRTY-FOUR. A BIRTHDAY IN MAY. MAY 15—HOW STRANGE TO REMEMBER...

I REMEMBERED THE FEEL OF HER SKIN...PALE AS PORCELAIN BUT WARM, ALWAYS WARM. I CRANED TO GET A BETTER VIEW.

NO WEDDING RING. SO WHAT? WITH ROBIN AT MY SIDE I WOULD HAVE TAKEN BRIEF NOTICE. OR SO I TRIED TO CONVINCE MYSELF.

SHARON AT A PARTY; IT DIDN'T FIT. SHE'D HATED THEM AS MUCH AS I HAD. BUT THAT HAD BEEN A LONG TIME AGO. PEOPLE CHANGE. LORD KNEW THAT APPLIED TO HER.

I COULDN'T KEEP MY EYES OFF HER. SHE HAD HER EYES ON ONE MAN—ONE OF THE SWANS, OLD ENOUGH TO BE HER FATHER. ODDLY BOYISH, ONE OF THOSE YOUTHFUL OLDER MEN WHO POPULATE THE BETTER CLUBS AND ARE ABLE TO BED YOUNGER WOMEN WITHOUT INCURRING SNICKERS.

WAS HE BEDDING SHARON? WHAT BUSINESS WAS IT OF MINE?

I RAISED MY GLASS TO MY LIPS, WATCHED HER TUG ON ONE EARLOBE—SOME THINGS STAYED THE SAME.

SUDDENLY SHE TURNED HER HEAD AND SAW ME. SHE PINKENED WITH RECOGNITION AND HER LIPS PARTED.

WE LOCKED IN ON EACH OTHER. AS IF DANCING.

I FELT DIZZY, BUMPED INTO SOMEONE. APOLOGIES.

SHARON KEPT LOOKING STRAIGHT AT ME.

I RETREATED FARTHER, ALL BUT RUNNING BACK DOWN THE PATH OUT OF SKYLARK, TOWARD HOME.

ALEX!

ALEX!

I ALMOST MADE IT.

ALEX! IT REALLY **IS** YOU. I CAN'T **BELIEVE** IT!

HELLO, SHARON. HOW'VE YOU BEEN?

SMOOTH. DR. WITTY.

JUST FINE.

NO, YOU'RE THE ONE PERSON WITH WHOM I DON'T HAVE TO PRETEND. NO, I **HAVEN'T** BEEN FINE. NOT AT ALL.

THE EASE WITH WHICH SHE'D SLIPPED INTO FAMILIARITY, THE EFFORTLESS ERASURE OF ALL THAT HAD PASSED BETWEEN US...

...RAISED MY DEFENSES.

I'M SORRY TO HEAR THAT.

OH, ALEX.

HER PERFUME—SOAP AND WATER TINGED WITH FRESH GRASS AND SPRING FLOWERS.

I FELT HER HEAT, WAS JOLTED BY A RUSH OF ENERGY BELOW MY WAIST. ALL AT ONCE I WAS ROCK-HARD. AND FURIOUS ABOUT IT.

BUT ALIVE, FOR THE FIRST TIME IN A LONG WHILE.

IT'S SO **GOOD** TO SEE YOU, ALEX.

GOOD TO SEE YOU, TOO.

IT CAME OUT THICK AND INTENSE, NOTHING LIKE THE INDIFFERENCE I'D AIMED FOR. HER FINGERS WERE BURNING A HOLE IN MY WRIST.

IT'S SO FUNNY WE SHOULD RUN INTO EACH OTHER LIKE THIS—PURE ESP. I'VE BEEN WANTING TO CALL YOU.

SOME ISSUES HAVE...COME UP. NOW'S NOT A GOOD TIME, BUT IF YOU COULD FIND SOME TIME TO TALK, I'D APPRECIATE IT.

WHAT ISSUES WOULD WE HAVE TO TALK ABOUT AFTER ALL THESE YEARS?

I WAS HOPING YOU WOULDN'T STILL BE ANGRY.

I'M NOT ANGRY, SHARON. JUST PUZZLED.

YOU'RE A GOOD GUY, DELAWARE. YOU ALWAYS WERE. BE WELL.

SHARON, I'M SORRY THINGS AREN'T GOING WELL FOR YOU.

NO...THEY REALLY AREN'T, BUT THAT'S NOT YOUR PROBLEM.

SHE CAME CLOSER, KEPT COMING. I REALIZED I WAS PULLING HER TOWARD ME, BUT WITH ONLY THE FAINTEST PRESSURE; SHE WAS ALLOWING HERSELF TO BE REELED IN.

THE JOY OF BEING NEEDED, AT LAST.

A STRANGER USING MY VOICE MADE A LUNCH DATE WITH HER FOR MONDAY.

I KNEW AT THAT MOMENT THAT SHE'D DO ANYTHING I WANTED, AND HER PASSIVITY TOUCHED OFF A STRANGE MELANGE OF FEELINGS WITHIN ME. PITY. GRATITUDE.

LATER, STRANGER!

CHEAP SONOFABITCH...

BACK HOME, I CHECKED IN WITH MY ANSWERING SERVICE. I THOUGHT I DETECTED PITY IN THE OPERATOR'S VOICE WHEN SHE TOLD ME I HAD NO MESSAGES.

TOLD MYSELF I WAS GETTING PARANOID.

MY HEAD WAS FULL OF EROTIC IMAGES. SLEEP WAS SHORT-LIVED.

SOME TIME DURING THE EARLY MORNING HOURS I HAD A WET DREAM. I WOKE STICKY, CRANKY...

...AND KNOWING, WITHOUT HAVING TO REASON IT OUT, THAT I WAS GOING TO BREAK THE DATE WITH SHARON.

LATE IN A MORNING SPENT FULL OF DIVERSIONS BEFORE CALLING SHARON, DENISE BURKHALTER'S LAWYER, MAL WORTHY, PROVIDED ANOTHER ONE.

WORKING ON SUNDAY, MAL?

THE DEPOSITION WAS SCHEDULED FOR WEDNESDAY AFTERNOON. MAL WARNED ME THERE WOULD BE SEVEN LAWYERS THERE, REPRESENTING VARIOUS CORPORATE FACTIONS.

HE OFFERED ONE TOO MANY EXHORTATIONS ABOUT HOW MY TESTIMONY COULD HELP PROVIDE DENISE AND DARREN WITH ENOUGH MONEY TO PUT THEIR LIVES BACK TOGETHER. MY SHORT FUSE BURNED TO THE NUB.

YEAH, I GET IT, MAL. YOU'RE A REGULAR WHITE KNIGHT.

NO, EVERY-THING'S FINE. JUST A LITTLE TIRED.

I'M SURE. I'LL BE THERE, MAL. I'LL BE READY.

I MANAGED TO WAIT UNTIL JUST AFTER NOON TO CALL SHARON.

GOT HER MACHINE. EVEN ON TAPE THE SOUND OF HER VOICE BROUGHT BACK MEMORIES... THE FEEL OF HER FINGERS ON MY CHEEK.

SHARON, THIS IS ALEX. CAN'T MAKE MONDAY. GOOD LUCK.

SHORT AND SWEET. DR. HEARTBREAKER.

HEARING HER VOICE PUT HER FACE IN MY MIND AGAIN. A PALE, LOVELY MASK DRIFTING IN AND OUT OF MY CONSCIOUSNESS.

HOPING TO EXCHANGE ONE LOVELY MASK FOR ANOTHER, I PHONED SAN LUIS OBISPO. ROBIN'S MOTHER ANSWERED.

THIS IS ALEX, ROSALIE.

IS ROBIN THERE?

DO YOU KNOW WHEN SHE'LL BE BACK?

I SEE.

SO, HOW'S THE BABY?

OKAY, THEN. PLEASE TELL HER I CALLED. BYE.

CLICK.

THE PRIVILEGE OF OWNING A MOTHER-IN-LAW WITHOUT HAVING TO DO THE PAPERWORK.

MONDAY, I STRUGGLED THROUGH THE MORNING PAPER, HOPING THE VENALITY AND LOW-MINDEDNESS OF INTERNATIONAL POLITICS WOULD CAST MY PROBLEMS IN A TRIVIAL LIGHT.

I FED THE FISH, CLEANED THE HOUSE, FILLED THE SEVILLE WITH GAS.

HOPING THE EVENING EDITION WOULD HAVE THE SAME DISTRACTING POWERS AS THE MORNING, I CLIMBED INTO BED EARLY WITH THE NEWS AND A CUP OF INSTANT COFFEE.

IT PROVED EFFECTIVE, UNTIL I FINISHED THE PAPER. THEN THAT OLD EMPTY FEELING RETURNED.

I DID WHATEVER IT TOOK TO FILL THE DAY. TO GET THROUGH IT.

SLOW NEWS DAY; MOST OF THE EVENING SPECIAL WAS A REHASH OF THE MORNING EDITION. I STUFFED MYSELF ON SWINDLES AND SUBTERFUGE. FOUND MY EYES BLURRING. PERFECT.

Psychologist's Death Possible Suicide

(LOS ANGELES) Police sources said the death of a local psychologist, found this morning in her Hollywood Hills home, probably resulted from a self-inflicted gunshot wound. The body of Sharon Ransom, 34, was discovered this morning in the bedroom of her Nichols Canyon home. She had apparently died sometime Sunday night.

Ransom lived alone in the Jalmia Drive house, which also doubled as an office. A native of New York City, she was educated and trained in Los Angeles, receiving her Ph.D. in 1981. No next of kin have been located.

I WAS BROUGHT ABRUPTLY BACK TO FOCUS BY A STORY ON PAGE TWENTY.

SUNDAY NIGHT. JUST HOURS AFTER I'D CALLED HER.

"NO, I HAVEN'T BEEN FINE. NOT AT ALL."

"I'M SORRY TO HEAR THAT."

VENDING MACHINE EMPATHY. I'D REELED HER IN, NOT GIVING HALF A SHIT. ENJOYED THE FEELING OF POWER AS SHE FLOATED TOWARD ME, PASSIVE.

"IF IT MEANS THAT MUCH TO YOU, WE CAN GET TOGETHER AND TALK..."

...AND LET ME FUCK YOUR EARS OFF.

CLOSING MY EYES, I TRIED TO LET MYSELF CRY. FOR HER, FOR ME, FOR ROBIN. FOR FAMILIES THAT FELL APART, A WORLD FALLING APART. LITTLE BOYS WHO WATCHED THEIR FATHERS DIE. ANYONE IN THE WORLD WHO GODDAM DESERVED IT.

THE TEARS WOULDN'T COME.

WAIT FOR THE BEEP.

PULL THE TRIGGER.

LATER, AFTER SOME OF THE SHOCK WORE OFF, I REALIZED THAT I'D RESCUED HER ONCE BEFORE. PERHAPS SHE'D REMEMBERED IT, HAD CONSTRUCTED A TIME-MACHINE FANTASY OF HER OWN.

SO, HAVE YOU PRESENTED ANYTHING THIS SEMESTER?

THE FALL OF '74. I WAS TWENTY-FOUR, A BRAND-NEW PH.D., CAUGHT UP IN THE NOVELTY OF BEING ADDRESSED AS DOCTOR BUT STILL AS POOR AS A STUDENT.

I WAS SUBBING FOR A CLINICAL PRACTICUM COURSE. THE STUDENTS WERE A LOVELY GROUP OF ACADEMIC STEREOTYPES. A NASTY LITTLE COLLECTION OF VIPERS, USUALLY TENDED TO AND STIRRED UP BY NONE OTHER THAN DR. PAUL KRUSE.

AND THEN THERE WAS SHARON.

NO. I—

THEN GO AHEAD, PLEASE.

I WAS A ROOKIE. I LET THE OTHER STUDENTS GOAD ME INTO PRESSING HER.

THERE'S ONE CASE I CAN TALK ABOUT, I SUPPOSE. A NINETEEN-YEAR-OLD WOMAN.

INITIAL TESTS SHOWED HER WITHIN NORMS ON EVERY PSYCHOLOGICAL MEASURE.

SHE AND HER BOYFRIEND ARE HAVING PROB-LEMS... IN THEIR RELATIONSHIP.

WHAT KIND OF PROBLEMS?

I'M NOT SURE WHAT YOU—

ARE THEY FUCKING?

THEY PERCEIVED HER AS KRUSE'S PET. WAS SHE? WAS SHE MORE? I ONLY KNEW THEY WERE DELIGHTING IN MAKING HER UNCOMFORTABLE.

A GENUINE, OLD-FASHIONED BLUSH— I HADN'T THOUGHT IT STILL EXISTED.

THEY'RE... HAVING RELATIONS. THEY—

HOW OFTEN. THAT COULD BE AN IMPORTANT PARAMETER OF—

HOLD ON. GIVE HER A CHANCE TO FINISH.

SHARON DISCUSSED HER CASE, RECOUNTING THE SEXUAL ISSUES OF HER YOUNG PATIENT, PUSHED TO REVEAL MORE THAN SHE WAS COMFORTABLE WITH BY THE VIPERS.

EACH TIME SHE TRIED TO DEMURE ON FACTS OF THE CASE THAT EMBARRASSED HER, THEY INTERJECTED, PUSHING HER ON.

A PREDATORY BUNCH. I PICTURED THEM ALL AS FULL-FLEDGED THERAPISTS IN A FEW YEARS. SCARY.

I CONSIDERED THE VALUE OF INTERVENING, OF SHUTTING THIS DOWN. WONDERED IF PROTECTING SHARON WOULD DO HER MORE HARM THAN GOOD IN THE LONG RUN.

I LOOKED AT HER, STARING AT THE FLOOR, FIGHTING A LOSING BATTLE WITH HER HANDS...

...AND I SUDDENLY DIDN'T CARE.

THAT'S ENOUGH. CLASS DISMISSED.

I CAUGHT UP WITH HER JUST AS SHE REACHED THE SIDEWALK.

SHARON? WAIT A SECOND, PLEASE.

I'M SORRY.

NO, IT WAS MY FAULT. I ACTED LIKE A BABY, TOTALLY INAPPROPRIATE.

THERE'S NOTHING INAPPROPRIATE ABOUT NOT WANTING TO BE BLUDGEONED. THEY'RE SOME BUNCH. I SHOULD HAVE KEPT A TIGHTER REIN ON THINGS. IS IT LIKE THAT ALL THE TIME?

DR. KRUSE SAYS WE HAVE TO CONFRONT OUR OWN DEFENSE SYSTEMS BEFORE BEING ABLE TO HELP OTHERS. I GUESS I HAVE A WAYS TO GO.

"YOU'LL DO FINE."

"THAT'S NICE OF YOU TO SAY, DR. DELAWARE."

"ALEX."

I PICKED HER UP OUTSIDE HER DORM THE FOLLOWING SATURDAY.

SHE LET ME HOLD THE CAR DOOR OPEN FOR HER.

THE SECOND MY HAND TOUCHED THE STEERING WHEEL, HERS WAS UPON IT, WARM AND FIRM.

WE HAD DINNER AT ONE OF THE SMOKY, NOISY, BEER-AND-PIZZA JOINTS THAT CLING TO EVERY COLLEGE CAMPUS—THE BEST I COULD AFFORD.

I COULDN'T KEEP MY EYES OFF HER, WANTED TO KNOW MORE ABOUT HER, TO FORGE AN IMPOSSIBLE, INSTANT INTIMACY.

SHE FED ME NIBBLES OF INFORMATION ABOUT HERSELF: SHE WAS TWENTY-ONE, HAD GROWN UP ON THE EAST COAST, GRADUATED FROM A SMALL WOMEN'S COLLEGE, CAME WEST FOR GRADUATE SCHOOL.

I ASKED ABOUT HER ASSOCIATION WITH KRUSE. SHE SAID HE WAS HER FACULTY ADVISER, MADE IT SOUND UNIMPORTANT. WHEN I ASKED WHAT HE WAS LIKE, SHE SAID HE WAS DYNAMIC AND CREATIVE, THEN CHANGED THE SUBJECT, AGAIN.

I TRIED TO LEARN MORE. SHE DANCED NIMBLY AWAY FROM MY QUESTIONS, KEPT SHIFTING THE FOCUS TO ME.

I HAD TO REMIND MYSELF WE'D JUST MET. HER DEMEANOR SUGGESTED A CONSERVATIVE, SHELTERED BACKGROUND. PRECISELY THE KIND OF UPBRINGING THAT WOULD STRESS THE DANGERS OF INSTANT INTIMACY.

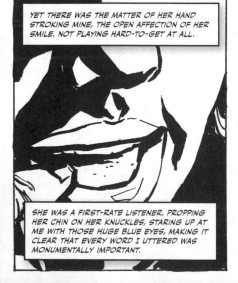

YET THERE WAS THE MATTER OF HER HAND STROKING MINE, THE OPEN AFFECTION OF HER SMILE. NOT PLAYING HARD-TO-GET AT ALL.

SHE WAS A FIRST-RATE LISTENER, PROPPING HER CHIN ON HER KNUCKLES, STARING UP AT ME WITH THOSE HUGE BLUE EYES, MAKING IT CLEAR THAT EVERY WORD I UTTERED WAS MONUMENTALLY IMPORTANT.

WHATEVER PROBLEMS SHE MIGHT HAVE, SHE'D CLEAN UP AS A THERAPIST.

I SURRENDERED TO THE CHEAP THRILLS OF AUTOBIOGRAPHY. SHE MADE IT EASY.

FOR HALF A DOZEN DATES IT REMAINED CHASTE: HAND-HOLDS AND GOODNIGHT PECKS, A NOSEFUL OF THAT LIGHT, FRESH PERFUME. I'D DRIVE HOME SWOLLEN BUT ODDLY CONTENT, SUBSISTING ON RECOLLECTIONS.

FROM THE BEGINNING I WANTED HER PHYSICALLY WITH AN INTENSITY THAT SHOOK ME. BUT SOMETHING ABOUT HER—A FRAGILITY THAT I SENSED OR IMAGINED—HELD ME BACK.

AS WE HEADED TOWARD THE DORM AFTER OUR SEVENTH EVENING TOGETHER, SHE INSTRUCTED ME TO DRIVE ON, AROUND THE CORNER.

COME.

OH, GOD.

COME TO ME.

I OBEYED.

THE LOW MOOD GATHERED STRENGTH AND HIT ME FULL FORCE. I GAVE UP ON SLEEP, OPTING FOR AN EARLY MORNING DRIVE.

HAVING SOMEONE TO TALK TO WOULD HAVE HELPED. MY LIST OF CONFIDANTS WAS DAMNED SHORT. ROBIN AT THE TOP. THEN MILO.

HE WAS OFF WITH RICK, ON A FISHING TRIP IN THE SIERRAS. BUT EVEN IF HIS SHOULDER HAD BEEN AVAILABLE I WOULDN'T HAVE CRIED ON IT.

OVER THE YEARS, OUR FRIENDSHIP HAD TAKEN ON A CERTAIN RHYTHM: WE TALKED ABOUT MURDER AND MADNESS OVER BEER AND PRETZELS, DISCUSSED THE HUMAN CONDITION WITH THE APLOMB OF A PAIR OF ANTHROPOLOGISTS OBSERVING A COLONY OF SAVAGE BABOONS.

WHEN THE HORRORS PILED UP TOO HIGH, MILO BITCHED AND I LISTENED. WHEN HE WENT OFF THE WAGON, I HELPED TALK HIM BACK ON IT.

SAD-SACK COP, SUPPORTIVE SHRINK. I WASN'T READY TO REVERSE THE ROLES.

I GUIDED THE SEVILLE TOWARD NICHOLS CANYON.

THE OLD DAYS. WHAT THE HELL WAS I EXPECTING TO GAIN BY EXHUMING THEM? BY DRIVING PAST HER HOUSE LIKE SOME MOONY TEENAGER HOPING TO CATCH A GLIMPSE OF HIS BELOVED? STUPID. NEUROTIC.

BUT I CRAVED SOMETHING TANGIBLE, SOMETHING REAL TO ASSURE ME THAT SHE'D BEEN REAL. THAT I WAS REAL.

I ENDED UP IN THE DRIVEWAY OF HER HOUSE. IT WAS REAL ENOUGH.

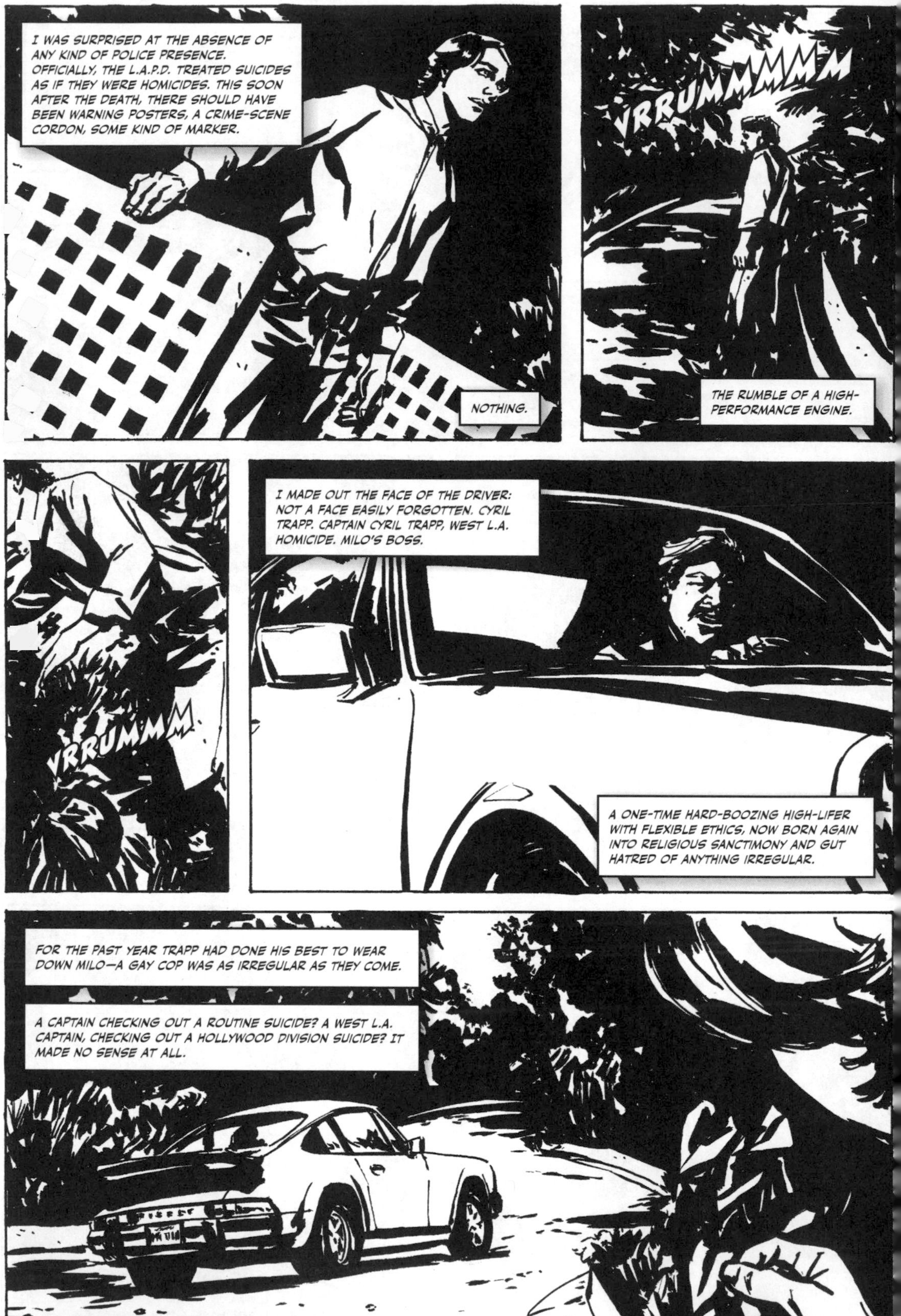
I WAS SURPRISED AT THE ABSENCE OF ANY KIND OF POLICE PRESENCE. OFFICIALLY, THE L.A.P.D. TREATED SUICIDES AS IF THEY WERE HOMICIDES. THIS SOON AFTER THE DEATH, THERE SHOULD HAVE BEEN WARNING POSTERS, A CRIME-SCENE CORDON, SOME KIND OF MARKER.
NOTHING.
VRRUMMMMMM
THE RUMBLE OF A HIGH-PERFORMANCE ENGINE.
VRRUMMM
I MADE OUT THE FACE OF THE DRIVER: NOT A FACE EASILY FORGOTTEN. CYRIL TRAPP. CAPTAIN CYRIL TRAPP, WEST L.A. HOMICIDE. MILO'S BOSS.
A ONE-TIME HARD-BOOZING HIGH-LIFER WITH FLEXIBLE ETHICS, NOW BORN AGAIN INTO RELIGIOUS SANCTIMONY AND GUT HATRED OF ANYTHING IRREGULAR.
FOR THE PAST YEAR TRAPP HAD DONE HIS BEST TO WEAR DOWN MILO—A GAY COP WAS AS IRREGULAR AS THEY COME.
A CAPTAIN CHECKING OUT A ROUTINE SUICIDE? A WEST L.A. CAPTAIN, CHECKING OUT A HOLLYWOOD DIVISION SUICIDE? IT MADE NO SENSE AT ALL.

OR WAS THE VISIT SOMETHING PERSONAL? THE USE OF THE PORSCHE INSTEAD OF AN UNMARKED SUGGESTED JUST THAT.

TRAPP AND SHARON INVOLVED? TOO GROTESQUE TO CONTEMPLATE. TOO *LOGICAL* TO DISMISS.

NOTHING HAD CHANGED. AT FIRST GLANCE, AN UGLY PIECE OF WORK. ONE OF THOSE "MODERNE" STRUCTURES THAT SPREAD OVER POSTWAR L.A., AGING POORLY. BUT I KNEW THERE WAS BEAUTY WITHIN.

A FREE-FORM CLIFF-TOP POOL THAT WRAPPED ITSELF AROUND THE NORTH SIDE OF THE HOUSE AND GAVE THE ILLUSION OF BLEEDING OFF INTO SPACE. WALLS OF GLASS THAT AFFORDED A BREATHTAKINGLY UNINTERRUPTED CANYON VIEW.

THE DOOR WAS LOCKED. AS I TURNED AWAY I NOTICED SOMETHING ATTACHED TO THE TRUNK OF ONE OF THE PALMS.

FOR SALE. ON THE MARKET BEFORE THE BODY WAS COLD.

FOR SALE

ROUTINE SUICIDE NOTWITHSTANDING, IT HAD TO BE THE FASTEST PROBATE IN CALIFORNIA HISTORY. UNLESS THE HOUSE HADN'T BELONGED TO HER. BUT SHE'D TOLD ME IT DID.

SHE'D TOLD ME *LOTS* OF THINGS.

I MEMORIZED THE REALTOR'S NUMBER.

SHE WAS ALWAYS AVAILABLE WHEN I ASKED HER OUT, EVEN ON THE SHORTEST NOTICE. WHEN A PATIENT CRISIS CAUSED ME TO BREAK A DATE, SHE NEVER COMPLAINED. NEVER PUSHED OR PRESSURED ME FOR COMMITMENT OF ANY SORT—THE LEAST DEMANDING HUMAN BEING I'D EVER KNOWN.

WE MADE LOVE NEARLY EVERY TIME WE WERE TOGETHER, THOUGH WE NEVER SPENT THE NIGHT TOGETHER. SHE WOULDN'T COME BACK TO MY PLACE. ALWAYS THE BACKSEAT OF MY CAR.

I ACCOMMODATED MYSELF TO HER NEEDS: RUT AND RUN. SOME OF THE EDGE WAS TAKEN OFF MY PLEASURE, BUT ENOUGH REMAINED TO KEEP ME COMING BACK FOR MORE.

HER PLEASURE—THE LACK OF IT—PREYED ON MY MIND. SHE WENT THROUGH PASSIONATE MOTIONS, MOVING ENERGETICALLY, FUELED BY AN ENERGY THAT I WASN'T SURE WAS EROTIC, BUT SHE NEVER CAME.

SHE WAS ALWAYS WILLING, SEEMED TO ENJOY THE ACT. BUT CLIMAX WASN'T PART OF HER AGENDA. WHEN I WAS FINISHED, SHE WAS, HAVING GIVEN SOMETHING TO ME, BUT NOT HERSELF.

WAS I TOO QUICK? I WORKED AT ENDURANCE. SHE RODE ME OUT, TIRELESS, AS IF WE WERE ENGAGED IN SOME SORT OF ATHLETIC COMPETITION. I TRIED BEING GENTLE, GOT NOWHERE, SWITCHED AND DID THE CAVEMAN BIT.

EVENTUALLY IT STARTED TO NAG AT ME. I WANTED TO GIVE AS MUCH AS I WAS GETTING, BECAUSE I REALLY CARED FOR HER. ON TOP OF THAT, OF COURSE, MY MALE EGO WAS CRYING OUT FOR REASSURANCE.

WORKED OVER HER AND UNDER HER UNTIL I DRIPPED WITH SWEAT AND MY BODY ACHED, WENT DOWN ON HER WITH BLIND DEVOTION.

NOTHING WORKED.

I STRUGGLED TO FIND A WAY TO COMMUNICATE MY CONCERNS, FINALLY OPENING UP AS WE LAY SPRAWLED IN THE BACKSEAT OF MY RAMBLER, STILL CONNECTED.

DON'T WORRY ABOUT ME, ALEX. I'M JUST FINE.

OH, I DO, ALEX. I LOVE IT.

I WANT YOU TO ENJOY IT, TOO.

NO MORE WORDS. SHE BEGAN ROCKING HER HIPS, WRAPPING HER ARMS AROUND ME AS I CONTINUED TO SWELL INSIDE HER.

SHE TOOK CHARGE...

...IMPRISONING ME...

...COMPLETELY.

...BUT IT STILL ALWAYS FELT LIKE THE BACKSEAT.

SHARON? WHAT'S WRONG?

NOTHING. I'M JUST RESTLESS—ALWAYS HAVE BEEN. I HAVE TROUBLE SLEEPING ANYWHERE BUT MY OWN BED. ARE YOU ANGRY?

SHE EVENTUALLY RELENTED, AGREED TO SPEND THE NIGHT AT MY APARTMENT...

NO, OF COURSE NOT. IS THERE ANY-THING I CAN DO?

TAKE ME HOME. WHEN YOU'RE READY.

SUMMER CAME AND MY FELLOWSHIP ENDED. SHARON HAD COMPLETED THE FIRST YEAR OF GRAD SCHOOL WITH TOP GRADES. I'D PASSED MY LICENSING EXAM AND HAD A JOB LINED UP AT WESTERN PEDIATRIC COME AUTUMN. TIME TO CELEBRATE, BUT NO INCOME UNTIL AUTUMN.

AN OPPORTUNITY TO EARN SOME REAL CASH CAME ALONG: AN EIGHT-WEEK DANCE-BAND GIG IN SAN FRANCISCO.

I ASKED HER TO COME NORTH WITH ME, SPUN VISIONS OF BREAKFAST IN SAUSALITO, GOOD THEATER, THE PALACE OF FINE ARTS, HIKING ON MT. TAMALPAIS.

I'D LOVE TO, ALEX, BUT I HAVE SOME THINGS TO TAKE CARE OF.

FAMILY BUSINESS.

PROBLEMS BACK HOME?

OH, NO, JUST THE USUAL.

THAT DOESN'T TELL ME A THING. I HAVE **NO** IDEA WHAT YOUR USUAL IS, BECAUSE YOU **NEVER** TALK ABOUT YOUR FAMILY.

THEY'RE JUST LIKE ANY OTHER FAMILY.

OH, YEAH, I CAN SEE IT NOW. IN A FEW WEEKS I'LL PICK UP THE PAPER AND SEE YOUR PICTURE IN THE SOCIETY PAGES, ENGAGED TO SOME GUY WITH THREE LAST NAMES AND A CAREER IN INVESTMENT BANKING.

HAH... I DON'T THINK SO, MY DEAR.

AND WHY'S THAT?

BECAUSE MY HEART BELONGS TO YOU.

DOES IT, SHARON? AFTER ALL THIS TIME, I STILL DON'T KNOW YOU VERY WELL.

YOU KNOW ME AS WELL AS ANYONE, ALEX.

I REALLY CARE ABOUT YOU.

THEN LIVE WITH ME WHEN WE GET BACK. I'LL GET A BIGGER PLACE, A BETTER ONE.

IT'S NOT THAT SIMPLE. THINGS ARE... COMPLICATED. PLEASE, LET'S NOT TALK ABOUT THIS RIGHT NOW.

ALL RIGHT, BUT CONSIDER IT.

WE'LL HAVE FUN IN SEPTEMBER. NOW...

...CONSIDER THIS.

DOCTOR? I'M MICKEY.

ALEX DELAWARE.

SELHOUS

IT IS DR. DELAWARE?

YES.

MICKEY EYED THE COAT OF DIRT ON THE SEVILLE, THEN MY CLOTHES. RUNNING A MENTAL DUN AND BRADSTREET ON ME: "SAYS HE'S A DOCTOR. DRIVES A CADDY BUT IT'S EIGHT YEARS OLD. THE CITY'S FULL OF BULLSHIT ARTISTS..."

THERE'S A **FABULOUS** VIEW FROM THE INSIDE. IT'S REALLY A CHARMER, GREAT BONES—I THINK IT WAS DESIGNED BY ONE OF NEUTRA'S STUDENTS.

INTERESTING.

I STRUGGLED TO FOCUS ON ANYTHING MICKEY SAID AS THE MEMORIES FLOODED MY BRAIN.

I ALWAYS LIKED NICHOLS CANYON. A FRIEND WHO LIVES NEARBY SAID THERE WAS A SALE SIGN UP HERE.

YES. IT JUST CAME ON THE MARKET, DOCTOR. WE HAVEN'T EVEN RUN ADS YET.

OH, WHAT KIND OF A DOCTOR ARE YOU?

PSYCHOLOGIST. TAKING A DAY OFF. A HALF DAY, ACTUALLY.

AS MICKEY GUIDED ME, I PRETENDED TO LISTEN, NODDING AND SAYING "UH HUH" AT THE RIGHT TIMES.

I FORCED MYSELF TO FOLLOW, RATHER THAN LEAD; I KNEW THE PLACE BETTER THAN SHE DID.

THE INTERIOR SMELLED OF CARPET CLEANING FLUID AND PINE DISINFECTANT. SPARKLY CLEAN, EXPUNGED OF DEATH AND DISORDER. BUT TO ME IT SEEMED MOURNFUL AND FORBIDDING—A BLACK MUSEUM.

MICKEY GUSHED ABOUT THE TERRACE. SOMETHING ABOUT THE VIEW. I JUST BARELY HEARD HER.

I FELT DIZZY.

"SOMETHING TO SHOW YOU, ALEX."

LATE SEPTEMBER. I GOT BACK TO L.A. BEFORE SHARON DID, $4,000 MORE SOLVENT, AND LONELY AS HELL. SHE WAS GONE. WE HADN'T EXCHANGED AS MUCH AS A POSTCARD.

I SHOULD HAVE BEEN ANGRY, YET SHE WAS ALL I THOUGHT ABOUT AS I DROVE DOWN THE COAST. I HEADED STRAIGHT FOR HER DORM. SHE WASN'T RETURNING THIS SEMESTER. NO FORWARDING ADDRESS OR NUMBER.

VRUMM-RMMM

I'D BEEN RIGHT: SHE'D BEEN SEDUCED BACK TO THE GOOD LIFE, PLIED WITH RICH BOYS, NEW TOYS. SHE WAS NEVER COMING BACK.

ERRT

FREE FOR LUNCH, DOCTOR?

YOU LIKE THE CAR?

SURE, IT'S GREAT.

YOU DRIVE.

AFTER LUNCH AT AN ITALIAN PLACE IN LOS FELIZ, SHE GUIDED ME HERE...TO HER NEW HOME.

SO, WHAT DO YOU THINK, DOC?

WHO LIVES HERE?

YOURS TRULY.

YOU'RE RENTING IT?

NO... IT'S MINE!

I WAS SURPRISED TO FIND THE HOUSE FURNISHED, EVEN MORE SURPRISED BY THE DATED, FIFTIES LOOK OF THE PLACE. NOT A STUDENT'S PAD BY A LONG SHOT.

I THOUGHT: AN ARRANGEMENT. SOMEONE HAD SET THE PLACE UP FOR HER. SOMEONE OLD ENOUGH TO HAVE BOUGHT FURNITURE IN THE FIFTIES.

KRUSE? SHE'D NEVER REALLY CLARIFIED THEIR RELATIONSHIP...

YOU DON'T LIKE IT.

NO, NO, I DO. IT'S FANTASTIC.

I WAS JUST WONDERING HOW YOU MANAGED IT. FINANCIALLY.

I HAF SECRET LIFE, MY DAHLINK!

AHA... FIGURED AS MUCH.

I JUST WASN'T PREPARED. I DON'T HEAR FROM YOU ALL SUMMER— NOW THIS. IT'S GORGEOUS. NOT AS GORGEOUS AS YOU...

YOU'RE SWEET.

I'LL EXPLAIN EVERYTHING. BUT FIRST, COME...

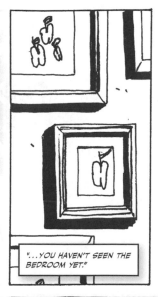

NOW, I'LL EXPLAIN, ALEX.

I'M AN ORPHAN. BOTH OF MY PARENTS DIED LAST YEAR.

THEY WERE WONDERFUL PEOPLE. GLAMOROUS. DADDY WAS AN ART DIRECTOR. MOMMY WAS AN INTERIOR DESIGNER. WE LIVED ON PARK AVENUE, WITH A PLACE IN PALM BEACH AND ANOTHER ON LONG ISLAND. I WAS THEIR ONLY LITTLE GIRL.

I'M SORRY—

SHE COULD HAVE BEEN TALKING ABOUT THE WEATHER. I LISTENED FOR A CATCH IN HER VOICE, RAPID BREATHING, SOME EVIDENCE OF SORROW.

NOTHING.

THEY WERE ACTIVE PEOPLE. LAST YEAR, THEY WERE IN SPAIN, ON HOLIDAY. THEY WERE DRIVING HOME FROM A PARTY WHEN THEIR CAR WENT OFF A CLIFF.

I'M SO SORRY FOR YOU, SHARON.

THANK YOU. YOU'RE SO RIGHT FOR ME, ALEX.

PAUL EVEN—I MEAN, I ALWAYS TALK ABOUT HOW WONDERFUL YOU ARE AND HE SAYS HE'S GLAD I'VE FOUND SOME-ONE SO GOOD FOR ME. HE LIKES YOU.

SHARON...

"...I'VE NEVER *MET* THE MAN."

I PUSHED SHARON ABOUT KRUSE. WAS HE MORE THAN HER ADVISER? DID HE HAVE SOMETHING TO DO WITH THE HOUSE?

INHERITANCE, SHE SAID. IT'S WHY SHE WAS GONE SO LONG— SETTLING MATTERS OF THE ESTATE. NOW SHE HAD A HOUSE AND A TRUST FUND AND AN ALFA ROMEO. SO, WHAT DID I THINK?

I TOLD HER IT WAS WONDERFUL.

...GOOD SIZED, **ESPECIALLY** BY TODAY'S STANDARDS.

MICKEY WAS REALLY HITTING HER STRIDE. MY EYES WERE DRAWN TO A SWIRL OF ACTION IN THE MIDDLE OF THE ROOM. GNATS, CIRCLING...

...PINPOINTING THE SPOT.

...MOTIVATED SELLER. A CORPORA- TION. THEY OWN LOTS OF PROPERTIES, TURN THEM OVER REGULARLY.

WHO LIVES HERE NOW?

RRSHH- RUUSHLLL

NO ONE. A TENANT MOVED OUT RECENTLY. I BELIEVE IT WAS A WOMAN. YOU KNOW L.A., PEOPLE COMING AND—

HURKK...

EXCUSE ME!

WHAT THE... DO YOU **KNOW** THAT MAN?

NO... ...NOT YET.

AS CAR CHASES GO, IT WASN'T ESPECIALLY THRILLING.

GRR-RONKK

THE GUY IN THE TRUCK MANAGED TO PUT SOME DISTANCE BETWEEN US AND THE HOUSE, BUT HE WAS CLEARLY INCAPACITATED. DRUNK? HIGH? BOTH?

HE CAN'T GET IT INTO GEAR. THE TRUCK STALLED. STARTED. STALLED AGAIN.

KRUNNK

VRRUUMMMM

HE GAVE UP ON THE GEARBOX, SLAMMING HIS FOOT ON THE ACCELERATOR. THE ENGINE RACED INEFFECTUALLY.

KLUNK

THUP

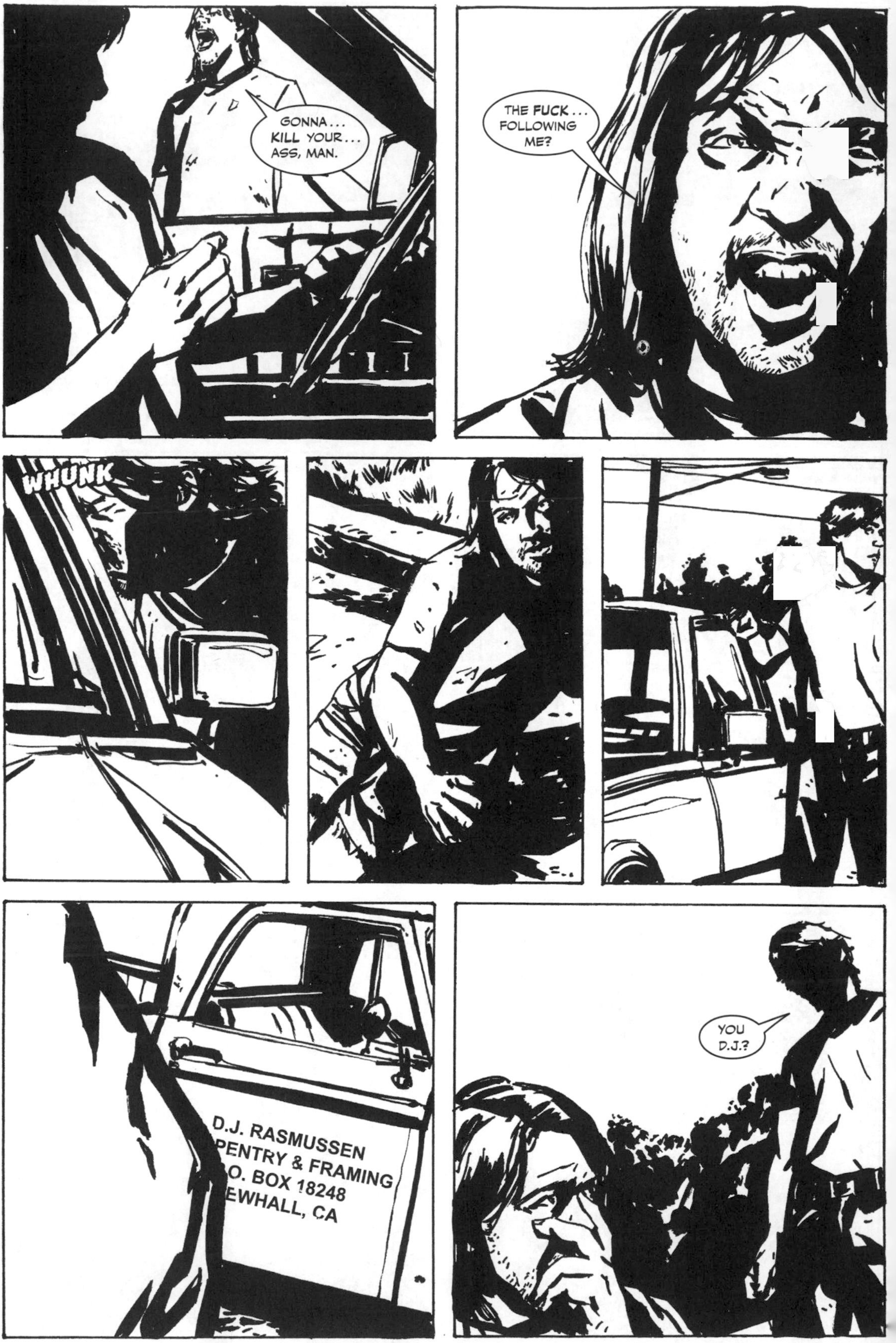
GONNA... KILL YOUR... ASS, MAN.
THE FUCK... FOLLOWING ME?
WHUNK
D.J. RASMUSSEN
PENTRY & FRAMING
O. BOX 18248
EWHALL, CA
YOU D.J.?

WHAT WERE YOU DOING UP THERE? PAYING LAST RESPECTS?

UP CLOSE HE SMELLED OF FERMENT AND VOMIT.

TO DR. RANSOM?

THE GAZE MELTED FAST. RIGHT TRACK.

I WAS A FRIEND OF HERS. HOW ABOUT YOU? D.J.?

FU-UCK YOU.

OH, MAN... YOU'RE...FUCKING... WITH...MY HEAD.

I'M NOT TRYING TO. JUST TRYING TO UNDER-STAND WHY SHE'S DEAD.

IF SHE WAS MORE THAN JUST A FRIEND, IT COULD BE HARDER ON YOU. LOSING A THERAPIST CAN BE LIKE LOSING A PARENT.

FUCK YOU!

HEY, MAN... WHAT THE...

YOU'RE IN NO SHAPE TO DRIVE. I'M HOLDING ON TO THESE UNTIL YOU SHOW ME YOU'VE GOT IT TOGETHER.

TALK TO ME, D.J., THEN I'LL BE OUT OF YOUR HAIR.

WERE YOU DR. RANSOM'S PATIENT?

UH-UH... NOT... CRAZY.

SO, WHAT'S YOUR CONNECTION TO HER?

BAD BACK. HURT...*FUCKING* JOB. PAIN...AND AFTER...

SHE HELPED YOU WITH THE PAIN? AND AFTER? THEN WHAT?

SHE HELPED YOU WITH THE PAIN, D.J. AND **THEN** WHAT?

FUCK YOU!

I'D PRESSED A BUTTON. GAVE ME AN IDEA.

D.J., WHO REFERRED YOU TO SEE DR. RANSOM FOR THE PAIN?

FUCK... YOU...

D.J., WHO REFERRED YOU?

LES... LESLIE...

LESLIE WHO? DOCTOR LESLIE, D.J.?

HUH...HAH... DOCTOR LESLIE.

DOCTOR WEINGARDEN.

BIG... MOUTH JEW.

I POURED OUT WHAT WAS LEFT OF HIS BOTTLES OF WHISKEY, LET THE AIR OUT OF TWO TIRES, AND HID THEY KEYS UNDER A PILE OF BLANKETS.

IF HE COULD WORK ALL THAT OUT, HE'D BE SOBER ENOUGH TO DRIVE HOME.

I DROVE AWAY TELLING MYSELF I'D USE THE POST OFFICE BOX WRITTEN ON HIS TRUCK TO REACH HIM IN A FEW DAYS. ENCOURAGE HIM TO GET A NEW THERAPIST.

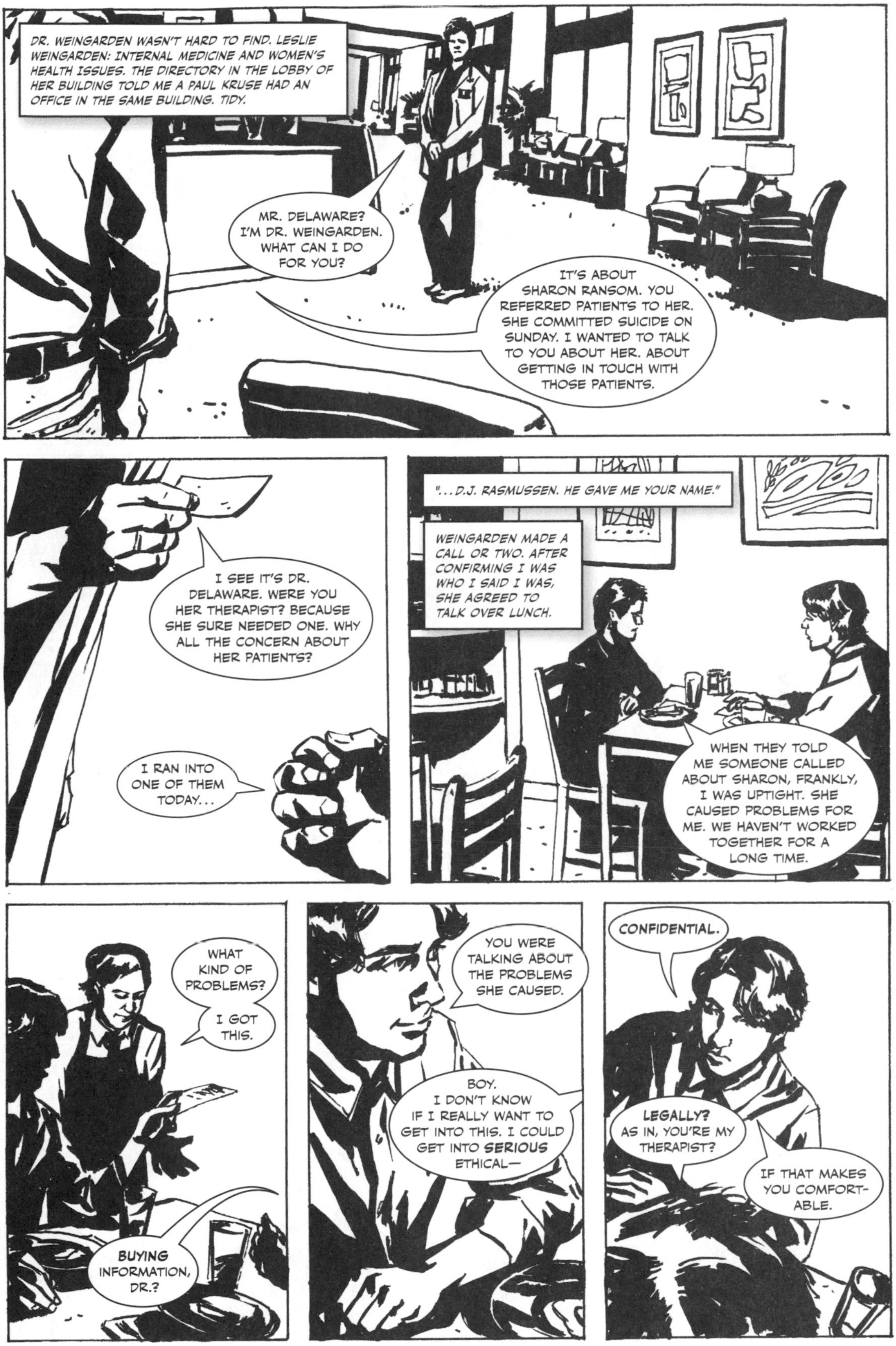
DR. WEINGARDEN WASN'T HARD TO FIND. LESLIE WEINGARDEN: INTERNAL MEDICINE AND WOMEN'S HEALTH ISSUES. THE DIRECTORY IN THE LOBBY OF HER BUILDING TOLD ME A PAUL KRUSE HAD AN OFFICE IN THE SAME BUILDING. TIDY.
MR. DELAWARE? I'M DR. WEINGARDEN. WHAT CAN I DO FOR YOU?
IT'S ABOUT SHARON RANSOM. YOU REFERRED PATIENTS TO HER. SHE COMMITTED SUICIDE ON SUNDAY. I WANTED TO TALK TO YOU ABOUT HER. ABOUT GETTING IN TOUCH WITH THOSE PATIENTS.
I SEE IT'S DR. DELAWARE. WERE YOU HER THERAPIST? BECAUSE SHE SURE NEEDED ONE. WHY ALL THE CONCERN ABOUT HER PATIENTS?
I RAN INTO ONE OF THEM TODAY...
"...D.J. RASMUSSEN. HE GAVE ME YOUR NAME."
WEINGARDEN MADE A CALL OR TWO. AFTER CONFIRMING I WAS WHO I SAID I WAS, SHE AGREED TO TALK OVER LUNCH.
WHEN THEY TOLD ME SOMEONE CALLED ABOUT SHARON, FRANKLY, I WAS UPTIGHT. SHE CAUSED PROBLEMS FOR ME. WE HAVEN'T WORKED TOGETHER FOR A LONG TIME.
WHAT KIND OF PROBLEMS?
I GOT THIS.
BUYING INFORMATION, DR.?
YOU WERE TALKING ABOUT THE PROBLEMS SHE CAUSED.
BOY. I DON'T KNOW IF I REALLY WANT TO GET INTO THIS. I COULD GET INTO **SERIOUS** ETHICAL—
CONFIDENTIAL.
LEGALLY? AS IN, YOU'RE MY THERAPIST?
IF THAT MAKES YOU COMFORT-ABLE.

SHE SHAFTED ME. *GOOD.* I'M SORRY SHE'S DEAD, BUT I JUST CAN'T FEEL ANY GRIEF. SHE USED ME.

SHE WALKED IN LAST YEAR, HUSTLING REFERRALS. SHE WAS BRIGHT, ARTICULATE. HER RESUME LOOKED TERRIFIC, AND SHE WAS RIGHT HERE, IN THE BUILDING.

ON THE THIRD FLOOR, WITH DR. KRUSE?

THAT'S THE ONE. KRUSE WROTE HER THIS TERRIFIC LETTER OF RECOMMENDATION. SILLY ME...I FIGURED THAT COUNTED FOR SOMETHING.

SO, HOW DID SHE SHAFT YOU?

YOU MEAN YOU HAVEN'T FIGURED IT OUT?

MY GUESS WOULD BE SEXUAL MISCONDUCT—SLEEPING WITH HER PATIENTS. BUT MOST OF YOUR PATIENTS ARE WOMEN. WAS SHE GAY?

GAY? I DON'T REALLY KNOW WHAT SHE WAS, BUT NOT AS FAR AS I KNOW. MEN. HUSBANDS OF PATIENTS. BOYFRIENDS. MEN WON'T GO INTO THERAPY WITHOUT PRODDING. THE WOMEN HAVE TO GET THE REFERRALS AND MAKE THE APPOINTMENTS.

MY PATIENTS ASKED ME FOR REFERRALS, I SENT THEM TO SHARON. SHE THANKED ME BY SLEEPING WITH THEM. CHRIST, DON'T YOU THERAPISTS GO THROUGH *ANY* SCREENING?

NOT ENOUGH. HOW DID SHE REACT WHEN YOU CONFRONTED HER?

JUST LOOKED AT ME WITH THOSE BIG BLUES, ALL INNOCENT, AS IF SHE DIDN'T KNOW WHAT I WAS TALKING ABOUT THEN SHE SAID 'SORRY,' AND JUST WALKED AWAY. NO *EXPLANATION,* NO *NOTHING.*

AS HER SUPERVISOR, KRUSE WAS LEGALLY RESPONSIBLE FOR HER. DID YOU TALK TO HIM?

I TRIED. CALLED HIM TWENTY TIMES, SLIPPED MESSAGES UNDER THE DOOR. NOTHING. SHE WAS PROBABLY SCREWING HIM TOO.

LISTEN, I WANT TO MAKE MYSELF VERY CLEAR. I WANT *OUT*—FREE OF ALL THIS GARBAGE. *GOT THAT?* IF YOU USE ANYTHING I'VE SAID TO CONNECT ME WITH HER, I'LL DENY SAYING IT. MENTION MY NAME, AND I'LL SUE YOU FOR BREACH OF CONFIDENTIALITY.

EASY. YOU'VE MADE YOUR POINT. I CAN GET THE CHECK.

I'LL PAY MY OWN WAY, THANK YOU.

DRIVING HOME, I RAN SCENARIOS, WONDERING HOW MANY MEN SHARON HAD VICTIMIZED, HOW LONG IT HAD BEEN GOING ON. IT WAS IMPOSSIBLE NOW FOR ME TO IMAGINE A MAN IN HER LIFE WITHOUT A CARNAL LINK.

TRAPP.

THE SHEIK.

D.J. RASMUSSEN.

ME. VICTIMS **ALL?**

I HADN'T SCREENED HER OUT OF MY LIFE, HAD LONG RATIONALIZED IT BY TELLING MYSELF I'D BEEN YOUNG AND NAÏVE, TOO GREEN TO KNOW ANY BETTER. YET THREE DAYS AGO I'D BEEN JACKED UP AND READY TO SEE HER AGAIN. READY TO START...WHAT?

BRINNG-RINNG

HELLO, ALEX.

HI, ROBIN.

THANKS FOR CALLING BACK. YOUR MOTHER AND I HAD A LOVELY CHAT.

JUST THOUGHT I'D CALL AND SEE HOW YOU WERE DOING.

JUST DANDY.

YEAH, WELL... WOULD YOU BELIEVE SEMI-DANDY?

IT'S NOTHING. IT JUST HASN'T BEEN A GREAT WEEK, SO FAR.

NO, IT HAS NOTHING TO DO WITH YOU. SOMEONE I KNEW BACK IN SCHOOL COMMITTED SUICIDE.

OH, MY GOD. HOW AWFUL.

DID YOU KNOW THIS PERSON WELL?

NO.

NOT REALLY.

THAT SECOND AUTUMN, WE REMAINED LOVERS, OF SORTS. WHEN I MANAGED TO REACH HER SHE ALWAYS SAID YES, ALWAYS HAD SWEET THINGS TO SAY. SHE WHISPERED IN MY EAR, RUBBED MY BACK, SPREAD HER LEGS FOR ME WITH THE EASE OF APPLYING HER LIPSTICK, INSISTING I WAS HER GUY, THE ONLY MAN IN HER LIFE.

BUT REACHING HER WAS THE CHALLENGE. SHE WAS SELDOM HOME, NEVER LEFT A CLUE TO HER WHEREABOUTS.

LATE ONE SATURDAY NIGHT, AFTER A WRENCHING SESSION WITH THE PARENTS OF A MERCILESSLY DEFORMED NEWBORN, I WANTED A SHOULDER TO CRY ON.

SHARON?

I MOVED TOWARD HER BEDROOM, HALF EXPECTING TO FIND HER WITH ANOTHER MAN. HALF WANTING TO.

SHARON?

I'D ENTERED HER BODY SO MANY TIMES, BUT THIS WAS THE FIRST TIME I'D SEEN IT COMPLETELY UNCLOTHED. SHE WAS FLAWLESS, UNBELIEVABLY RICH. I RESTRAINED MYSELF FROM TOUCHING HER.

SHARON.

49

I WONDERED IF SHE WAS ENGAGING IN SOME KIND OF SELF-HYPNOSIS. I'D HEARD KRUSE WAS A MASTER HYPNOTIST. HAD HE BEEN GIVING HER PRIVATE LESSONS?

BUT SHE LOOKED STRICKEN RATHER THAN ENTRANCED—FROWNING, BREATHING RAPIDLY AND SHALLOWLY. HER HANDS BEGAN TO TREMBLE.

I NOTICED SOMETHING IN THE LEFT ONE.

TWIN GIRLS IN IDENTICAL COWGIRL COSTUMES. A PERFECT PHOTOGRAPHER'S BACKDROP BEHIND THEM.

CARBON COPIES OF EACH OTHER EXCEPT FOR ONE SMALL DETAIL. ONE GIRL CLUTCHED HER ICE CREAM CONE IN HER RIGHT HAND; THE OTHER, IN HER LEFT. MIRROR-IMAGE TWINS. THEIR FEATURES WERE SET, HYPER-MATURE. SHARON'S FEATURES, TIMES TWO.

"I WAS THEIR ONLY LITTLE GIRL."

SURPRISE, SURPRISE.

SHARON...

NO, NO, NO! GIMME, GIMME!

S and S.
Silent Partners.

NO!

THE LOOK IN HER EYES WAS MURDEROUS.

I BACKED OUT OF THE ROOM, RAN FROM THE HOUSE, FEELING DIZZY, SICK, SUCKER-PUNCHED.

CERTAIN THAT WHATEVER WE HAD WAS OVER.

NOT KNOWING IF THAT WAS GOOD OR BAD.

51

WITH MILO AWAY, MY ONLY OTHER POLICE CONTACT WAS DELANO HARDY. A FEW YEARS AGO HE'D SAVED MY LIFE. I'D BOUGHT HIM A GUITAR, A CLASSIC FENDER STRATOCASTER, THAT ROBIN HAD RESTORED, AS THANKS. IT WAS CLEAR WHO OWED WHO, BUT I'D CALLED HIM ANYWAY.

DOCTOR? I GOT SOME STUFF FOR YOU, IF YOU'RE IN ANY MOOD TO HEAR IT.

"I DROPPED BY THE CORONER'S. SPOKE TO A BUDDY THERE."

"TIME OF DEATH: BETWEEN EIGHT P.M. AND THREE A.M. SUNDAY. CAUSE: 22 CALIBER BULLET TO THE BRAIN. IT BOUNCED AROUND IN THERE. SMALL CALIBER BULLETS DO THAT."

"HEAVY AMOUNTS OF ALCOHOL AND BARBITURATES IN HER SYSTEM— BORDERLINE LETHAL DOSAGE. THEY ALSO FOUND SOME OLD SCARS BETWEEN HER TOES...OLD TRACKS. YOU EVER KNOW THIS LADY TO BE INTO DRUGS?"

NO, BUT IT WAS A LONG TIME AGO.

YEAH. PEOPLE CHANGE. KEEPS US BUSY.

HERE'S THE INTER- ESTING PART: CORONER TOLD ME THEIR OFFICE PROCESSED THE CASE QUICKLY, ORDERS OF THE BOSS. THEIR AVERAGE IS SIX TO EIGHT WEEKS. THEY ALSO GOT ORDERS NOT TO DISCUSS THE CASE WITH ANYONE.

PATHOLOGIST GOT THE CLEAR IMPRES- SION IT WAS A RICH-FOLKS CASE, GREASE THE SKIDS TO THE MAX, KEEP IT HUSHED. THE CASE CLOSED. GOT ONE MORE THING. YOU KNOW ENOUGH TO KNOW SHE WASN'T ANY SAINT?

WELL, RUMOR IS A PORN LOOP WAS FOUND IN HER ROOM...A LOOP WITH **HER IN IT.** DOCTOR/PATIENT THING, WHERE THE CHECKUP LEADS TO SEX. SHE WAS THE PATIENT.

I HEAR SHE HAD SOME... **TALENTS.**

THE LOOP DISAP- PEARED AROUND THE OFFICE, IF YOU KNOW WHAT I MEAN. IT'S NOT GOING TO SHOW UP, DOC. OH, AND NOTHING ON THE SISTER YOU ASKED ABOUT. NO SHIRLEE RANSOM WITH US OR THE DMV.

NO PROBLEM, DOC. GLAD TO GIVE IT. WHEN I HAVE IT.

THE OUTFIT WAS NEW, AS WAS THE COCKTAIL, PINK AND REDOLENT. IT OBSCURED HER PERFUME— NO SPRING FLOWERS.

THE SCENE WITH THE TWIN PHOTO LEFT ME ADDLED, IN PAIN, UNABLE TO CONCENTRATE ON WORK. THREE DAYS LATER I STARTED CALLING HER, GOT NO ANSWER. I TRIED CORNERING KRUSE, GOT STONEWALLED—LIKE HE NEVER HEARD MY NAME BEFORE.

SHE LEFT A MESSAGE. OFFERING TO EXPLAIN EVERYTHING... AGAIN. I WENT TO THE HOUSE PREPARED TO ASK HARD QUESTIONS.

HER BREATH WAS SHARP WITH ALCOHOL.

DON'T THINK I'VE EVER SEEN YOU DRINK ANY-THING BUT 7-UP.

STRAWBERRY DAIQUIRI, DARLING. I GUESS I'M IN A TROPICAL MOOD.

HER VOICE WAS HUSKY, INEBRIATED.

I OPENED MY EYES TO FIND HER PEELING OUT OF THE RED DRESS, SHIMMYING AND LICKING HER LIPS.

IN THE ABSTRACT IT WAS X-RATED COMEDY, FREDERICK'S OF HOLLYWOOD, A LAMPOON. BUT SHE WAS ANYTHING BUT ABSTRACT AND I STOOD THERE, TRANSFIXED.

TO HELL WITH THAT. I DIDN'T CARE—I WANTED HER.

I LET HER STRIP ME DOWN IN A PRACTICED MANNER THAT EXCITED AND FRIGHTENED ME.

TOO NIMBLE. TOO PROFESSIONAL. HOW MANY OTHER TIMES? HOW MANY OTHER MEN? WHO'D TAUGHT HER—

NO. KEEP IT BRIGHT. I WANT TO SEE IT, SEE EVERYTHING.

THAT'S IT. THE LIGHTS. I WANT TO SEE IT.

NO...THE BEDROOM.

I NEED YOU INSIDE ME, BUT NOT HERE...

"...THE BATHROOM."

THE BATHROOM WAS MIRRORED ON THREE SIDES. SHE PLACED HERSELF ON TOP OF ME, WITH A CLEAR VIEW OF EVERYTHING.

FINALLY SATISFIED WITH HER ARRANGEMENT, SHARON LOST HERSELF IN THE PLEASURE, HEAVING...NEARLY SOBBING.

THEN, FOR THE FIRST TIME IN OUR TIME TOGETHER...SHE CAME.

HI.

SHARON?

OKAY, YOU GOT WHAT YOU WANTED, YOU SCUMMY **PRICK.** NOW GET THE **FUCK** OUT OF HERE.

GET THE **FUCK OUT OF** MY **LIFE**...

"...GET OUT!"

I DRESSED HURRIEDLY, FEELING AS WORTHWHILE AS A SCAB. I RUSHED PAST HER, SHAKING. I STARTED THE CAR AND HURTLED DOWN JALMIA. ONLY WHEN I WAS BACK ON HOLLYWOOD BOULEVARD DID I TAKE THE TIME TO BREATHE.

BUT BREATHING HURT, AS IF I'D BEEN POISONED. I WANTED SUDDENLY TO DESTROY HER. TO LEACH HER TOXIN FROM MY BLOOD.

I GOT ONTO SUNSET, PASSED NIGHTCLUBS AND DISCO JOINTS, SMILING FACES THAT SEEMED TO MOCK MY OWN MISERY. BUT BY THE TIME I REACHED DOHENY, MY **RAGE** HAD FADED TO GNAWING **SADNESS. DISGUST.**

FA-UUUCCKKK!!!

THIS WAS IT—NO MORE MINDFUCKS.

THIS WAS IT!

221...222...

FINALLY I FORCED MYSELF TO TAKE A SINGLE STEP FORWARD...A BABY STEP.

MOTHER, MAY I? PLEASE?

SOLID GROUND. NO FIREWORKS.

ANOTHER STEP. I SWUNG ONE FOOT OUT IN A SLOW ARC, TESTING...NO TRIPWIRES...WAS INCHING FORWARD...

...WHEN AN ELECTRIC WHINE SOUNDED FROM SOMEWHERE BEHIND ME.

YEAH. YEAH... I'M FINE, MAL.

HAS DARREN'S MOTHER TAKEN HIM FOR MORE SESSIONS?

ALEX?

ALEX... YOU WITH ME, BROTHER?

SHE SAYS SHE WANTS TO HANDLE THINGS BY HERSELF.

BUT THAT'S OFF THE RECORD. AS FAR AS THE OTHER SIDE'S CONCERNED, THE KID WILL BE IN TREATMENT THE REST OF HIS LIFE. AND BEYOND. NOW...

"...YOU **SURE** YOU'RE READY FOR THIS?"

...YOUR OWN REPORT, DR. DELAWARE, SHOWS THAT EVEN CHILDREN WITH CHRONIC ILLNESSES WERE NO MORE NERVOUS OR MALADJUSTED THAN THEIR HEALTHY PEERS.

DARREN BURKHALTER ISN'T CHRONICALLY ILL. HE'S A ONE-SHOT DEAL. HE'D BE EVEN LESS VULNERABLE TO PROBLEMS THAN—

GOOD POINT, MR. MORETTI. CHRONICALLY ILL AND TRAUMATIZED CHILDREN ARE VERY DIFFERENT. THAT'S WHY I WONDERED WHY YOU CITED THAT ARTICLE IN THE FIRST PLACE.

A BLOODY, VIOLENT SCENE LIKE DARREN WAS SUBJECTED TO BURIES ITSELF IN THE SUBCONSCIOUS. IT—

WHAT DOES A SUBCONSCIOUS **LOOK** LIKE, DOCTOR? I'VE NEVER SEEN ONE.

NEVERTHELESS, YOU HAVE ONE. WE ALL DO. IT'S LIKE A BIN IN OUR BRAINS WHERE WE PUT EXPERIENCES AND FEELING WE DON'T WANT TO DEAL WITH.

WHEN OUR DEFENSES ARE DOWN, THE BIN TIPS OVER AND SOME OF THE STORED MATERIAL SPILLS OUT—RESULTING IN THE SEEMINGLY IRRATIONAL OR EVEN SELF-DESTRUCTIVE BEHAVIORS WE CALL SYMPTOMS.

THE SUBCONSCIOUS IS REAL, MR. MORETTI. IT'S WHAT MAKES *YOU* DREAM OF *WINNING.*

A BIG PART OF WHAT MOTIVATED YOU TO BECOME A LAWYER.

THANK YOU FOR THAT INSIGHT, DOCTOR. SEND ME A BILL...

THOUGH JUDGING FROM WHAT YOU'RE CHARGING MR. WORTHY, I DON'T KNOW IF I CAN AFFORD YOU.

IN THE MEANTIME, LET'S STICK TO THE ACCIDENT—

ACCIDENT DOESN'T BEGIN TO DESCRIBE WHAT DARREN BURKHALTER EXPERIENCED. *DIS-ASTER* WOULD BE MORE ACCURATE.

HE WAS NAPPING IN HIS CAR AT THE MOMENT OF IMPACT. THE FIRST THING HE SAW WHEN HE WOKE UP WAS HIS FATHER'S DECAPITATED HEAD FLYING OVER THE FRONT SEAT AND LANDING NEXT TO HIM...

...THE FEATURES STILL *TWITCHING.*

RIGHT IN THE *COJONES,* ALEX...ABSOLUTELY *BEAUTIFUL!* I SHOULD BE GETTING THEIR OFFERS THIS AFTERNOON.

I MADE A STRONGER CASE THAN I INTENDED. BASTARD GOT TO ME.

YOU *SURE* ABOUT THE OFFERS? MORETTI SEEMED CONFIDENT, EVEN AFTER THE VIDEO OF DARREN'S SESSION.

PURE CRAPOLA. SAVING FACE IN FRONT OF HIS PARTNERS. HE MAY NOT WANT TO SETTLE, BUT HE'LL SETTLE.

YOU THINK HE WANTS A *JURY* HEARING ABOUT DADDY'S HEAD LANDING IN LITTLE DARREN'S LAP?

YOUR JIBE ABOUT THE SUBCONSCIOUS WAS *PERFECT!* YOU GOT A *REAL* FUCKING MEAN STREAK, DELAWARE...YOU KNOW THAT?

SORRY. I—

HEY, DON'T GET ME *WRONG,* ALEX. I LIKE IT.

I MEAN I *REALLY* LIKE IT.

MAL'S GLEE DIDN'T DO MUCH TO DISTRACT ME. BY FOUR, I FOUND MYSELF REACHING FOR THE PHONE...FOR ROBIN. THE LAST PERSON I WANTED TO TALK TO ANSWERED...HER MOTHER.

IT'S ME, ROSALIE.

WHEN ARE YOU EXPECTING HER BACK? OKAY, WOULD YOU PLEASE TELL HER—

I'M NOT TELLING HER ANYTHING. WHY DON'T YOU JUST QUIT? SHE DOESN'T WANT TO BE WITH YOU. ISN'T THAT PLAIN TO SEE?

YOU'RE NOT AS SMART AS YOU THINK. YOU THINK YOU'RE ALL GROWN UP, GOT EVERYTHING FIGURED OUT, DON'T NEED ADVICE FROM NO ONE.

SHE'S STILL MY KID AND I DON'T LIKE PEOPLE PUSHING HER AROUND.

IF THE SHOE FITS, MISTER. YESTERDAY, AFTER SHE TALKED TO YOU, WE WAS MOPEY ALL DAY. SHE DOESN'T NEED THAT KIND OF MISERY.

SO WHY DON'T YOU JUST FORGET IT.

I'M NOT ABOUT TO FORGET ANYTHING. I LOVE HER.

JUST GIVE HER THE MESSAGE, ROSALIE.

"DO YOUR OWN DAMN DIRTY WORK."

I BARELY MANAGED TO CUT OFF MY MOUNTING RAGE WITH A DROP OF REASON. OF COURSE, ROSALIE WOULD TRY TO PROTECT ROBIN. NORMAL MATERNAL INSTINCT.

THIS WASN'T GOING TO WORK OVER THE PHONE. I'D BOOK A FLIGHT TO SAN LUIS. WE COULD—

DIN-DONNNG!

FOUR DAYS EARLY, MILO? CRAVE CIVILIZATION?

FISH. TAKE 'EM. I HAVE TO SCRATCH.

YOU LOOK TERRIBLE, BY THE WAY.

GEE, THANKS. YOU LOOK LIKE STRAWBERRY YOGURT YOURSELF. STIRRED FROM THE BOTTOM.

SO, WHAT DO YOU THINK? PRETTY GODDAMNED ABERCROMBIE AND ITCH, HUH?

RICK FORCED ME TO GO SHOPPING. INSISTED WE HAD TO OUT-MACHO EVERYONE.

DID YOU SUCCEED?

OH, YEAH. WE WERE SO GODDAMNED TOUGH IT SCARED THE SHIT OUT OF THE FISH.

LITTLE SUCKERS JUMPED RIGHT OUT OF THE RIVER, LANDING IN OUR SKILLETS, LEMON SLICES IN THEIR MOUTHS.

SO, THE MAN DOES STILL REMEMBER HOW TO LAUGH.

WHAT'S THE MATTER, GUY. WHO *DIED*?

GIVE ME A FRY PAN, BUTTER, GARLIC, AND ONIONS...NO, EXCUSE ME, THIS IS AN UPSCALE HOUSEHOLD... *SHALLOTS*. GIVE ME SHALLOTS.

GOT ANY BEER?

GOING TEMPERATE ON ME?

JUST...NOT RIGHT NOW.

NO SHALLOTS. NO GARLIC EITHER, JUST THIS.

TSK, TSK, SLIPPING, DR. SUAVE. I'M REPORTING YOU TO THE FOODIE PATROL.

BETTER YET, WE PLAY HUNTERS AND GATHERERS. ME CATCH, *YOU* COOK.

NICE, HUH? PAYS TO TAKE A SURGEON ALONG.

WHERE IS RICK?

GETTING SOME SHUTEYE WHILE HE CAN. HE'S GOT A TWENTY-FOUR-HOUR COMING UP AT THE E.R., THEN A DAY OFF BEFORE ANOTHER TWENTY-FOUR...

THE SATURDAY NIGHT SHIFT. GUN-SHOTS AND MALICIOUS FOOLISHNESS.

AND HE'S STARTED HEADING OVER TO THE FREE CLINIC TO COUNSEL AIDS PATIENTS.

WHAT A GUY, HUH? ALL OF A SUDDEN I'M LIVING WITH THE GAY SCHWEITZER.

HOW WERE THE GREAT OUTDOORS?

TOO MUCH PRISTINE, UNSPOILED BEAUTY... COULDN'T TAKE IT. SEEMS BOTH OF US ARE URBAN SLEAZE-JUNKIES. ALL THAT CLEAN AIR AND CALM AND WE WERE GOING THROUGH THE SHAKES.

NOTHING IN HERE, ALEX. WHAT'S GOING ON?

I NEED TO SHOP.

UH-HUH. HOW'S THE LOVELY MS. CASTAGNA?

WORKING HARD.

UH-HUH.

OKAY, TELL ME WHAT THE HELL IS BOTHERING YOU.

I CONSIDERED TELLING HIM ABOUT ROBIN. TOLD HIM ABOUT SHARON INSTEAD.

MILO LISTENED, PERKING UP AS I RECOUNTED SEEING TRAPP SNEAKING AWAY FROM SHARON'S HOUSE IN THE MIDDLE OF THE NIGHT.

NOT HUNGRY?

TRAPP, HUH? YOU'RE SURE IT WAS HIM.

HE'S HARD TO MISS WITH THAT WHITE HAIR AND THAT SKIN.

YEAH. SOME SORT OF AUTO-IMMUNE CONDITION. BODY ATTACKS ITSELF BY LEECHING PIGMENT. NO ONE KNOWS WHAT CAUSES IT.

I THINK THE ASSHOLE IS SO FULL OF POISON THAT HIS OWN SYSTEM CAN'T STAND HIM. MAYBE WE'LL GET LUCKY AND HE'LL FADE AWAY COMPLETELY.

WHO KNOWS? MAYBE HE AND YOUR LATE FRIEND WERE GETTING IT ON AND HE WENT BACK TO MAKE SURE HE HADN'T LEFT ANY EVIDENCE. SLEAZY BUT NOT INDICTABLE.

WHAT DO YOU THINK ABOUT HIS BEING AT THE HOUSE?

IF SHE WAS GETTING IT ON WITH HIM SHE **MUST** HAVE BEEN NUTS.

WHAT ABOUT THE QUICK SALE ON THE HOUSE? AND THE TWIN SISTER? I KNOW SHE EXISTS...EXISTED. I MET HER SIX YEARS AGO.

SIX YEARS IS A LONG TIME, ALEX. AND WHO'S TO SAY SHE HASN'T BEEN FOUND? IT SMELLS LIKE COVER UP, BUT THAT DOESN'T MEAN WHAT'S BEING COVERED UP WAS ANY-THING JUICY.

WHEN RICH FOLK END UP IN AWKWARD SITUATIONS, THEY CAN PAY TO SWEEP IT UNDER THE RUG. HAPPENS ALL THE TIME.

SO YOU'RE SAYING FORGET ABOUT IT?

NOT SO FAST, LONE RANGER.

I'LL PURSUE IT, IF ONLY FOR SELFISH REASONS: THE CHANCE OF GETTING SOMETHING ON TRAPP.

I'VE GOT SOME TIME TO KILL, ANYWAY. IDLE HANDS MAKE THE DEVIL'S WORK, LAD. FAR BE IT FROM ME TO TEMPT SATAN.

'FESS UP, DOCTOR. THIS FRIEND WAS **MORE** THAN JUST A FRIEND.

A LONG TIME AGO, MILO.

BUT THE WAY YOU LOOK WHEN YOU TALK ABOUT HER, IT'S NOT **THAT** ANCIENT A HISTORY. DO CONSIDER ONE THING, ALEX. YOU READY TO HEAR MORE DIRT ABOUT HER?

FROM WHAT WE KNOW ALREADY, ONCE WE START DIGGING, IT AIN'T GONNA BE BURIED TREASURE TIME.

NO PROBLEM.

UH-HUH.

I SLEPT POORLY. I WAS GETTING USED TO IT. TRIED A RUN IN THE MORNING...BAGGED IT AFTER JUST ONE MILE, ALREADY OUT OF BREATH.

I KEPT THINKING ABOUT SHIRLEE RANSOM, THE SISTER I'D MET SIX YEARS BEFORE. A FRIEND OF MINE WAS A SOCIAL WORKER WITH THE DEPARTMENT OF SOCIAL SERVICES FOR THIRTY YEARS.

IF ANYONE COULD DIG UP RECORDS ON SHIRLEE, IT WAS OLIVIA.

ALEX! HELLO, DARLING.

NO, YOU DIDN'T CATCH ME IN THE MIDDLE OF ANYTHING, UNLESS YOU CONSIDER PRUNES AND OAT BRAN A HOT DATE.

AL? OH, HE'S STILL THE LIFE OF THE PARTY. I ONLY KEEP HIM AROUND FOR THE TORRID SEX.

SO, HOW ARE YOU?

A FAVOR? DAMN. HERE I THOUGHT YOU WERE JUST AFTER MY BODY.

YEAH...BIG TALK! WHAT DO YOU NEED, HANDSOME?

ACCESS? YOU KIDDING? I'VE GOT ACCESS TO MEDICAL, MEDICARE, AFDC, FDI... EVERY DAMN FILE YOU CAN IMAGINE.

IS THIS ABOUT A PATIENT OF YOURS?

AH...I SEE. DON'T WORRY ABOUT IT, GOODY TWO-SHOES. IT'S NOT LIKE YOU'RE ASKING ME TO COMMIT A CRIME. RIGHT?

OKAY, GIVE ME A NAME AND ANYTHING ELSE YOU KNOW. EVERYTHING WILL BE ON THE COMPUTER.

WE'RE ALL ON SOMEBODY'S LIST, DARLING. YOU, ME, AND WHAT WE HAD FOR BREAKFAST.

FRIDAY MORNING I BOOKED A SATURDAY FLIGHT TO SAN LUIS. I NEEDED TO SEE ROBIN.

LARRY DASCHOFF CALLED JUST AFTER. HE'D FOUND A COPY OF THE PORN LOOP. KRUSE HAD MADE THE THING AFTER ALL. IT WAS NOW IN THE COLLECTION OF A COUPLE OF... *ENTHUSIASTS.*

LARRY COULD MEET ME AT THEIR HOUSE TO WATCH THE LOOP OVER HIS LUNCH HOUR. HE GAVE ME A BEVERLY HILLS ADDRESS.

TURNING-OVER-THE-ROCK TIME. I FELT QUEASY, UNCLEAN.

PRETTY RECHERCHÉ, HUH, D.?

WHO **ARE** THESE PEOPLE?

THE FONTAINES... GORDON AND CHANTAL. BENEVOLENT MILLIONAIRES. THE GIVE TO CHARITY, HAND OUT THANKSGIVING TURKEYS ON SKID ROW, AND THEY **LOVE** PORN. DAMN NEAR WORSHIP IT.

THEY'RE THE PRIVATE DONORS I TOLD YOU ABOUT, THE ONES WHO FUNDED KRUSE'S RESEARCH.

GOOD SIMPLE FOLK, HUH?

WELL, THEY'RE JUST INTO GOOD OLD-FASHIONED, STRAIGHT SEX ON FILM. CLAIM IT SAVED THEIR MARRIAGE.

THEY GET DOWNRIGHT EVANGELICAL ABOUT IT.

THEY THOUGHT KRUSE WOULD HELP THEM SPREAD THE WORD ABOUT THE THERAPEUTIC BENE-FITS OF EROTICA.

I TOLD GORDON I WAS NO FAN OF KRUSE MYSELF...TOLD HIM THE STAR OF THE LOOP WAS DEA WE WERE OLD FRIENDS, AND WE WANTED TO REMEMBER HER FOR **EVERYTHING** SHE'D DONE.

THEY THOUGHT IT WOULD BE A DANDY MEMORIAL. BESIDES, LIKE **ALL** FANATICS, THEY LOVE TO SHOW OFF.

COLD FEET, D.?

IT SEEMS... GHOULISH.

SURE IT'S GHOULISH. SO ARE EULOGIES. IF YOU WANT TO CALL IT OFF, I'LL GO IN THERE AND TELL THEM.

NO...

...LET'S DO IT.

SCULPTURE. ORIGINAL LOMBARDO.

VERY EXPENSIVE.

NOK-NOK-NOK

COME.

THANK YOU, ROSA.

LITTLE ROSIE RAMOS...SHE WAS A REAL TALENT IN THE SIXTIES. *PX MAMAS. GINZA GIRLS.* CHOOSE ONE FROM COLUMN X.

GORDON FONTAINE. THIS IS MY WIFE, CHANTAL.

THANKS FOR SEEING US. THIS IS MY FRIEND I TOLD YOU ABOUT...DR. ALEX DELAWARE.

ALEX. CHARMED. YOU HAVE A PHOTOGENIC FACE, DOCTOR. EVER ACT?

PLEASED TO MEET YOU, CHANTAL. NO.

SO, I KNOW YOU'RE BOTH ON A SCHEDULE. LET'S GET BUSY SHOWING YOU WHAT TOOK DECADES AND I-WON'T-TELL-YOU-HOW-MANY DOLLARS TO PUT TOGETHER.

GENTLEMEN, OUR **COLLECTION!**

THE NEXT HALF HOUR WAS SPENT ON A TOUR OF THE BLACK ROOM.

EVERY GENRE OF PORNOGRAPHY WAS REPRESENTED, IN *ASTOUNDING* QUALITY AND VARIETY, CATALOGUED AND LABELED WITH SMITHSONIAN PRECISION.

THOSE RED ONES ARE FROM THE BORDELLO IN NEW ORLEANS WHERE SCOTT JOPLIN PLAYED PIANO.

IF ONLY THEY COULD TALK, EH?

ONWARD... TO THE PIÈCE DE RÉSISTANCE!

THE FONTAINES SEEMED TO KNOW MANY OF THE MODELS AND ACTRESSES PERSONALLY...DISCUSSING THEM WITH NEAR PARENTAL CONCERN.

THE CLEANEST PRINTS YOU'LL EVER SEE. *EVERY* IMPORTANT EXPLICIT FILM EVER MADE, ALL CONVERTED TO VIDEOTAPE DUPLICATE.

IMPRESSIVE.

WE'RE TRYING TO PRESERVE THE ORIGINALS. WE HOPE TO DONATE THEM TO A MAJOR MUSEUM ONE DAY.

NOW, YOU WANTED TO SEE SHAWNA'S LOOP.

SHAWNA?

SHAWNA BLUE... THE NAME PRETTY SHARON USED ON THE LOOP. WE ALWAYS CALLED HER PRETTY SHARON BECAUSE SHE WAS SUCH A LOVELY THING...

"...VIRTUALLY FLAWLESS."

CHECKUP. STARRING THE LATE MISS SHAWNA BLUE AND THE LATE MR. MICHAEL STARBUCK.

I SAT RIGID, HOLDING MY BREATH, TOLD MYSELF I'D BEEN AN IDIOT TO COME. THEN, THE IMAGES BEGAN TO FLASH BY AND I LOST MYSELF IN THEM.

NO SOUNDTRACK. SHODDY, CHEAP ALL AROUND.

BLACK AND WHITE, BUT I KNEW THE DRESS WAS FLAME-COLORED.

SHARON'S FACE. DESPITE THE WIG, NO DOUBT ABOUT IT.

SHE HAD COME BACK TO LIFE, WAS UP THERE, SMILING AND BECKONING... IMMORTALITY CONCEIVED IN LIGHT AND SHADOW.

I HAD TO RESTRAIN MYSELF FROM REACHING OUT TO TOUCH HER.

WANTED, SUDDENLY, TO YANK HER OUT OF THE SCREEN, TO PULL HER BACK IN TIME. RESCUE HER.

I CONCENTRATED ON THE CHOPPINESS, TRYING TO RESTORE HER TO SOMETHING TWO-DIMENSIONAL. I WATCHED HER HANDS MOVE...FELT THEM.

BUT SOMETHING WAS WRONG. SOMETHING ABOUT THE HANDS...OFF-KILTER.

THE MORE I TRIED TO FIGURE OUT WHAT IT WAS, THE FURTHER IT RECEDED: CHINESE FINGER-PUZZLE TIME.

I STOPPED TRYING, TOLD MYSELF IT WOULD COME TO ME.

RAPID THRUSTS, WITHDRAWAL, THE MILKY PROOF OF CLIMAX FLYING THROUGH THE AIR.

SHARON WINKING AT THE CAMERA AFTER LICKING HER FINGERS.

BLANK SCREEN. I FELT SUFFOCATED, ANGRY, SAD.

EXCUSE ME, I... I HAVE SOMETHING TO ATTEND TO.

I FOUND SOME WORDS THAT DIDN'T INVOLVE SHARON... FORCED THEM OUT.

YOU SAID "THE **LATE** MICHAEL STARBUCK." HOW DID HE DIE?

COCAINE OVERDOSE, SEVERAL YEARS AGO. HE WANTED TO BREAK INTO STRAIGHT FILMS BUT COULDN'T. THERE'S **TERRIBLE** DISCRIMINATION AGAINST EXPLICIT STARS. ENDED UP DRIVING A CAB.

PRETTY SHARON JUST MADE THE ONE FILM, OF COURSE. IT WAS **SUPPOSED** TO BE FOR EDUCATIONAL PURPOSES. THAT'S WHY WE AGREED TO PUT UP THE MONEY.

THAT COCKROACH KRUSE ASSURED US IT WAS ON THE UP-AND-UP. WHEN I SAW THE FINISHED PRODUCT I KNEW **PRECISELY** WHAT HE'D DONE.

WHAT HE'D DONE?

YES. SIT BACK DOWN...

"...I'LL SHOW YOU."

THIS ONE HAD NO TITLE, NO CREDITS. JUST GRAINY, JUMPY ACTION, THE CAMERA WORK EVEN MORE AMATEURISH THAN THE FIRST...

...BUT CLEARLY ITS INSPIRATION.

THE STAR: SEVERAL INCHES SHORTER THAN SHARON, THE BONES SMALLER, THE FACE SLIGHTLY FULLER. SIMILAR ENOUGH TO BE HER TWIN.

TWIN SISTER. NO, THAT WAS IMPOSSIBLE. COULDN'T BE THE SHIRLEE I'D MET.

IF SHARON HAD TOLD THE TRUTH. BIG IF.

A CRUDE RESEMBLANCE TO MICKEY STARBUCK, BUT NOTHING STRIKING. AND NO LEER. GENUINE SURPRISE.

THE SAME PROGRESSION AS IN SHARON'S FILM. BUT DIFFERENT.

BECAUSE THIS ONE WASN'T STAGED. THE DOCTOR WASN'T ACTING.

NO MUGGING FOR THE CAMERA BECAUSE HE DIDN'T KNOW THERE WAS A CAMERA.

1952.

WHEN WAS THAT ONE MADE?

SHARON'S MOTHER.

I CAN'T PROVE IT, BUT WITH THE RESEMBLANCE SHE'D HAVE TO BE, WOULDN'T SHE?

WHEN I SAW KRUSE'S FINAL PRODUCT, I KNEW WHAT HE—WELL, WE GAVE HIM FULL ACCESS TO OUR COLLECTION.

HE FOUND LINDA'S FILM AND SET OUT TO APE IT.

MOTHER AND DAUGHTER. AN **INTRIGUING** THEME, BUT HE SHOULD HAVE BEEN TRUTHFUL ABOUT IT.

LINDA WHO?

LINDA LANIER. ONE OF THE PRETTY LITTLE THINGS THAT FLOODED HOLLYWOOD AFTER THE WAR. STILL DO, I GUESS.

SHE HAD A CONTRACT FOR A STUDIO OWNED BY LELAND BELDING. NEVER WORKED, THOUGH. BECAME ONE OF BELDING'S PARTY GIRLS.

THE BASKET-CASE BILLIONAIRE... THE MAGNA COR-PORATION.

YES. QUITE A RENAISSANCE MAN IN HIS DAY. AEROSPACE, ARMAMENTS, SHIPPING, MINING, MOVIES.

HE USED TO THROW A LOT OF PARTIES. OWNING A STUDIO GAVE HIM EASY ACCESS TO BEAUTIFUL GIRLS. HE HIRED THEM AS HOSTESSES.

THE MAN IN THE FILM WAS A REAL DOCTOR. THE FILM WAS REAL, TOO— THE **VÉRITÉ** IS ALMOST OVERWHELMING, ISN'T IT?

THIS IS THE ORIGINAL AND ONLY SURVIVING PRINT. COST ME PLENTY. I COULD MAKE COPIES AND SELL THEM, BUT THAT WOULD DILUTE THE VALUE OF THE ORIGINAL. I REFUSE TO BEND MY PRINCIPLES.

WHO WAS THE DOCTOR?

OH, I DON'T KNOW.

A LIE? WOULD A FANATIC AND VOYEUR LIKE FONTAINE HAVE RESTED BEFORE GLEANING EVERY LAST DETAIL ABOUT HIS TREASURE?

THE FILM WAS PART OF A **BLACKMAIL** PLOY, WASN'T IT? THE DOCTOR WAS THE VICTIM.

NONSENSE. JUST A HOLLYWOOD PRACTI-CAL JOKE. OLD ERROL FLYNN BORED PEEPHOLES IN THE WALLS OF HIS BATHROOMS, USED A HIDDEN CAMERA TO FILM HIS LADY FRIENDS ON THE COMMODE.

TACKY.

I'M **SORRY** YOU FEEL THAT WAY, DR. DASCHOFF. IT WAS ALL IN THE SPIRIT OF FUN.

NOW... I'M SURE YOU GENTLEMEN HAVE TO GET BACK TO YOUR PATIENTS.

POOR OLD GORDON. HIS BELIEF SYSTEM'S UNDER ASSAULT. HE AND CHANTAL LIKE TO THINK THEIR HOBBY IS BENIGN, LIKE STAMP COLLECTING.

YOU DON'T USE *STAMPS* FOR BLACKMAIL.

TWO FILMS. A LINK TO A DEAD BILLIONAIRE. AND KRUSE... HOVERING OVER THE WHOLE DAMNED THING.

KRUSE THE MANIPULATOR. DID HE CONVINCE SHARON THE LOOP WOULD BE A VALUABLE PART OF HER TREATMENT? WORKING THROUGH THE SINS OF HER MOTHER? OR WAS HE JUST CONTROLLING HER...USING HER FOR HIS OWN PURPOSES?

THE ILLUSTRIOUS DR. PAUL KRUSE... DEPARTMENT CHAIR. WONDER HOW THE UNIVERSITY WOULD REACT TO HIS—

HELLO, MAL. THERE MUST BE A PROVERB ABOUT ACCEPTING EXTRAVAGANT GIFTS FROM ATTORNEYS.

WHY THE GRATUITY?

SEVEN-FIGURE SETTLEMENT IS WHY. ALL THAT LEGAL TALENT GOT TOGETHER AND DECIDED TO DIVVY UP.

MORETTI DIDN'T EVEN BOTHER TO PLAY HARD TO GET. DENISE AND THE LITTLE DARREN HAVE WON THE LOTTERY, DOCTOR.

WELL, BEING RICH SHOULD HELP, BUT SURE, I'LL PUSH HER AGAIN ON THE THERAPY.

BY THE WAY, MORETTI ASKED FOR YOUR NUMBER. HE WAS IMPRESSED.

FLATTERED. DO ME A FAVOR. WHEN YOU GIVE IT TO HIM...

...TELL HIM WHERE HE CAN SHOVE IT.

I CALLED MY SERVICE AFTER MAL. LESLIE WEINGARDEN HAD LEFT A MESSAGE JUST BEFORE I GOT HOME.

SOMETHING ABOUT A CRISIS.

GOD, WISH I STILL SMOKED. THANKS FOR COMING.

WHAT'S UP?

D.J. RASMUSSEN. HE'S DEAD. HIS GIRLFRIEND'S INSIDE, TOTALLY COMING APART. SHE WALKED IN...BROKE DOWN IN THE WAITING ROOM.

I HUSTLED HER IN HERE AND GAVE HER A SHOT OF VALIUM.

HELPED FOR A WHILE, BUT NOW SHE'S COMING APART AGAIN. THINK YOU CAN DO ANYTHING BY TALKING TO HER?

HOW DID HE DIE?

"CARMEN, THE GIRLFRIEND, SAID HE'D BEEN DRINKING HEAVILY FOR A FEW DAYS. MORE THAN USUAL. SHE WAS AFRAID HE'D GET ROUGH WITH HER...THE USUAL PATTERN."

"BUT INSTEAD HE GOT WEEPY, DEEPLY DEPRESSED...STARTED TALKING ABOUT WHAT A BAD PERSON HE WAS, ALL THE TERRIBLE THINGS HE'D DONE. SHE TRIED TO TALK TO HIM BUT HE JUST GOT LOWER, KEPT DRINKING."

Goodbye -D.J.

"THIS MORNING HE'S GONE...LEFT A BUNCH OF CASH AND A NOTE. HE TOOK ALL HIS GUNS WITH HIM."

"CARMEN FOUND HIM IN THE DRIVEWAY, STINKING OF BOOZE. SHE TRIED TO STOP HIM BUT HE SHOVED HER AWAY AND DROVE OFF."

D.J. RASMUSSEN CARPENTRY & FRAM P.O. BOX 18248

"SHE FOLLOWED HIM AS BEST SHE COULD. HE WAS SPEEDING... WEAVING."

"HE WENT OVER AN EMBANKMENT."

"THE TRUCK ROLLED OVER AT THE BOTTOM AND EXPLODED. JUST LIKE ON TV, SHE SAID."

"CAN YOU IMAGINE?"

DO THE POLICE KNOW ABOUT THIS?

PRIVATE

SHE CALLED THEM. THEY TOOK HER STATEMENT AND SENT HER HOME. SHE HEARD ONE OF THEM MUTTER, "FUCKING STREETS ARE SAFER NOW."

CAN YOU HELP?

CARMEN, THIS IS DR. DELAWARE. DR. DELAWARE, CARMEN SEEBER.

CARMEN, DR. DELAWARE'S A PSYCHOLOGIST. YOU CAN TALK TO HIM.

HI, CARMEN. DR. WEINGARDEN TOLD ME ABOUT D.J. I'M VERY SORRY.

IS THERE ANYTHING I CAN DO FOR YOU, CARMEN? ANYTHING YOU NEED?

I MET D.J. ONCE. HE SEEMED A VERY TROUBLED PERSON.

IT MUST HAVE BEEN HARD FOR YOU, LIVING WITH HIM...ALL THE DRINKING. BUT EVEN SO, YOU MISS HIM TERRIBLY. IT'S HARD TO BELIEVE HE'S GONE.

OH, GOD! OH, GOD! OH, GOD, HELP ME! OH, GOD!

IT'S OKAY, CARMEN. IT'S OKAY TO HURT.

YOU'RE A NICE MAN.

THANK YOU.

MY PAPA WAS A NICE MAN. HE YA KNOW DIED.

HE LEFT A LONG TIME AGO, WHEN I WAS IN YA KNOW KINDERGARTEN. I CAME HOME WITH STUFF WE MADE FOR THANKS-GIVING...YA KNOW PAPER TURKEYS AND PILGRIM HATS...AND I SAW THEM TAKE HIM AWAY IN THE AMBULANCE.

HOW OLD ARE YOU, CARMEN?

TWENTY.

YOU'VE DEALT WITH A **LOT** IN TWENTY YEARS.

I GUESS SO. AND NOW DANNY. HE WAS YA KNOW NICE, TOO, EVEN THOUGH HE WAS A MEAN ONE WHEN HE DRANK. BUT DEEP DOWN, NICE.

HE DIDN'T YA KNOW GIVE ME NO HASSLES, TOOK ME PLACES, GOT ME YA KNOW ALL KINDS OF STUFF.

I NEVER, EVER THOUGHT HE'D REALLY YA KNOW DO IT.

WHEN HE DRANK AND GOT ALL P.O.'D, YA KNOW, HE'D GO ON ABOUT HOW YA KNOW LIFE SUCKED, IT WAS BETTER TO BE DEAD, YA KNOW, HE WAS GONNA DO IT SOME DAY, TELL EVERYONE THE F-WORD OFF.

THEN WHEN HE HURT HIS BACK...YA KNOW THE PAIN, OUT OF WORK...HE WAS REAL LOW. BUT I NEVER THOUGHT...

THERE WAS NO WAY TO KNOW, CARMEN. WHEN A PERSON MAKES UP HIS MIND TO KILL HIMSELF, THERE'S NO WAY TO STOP HIM.

DR. WEINGARDEN SAID HE TALKED ABOUT SOME BAD THINGS HE'D DONE.

HE WAS PRETTY BROKE UP. SAID HE WAS A SINNER. HE USED TO YA KNOW GET IN FIGHTS.

HE WAS LITTLE BUT TOUGH. **SCRAPPY.** HE'D DRINK AND SMOKE AND GET MORE SCRAPPY, BUT HE WAS A GOOD DUDE YA KNOW.

DO YOU HAVE FAMILY IN TOWN, CARMEN?

I DON'T GOT NO FAMILY. NEITHER DID DANNY. HIS PAPA BEAT HIM UP ALL THE TIME AND IT TURNED HIM YA KNOW ANGRY AT THE WORLD. THAT'S WHY HE...

HE WHAT, CARMEN?

OFFED HIM.

D.J. KILLED HIS FATHER?

WHEN HE WAS A KID...SELF-DEFENSE!

BUT THE COPS DID A NUMBER ON HIM—THEY SENT HIM TO YA KNOW CYA TILL HE WAS EIGHTEEN. HE GOT OUT AND DID HIS OWN THING BUT HE DIDN'T LIKE NO FRIENDS.

ALL HE LIKED WAS ME AND THE DOGS... WE GOT TWO ROTTWEILER MIXES, DANDY AND PACO. THEY LIKED HIM A LOT.

THEY BEEN CRYING ALL DAY, GOING TO MISS HIM SOMETHING BAD.

CARMEN, YOU'RE GOING THROUGH HARD TIMES. IT WILL HELP TO HAVE SOMEONE TO TALK TO.

I COULD TALK TO YOU.

I'M A CHILD PSYCHOLOGIST. I WORK WITH CHILDREN.

THE PERSON I WANT TO REFER YOU TO IS VERY NICE, VERY EXPERIENCED.

CARMEN, IF I TALK TO HER ABOUT YOU AND GET YOU HER NUMBER, WILL YOU CALL?

A HER? NO WAY! I DON'T WANT NO LADY DOCTOR.

DANNY HAD A LADY DOCTOR. SHE MESSED WITH HIM.

MESSED WITH HIM?

YA KNOW **BALLIN'** HIM. HE ALWAYS SAID, BULLSHIT, CARMEN, WE NEVER DONE IT.

BUT HE'D COME BACK FROM YA KNOW SEEIN' HER AND HAVE THAT YA KNOW LOOK IN HIS EYES AND HE'D SMELL ALL OF LOVIN'... DISGUSTIN'.

DR. SMALL, THE PERSON I WANT TO SEND YOU TO, IS IN HER FIFTIES, VERY KIND, WOULD NEVER DO ANYTHING DIS-HONEST.

CARMEN, I'VE SEEN HER MYSELF. SHE WAS MY DOCTOR.

YOU? WHAT FOR?

SOMETIMES I NEED TO TALK, TOO. EVERYONE DOES.

NOW PROMISE ME TO GO SEE HER ONCE. IF YOU DON'T LIKE HER, I'LL GET YOU SOMEONE ELSE.

I JUST DON'T THINK IT'S RIGHT... HER BALLING HIM. A DOCTOR SHOULD, YA KNOW, KNOW BETTER.

YOU'RE ABSOLUTELY RIGHT.

SOME DOCTORS SHOULDN'T BE DOCTORS.

CARMEN, I'LL STAY HERE WITH YOU AS LONG AS YOU NEED ME TO. ALL RIGHT?

ALL RIGHT, CARMEN?

AS LONG AS YOU NEED.

HOW'S SHE LOOK TO YOU?

PRETTY FRAGILE AND SHE'S STILL CUSHIONED BY SHOCK. THE NEXT FEW DAYS COULD GET REALLY BAD. SHE DOESN'T HAVE ANY SUPPORT SYSTEM.

IT'S **REALLY** IMPORTANT FOR HER TO BE SEEING SOMEONE.

I'LL DRIVE HER MYSELF. THE PERSON YOU'RE REFERRING TO IS GOOD?

THE **BEST**. I'VE SEEN HER MYSELF.

CALIFORNIA HONESTY.

JESUS, I'M SORRY. YOU'VE BEEN REALLY NICE, COMING HERE ON NO NOTICE. I'VE BECOME A TOTAL CYNIC. I KNOW IT'S NOT HEALTHY.

ALL THIS CRAP. RANSOM... **KRUSE**...

I KNOW. IT'S TOUGH.

LISTEN, I REALLY DO WANT TO THANK YOU FOR COMING DOWN HERE.

TELL ME WHAT YOUR FEE IS AND I'LL WRITE A CHECK RIGHT NOW.

NO WAY, LESLIE. I NEVER EXPECTED TO GET PAID.

AND, FOR WHAT IT'S WORTH, YOU'RE DOING THE RIGHT THING WITH CARMEN.

IT MEANS A LOT. THANK YOU.

THAT WAS STUPID.

SHE WAS OFF TO THE NEXT PATIENT BEFORE I COULD TELL HER IT WASN'T.

KRUSE.

I DROVE STRAIGHT TO HIS HOUSE AFTER LEAVING LESLIE'S OFFICE. IT WAS ALREADY DARK WHEN I GOT THERE. FEELING MY BLOOD PUMP AS I WALKED TO THE FRONT DOOR I WAS AWARE, SUDDENLY, THAT MY ENERGY HAD RETURNED.

FOR THE FIRST TIME IN A LONG WHILE I FELT IMBUED WITH **PURPOSE**, RIGHTEOUS WITH ANGER. NOTHING LIKE AN ENEMY TO CLEANSE ONE'S SOUL.

ALL THE CARS IN THE DRIVE, BUT NO LIGHTS INSIDE.

NOK-NOK-NOKK

KLICK

LIGHTS CLICKED ON AROUND THE POOL AND YARD.

TIMERS.

THE SOUR SMELL OF MILDEW...
AND SOMETHING STRONGER.

A SWIM INTERRUPTED...

I GAGGED, LOOKED AWAY, SAW HIGH, BEAMED CEILINGS, OVERSTUFFED FURNITURE.

TASTEFUL. GOOD DECORATOR.

THEN BACK DOWN TO THE HORROR...

I STARED AT THE CARPET. TRIED TO LOSE MYSELF IN THE DAMN THING. GOOD WEAVE. IMMACULATE.

EXCEPT FOR THE BLACKENING STAINS...

I BENT LOW, SMELLING THE FLOWERS' PERFUME. SWEET. TOO SWEET.

MY GUT CHURNED. I TRIED TO VOMIT BUT COULDN'T.

I STUMBLED ACROSS THE MANICURED LAWN WITH THE TIMED, COLORED LIGHTS. ORDERLY...PRECISE...BEAUTIFUL.

I FOUND A PHARMACY AND A PHONE BOOTH IN BRENTWOOD. GOT MILO ON THE FIRST RING. ALSO GOT SOME CHEAP PANATELAS.

STRONG ENOUGH TO DRIVE THE STENCH FROM MY MOUTH.

WHY'D YOU COME UP HERE, ALEX?

I TOLD HIM ABOUT THE PORN LOOPS, D.J. RASMUSSEN'S FATAL ACCIDENT, LELAND BELDING'S NAME POPPING UP.

KRUSE'S HAND RUNS THROUGH MOST OF IT.

NOT MUCH HAND LEFT. BODIES HAVE BEEN THERE FOR A WHILE.

WHAT'D YOU TOUCH IN THERE?

THE LIGHT SWITCH AND THE GATE. THAT'S IT.

ALL RIGHT. CRIME SCENE BOYS SHOULD BE HERE ANY MINUTE. GO ON. DISAPPEAR BEFORE THE PARTY BEGINS.

MILO—

GO ON, ALEX. LET ME DO THE DAMNED JOB.

EVERYTHING SHARON HAD TOUCHED WAS TURNING TO DEATH.

I FOUND MYSELF WONDERING WHAT HAD MADE HER THAT WAY. WHAT KIND OF EARLY TRAUMA.

THE WAY SHE'D ACTED THE NIGHT I'D FOUND HER WITH THE TWIN PHOTO. THRASHING, SCREAMING, COLLAPSING. SIMILAR TO DARREN BURKHALTER'S BEHAVIOR IN MY OFFICE. EARLY CHILDHOOD TRAUMA.

SHE'D EXPLAINED IT TO ME ONCE. FOLLOWED IT UP WITH A DISPLAY OF TENDER, LOVING KINDNESS. LOOKING BACK, A WELL-STAGED DISPLAY. ANOTHER ACT?

THE SUMMER OF '81, A HOTEL COCKTAIL LOUNGE IN NEWPORT BEACH, SWARMING WITH PSYCHOLOGIST CONVENTIONEERS.

IT'S GOOD TO SEE YOU AGAIN.

I WANTED TO SEE YOU.

WHAT ABOUT?

I WANTED TO EXPLAIN.

THERE'S NOTHING TO EXPLAIN, SHARON. ANCIENT HISTORY.

NOT TO ME.

BELIEVE ME, I KNOW I BLEW IT. BUT, AFTER ALL THIS TIME, YOU'RE STILL WITH ME.

GOOD MEMORIES. SPECIAL MEMORIES. POSITIVE ENERGY.

SELECTIVE PERCEPTION.

NO. WE DID HAVE SOME WONDERFUL TIMES, ALEX. I'LL NEVER LET GO OF THAT.

WHAT WE HAD WAS SPECIAL, ALEX, AND I ALLOWED IT TO BE DESTROYED.

ALLOWED IT? THAT SOUNDS PRETTY PASSIVE.

ALL RIGHT, I DESTROYED IT. I WAS CRAZY. IT WAS A CRAZY TIME IN MY LIFE.

DON'T THINK I HAVEN'T REGRETTED IT A THOUSAND TIMES.

ALEX, MEETING YOU HERE TODAY WAS NO ACCIDENT. I SAW YOUR NAME ON THE CONVENTION PROGRAM AND WANTED TO SEE YOU AGAIN.

I WANTED TO—

TO WHAT? YOU WANT TO BE FRIENDS? BURY THE PAST? CONSIDER IT DONE. MISSION ACCOMPLISHED.

PLEASE, ALEX, DON'T BE VINDICTIVE. LET ME SHOW YOU.

LET ME SHOW YOU SOMETHING I'VE NEVER SHOWN ANYONE.

I FOLLOWED HER TO AN ADDRESS ON THE SOUTH SIDE OF GLENDALE. SEPARATE CARS, "SO YOU CAN ESCAPE ANY TIME YOU WANT."

BZ-ZZZZZ

AFTERNOON, DR. RANSOM.

AFTERNOON, ELMO. THIS IS DR. DELAWARE, A FRIEND OF MINE.

PLEASED TO MEET YOU, SIR.

SHE'S ALL PRETTIED UP AND READY FOR YOU, DR. RANSOM.

THAT'S GREAT, ELMO. THANK YOU.

I'D BEEN SO FOCUSED ON MY RESENTMENT TOWARD SHARON THAT I HADN'T REALLY TAKEN TIME TO BUILD EXPECTATIONS FOR WHERE SHE WAS TAKING ME.

I WOULDN'T HAVE IMAGINED THIS...A SEA OF PANDEMONIUM. SCORES OF BODIES: TWITCHING, STUMBLING, BRUTALIZED BY NATURE AND THE LUCK OF THE DRAW.

AND EVERYWHERE, MOVEMENT. A RANDOM BALLET.

THE ATTENDANTS...FAR TOO ABSORBED IN THEIR AFTERNOON GAME SHOW TO NOTICE OUR PASSING.

THE PATIENTS NOTICED. AS IF MAGNETIZED, THEY SWARMED TOWARD SHARON.

SHARON HANDED OUT CANDY FROM HER PURSE. SHE'D BEEN PREPARED FOR THIS.

SHE LOOKED HAPPIER THAN I'D EVER SEEN HER... COMPLETE.

A STORYBOOK PRINCESS REIGNING OVER A KINGDOM OF THE MISSHAPEN.

THAT'S ALL, PEOPLE. GOTTA GO.

HERE, THE AIR WAS FRESH, WITH A TRACE OF FLOWERS.

SOFT MUSIC...THE BEATLES AS INTERPRETED BY A SOMNOLENT STRING ORCHESTRA.

AS WE LEFT THE LONG ROOM OF PATIENTS BEHIND, THE SMELLS OF THE FACILITY BEGAN TO SOFTEN.

HER SKIN WAS GRAY-WHITE. HER EYES DEEP BLUE...THE SAME COLOR AS SHARON'S, BUT FILMED AND IMMOBILE.

SOMEWHERE IN THE RUINS OF A FACE THAT WAS MORE JUST A SKETCH OF A FACE, RESEMBLANCE. A HINT OF SHARON.

THE ONLY SOUND FROM THE WOMAN ON THE BED WAS SHALLOW BREATHING THAT DISAPPEARED BEFORE BEING HERALDED AGAIN BY A FAINT SQUEEZE-TOY SQUEAK.

IT'S GOOD TO SEE YOU, DARLING. ELMO SAYS YOU'RE DOING JUST FINE.

SHIRLEE, WE HAVE A VISITOR. HIS NAME IS DR. ALEX DELAWARE. HE'S A NICE MAN. ALEX, MEET MISS SHIRLEE RANSOM.

MY SISTER. MY TWIN. MY SILENT PARTNER.

CLINICALLY, SHE'S DEAF AND BLIND... MINIMAL CORTICAL FUNCTIONING. BUT I KNOW SHE SENSES PEOPLE. I CAN *FEEL* IT. SHE GIVES OFF SMALL VIBRATIONS.

ISN'T THAT TRUE, DARLING? YOU *DO* KNOW WHAT'S GOING ON, *DON'T* YOU? YOU'RE FAIRLY *HUMMING* TODAY.

SAY SOME-THING TO HER, ALEX.

HELLO, SHIRLEE.

NOTHING.

THERE. SHE'S HUMMING.

ALEX *DELAWARE*, DARLING. THE ONE I'VE TOLD YOU ABOUT, SHIRL. SO *HANDSOME*, ISN'T HE? HANDSOME AND GOOD.

I WAITED AS SHARON TALKED TO A WOMAN WHO COULDN'T HEAR. SANG, PRATTLED ON ABOUT FASHION, MUSIC, RECIPES, CURRENT EVENTS.

SHE TURNED HER SISTER OVER, MASSAGING AND SEARCHING FOR BED SORES. BEFORE WE LEFT, SHE GAVE SHIRLEE'S HAIR A HUNDRED STROKES WITH A TORTOISESHELL BRUSH.

WE WERE BORN ABSOLUTELY IDENTICAL. NO ONE COULD TELL US APART. SOMETIMES WE COULDN'T TELL OUR-SELVES APART.

I REMEMBERED THE PHOTO OF THE TWO LITTLE GIRLS.

ONE DIFFERENCE: MIRROR-IMAGE IDENTICAL.

YES. THAT'S RIGHT... SHE'S A LEFTY, I'M A RIGHTY. AND OUR HAIR WHIRLS IN DIFFERENT DIRECTIONS.

CARBON COPIES. INSEPARABLE. WE LOVED EACH OTHER WITH A GUT INTEN-SITY. WE DID EVERYTHING TOGETHER, CRIED HYSTERICALLY WHEN ANYONE TRIED TO SEPARATE US, UNTIL FINALLY NO ONE TRIED.

I KNOW HOW IT SOUNDS, BUT WE WERE MORE THAN SISTERS... MORE THAN TWINS. PSYCHIC PARTNERS.

EACH OF US ONLY FELT WHOLE WHEN IN THE PRES-ENCE OF THE OTHER.

IT DOESN'T SOUND STRANGE. I'VE HEARD IT BEFORE.

"THANK YOU FOR SAYING THAT, ALEX."

"WHEN WE WERE LITTLE, WE HAD A WONDERFUL LIFE TOGETHER. PARK AVENUE, AND THE SUMMER HOUSE IN SOUTHAMPTON. THERE WAS A POOL WITH A HOUSE OVER IT. WE WERE SUPPOSED TO STAY AWAY FROM THERE WHEN IT WAS DRAINED. OF COURSE, WE NEVER DID."

"THE WATER LEFT IN THE POOL WAS MIXED WITH CLEANING CHEMICALS...ACID-GREEN AND BUBBLING. IT WREAKED OF SULFUR. IT WAS MONSTROUS. WE LOVED IT!"

"OUR GALOSHES WERE SLICK AND WE WERE SKIDDING ALL OVER THE PLACE, PRETENDING WE WERE AT AN ICE RINK. WE WERE HAVING A GREAT TIME, LOST IN THE MOMENT TOGETHER, AS IF WE WERE ONE SELF."

"THEN I SAW SHIRLEE TAKE A BIG SKID...AND JUST KEEP SKIDDING."

"THE NANNY WAS ASKING ME WHERE SHIRLEE WAS. I COULDN'T ANSWER."

"I COULDN'T EVEN SCREAM ANYMORE. I *KNEW* SHIRLEE WAS DROWNING BECAUSE *I* WAS DROWNING. *CHOKING* AND *SUFFOCATING* ON THE PUTRID WATER."

"SOMEHOW I MANAGED TO POINT TO THE POOL."

"DADDY PULLED HER OUT. LIMP, COVERED WITH FILTH, PALE AND DEAD-LOOKING."

EVERYONE WAS SCREAMING... SOBBING. THE CARETAKERS WERE STARING. AT ME, I THOUGHT. THEY WERE *BLAMING* ME!

"I STARTED TO HOWL AND CLAW AT THEM. SOMEONE SAID 'TAKE HER OUT' AND EVERYTHING WENT BLACK."

I WOKE UP BACK ON PARK AVENUE...THE NEXT DAY. SOMEONE MUST HAVE SEDATED ME. THEY TOLD ME SHIRLEE HAD DIED, HAD BEEN BURIED.

NOTHING MORE WAS EVER SAID ABOUT HER. MY LIFE WAS CHANGED, EMPTY...I HAD TO LEARN TO BE A NEW PERSON. A PARTNER WITHOUT A PARTNER.

I CAME TO ACCEPT, LIVED IN MY HEAD, AWAY FROM THE WORLD. EVENTUALLY I STOPPED THINKING ABOUT SHIRLEE...CONSCIOUSLY STOPPED. I WENT THROUGH THE MOTIONS, BEING A GOOD GIRL.

GETTING GOOD GRADES, NEVER RAISING MY VOICE. BUT I WAS EMPTY...MISSING SOMETHING.

I DECIDED TO BECOME A PSYCHOLOGIST, TO LEARN WHY.

I MOVED OUT HERE, MET YOU, STARTED TO REALLY LIVE.

THEN, EVERYTHING CHANGED—MUMMY AND DADDY DYING. I HAD TO GO BACK EAST TO TALK TO THEIR LAWYER.

HE TOOK ME OUT TO THE RUSSIAN TEA ROOM AND TOLD ME ABOUT MY TRUST FUND, THE HOUSE, TALKED A LOT ABOUT NEW RESPONSIBILITIES. WHEN I ASKED HIM WHAT HE MEANT, HE LOOKED UNEASY, CALLED FOR THE CHECK.

"THE NIGHT YOU FOUND ME HOLDING THE SNAPSHOT WAS SOON AFTER SHIRLEE HAD BEEN FLOWN OUT. I HADN'T SLEPT FOR DAYS, WAS WIRED **AND** FATIGUED. THE PHOTO HAD BEEN IN MUMMY'S PURSE THE DAY SHE DIED."

HE FINALLY TOLD ME ABOUT SHIRLEE. SHE'D NEVER DIED, HAD BEEN COMATOSE WHEN DADDY PULLED HER OUT OF THE POOL.

ALL THAT TIME SHE'D BEEN LIVING IN AN INSTITUTION. THEY JUST SENT HER AWAY. I WAS **FURIOUS.** I DEMANDED SHE BE FLOWN OUT HERE. I FOUND THIS PLACE.

"I STARTED STARING AT IT, **FELL** INTO IT LIKE ALICE DOWN THE HOLE. I FELT AS IF THE PHOTO WAS CAPTURING ME... EATING ME UP THE WAY THE POOL HAD EATEN SHIRLEE. I WAS HANGING BY A THREAD WHEN YOU CAME IN."

I'M SO SORRY.

I NEVER **HEARD** YOU, ALEX. NOT UNTIL YOU WERE STANDING OVER ME. AND YOU SEEMED **ANGRY**... JUDGING ME. DIS-APPROVING.

WHEN YOU TOOK THE PICTURE, IT FELT LIKE YOU'D **INVADED** ME...FORCED YOUR WAY INTO MY PRIVATE PAIN. IT WAS TOO MUCH. I JUST BLEW.

THE NEXT COUPLE OF WEEKS WERE **HORRIBLE**, JUST A **NIGHTMARE.** I WORRIED WHAT I'D DONE TO YOU AND ME, BUT I HAD SO MUCH TO DEAL WITH.

MY RAGE AT MY PARENTS FOR LYING. MY RAGE AT SHIRLEE FOR COMING BACK SO DAMAGED, FOR BEING UN-ABLE TO RESPOND TO MY LOVE. I DIDN'T REALIZE YET THAT SHE WAS VIBRATING, COMMUNI-CATING WITH ME.

SO MANY CHANGES. IT WAS LIKE A JUMBLE OF LIVE WIRES BURNING INTO MY BRAIN. I GOT HELP.

KRUSE.

WHATEVER YOU MAY THINK OF PAUL, HE **HELPED** ME, ALEX. HELPED PUT ME BACK TOGETHER AGAIN.

"I CARED ABOUT YOU—THAT'S WHY I FINALLY **FORCED** MYSELF TO GET TOGETHER WITH YOU, EVEN THOUGH PAUL SAID I WASN'T READY. HE WAS RIGHT."

"I CAME ON LIKE A NYMPHO BECAUSE I WAS FEELING **WORTHLESS**, OUT OF CONTROL. ACTING LIKE A SEXPOT MADE ME FEEL IN CHARGE. LATER, WHILE YOU SLEPT, I **DESPISED** WHAT I'D DONE, DESPISED YOU."

I DUMPED ON YOU BECAUSE YOU WERE THERE, AND BECAUSE YOU WERE GOOD. I RUINED WHAT WE HAD BECAUSE I WAS UNABLE TO TOLERATE GOODNESS, ALEX.

I DIDN'T FEEL I DESERVED GOODNESS. AND AFTER ALL THESE YEARS, I STILL REGRET THAT.

SHARON...

I KNOW. NOT AGAIN.

HOW COULD YOU **EVER** KNOW YOU'D BE SAFE WITH ME?

"NO REASON TO EXPLAIN, ALEX. ANCIENT HISTORY. I JUST WANTED TO SHOW YOU THAT I'M NOT ALL BAD."

MUMMY AND DADDY. GENTEEL CARDBOARD CUTOUTS. BUT I'D SEEN A FILM THAT SAID MUMMY WAS **ANYTHING** BUT GENTEEL.

IF SHE LOVED SHIRLEE SO MUCH, HOW COULD SHE KILL HERSELF. S & S, MIRROR-IMAGE TWINS. SUDDENLY IT HIT ME WHAT WAS OFF ABOUT THE PORN LOOP...THE INCONGRUITY THAT HAD STAYED UNDER MY SKIN.

SHARON WAS RIGHT-HANDED BUT IN THE FILM...STROKING, KNEADING... SHE'D FAVORED HER LEFT.

AND THE DETAIL OF THE DROWNING STORY... TOO VIVID FOR A TODDLER TO REMEMBER. PRACTICED? COACHED? HER MEMORY ENHANCED? HYPNOSIS...AS IN PAUL KRUSE?

I WAS CERTAIN NOW THAT HE'D KNOWN ENOUGH TO FILL IN LOTS OF BLANKS...HAD DIED HORRIBLY WITH THAT KNOWLEDGE. I WANTED, MORE THAN EVER, TO FIND OUT WHY.

"I'LL LET YOU GO NOW."

FEELING SOMEHOW INFECTED, I CANCELED MY FLIGHT TO SAN LUIS AND TURNED ON THE TV, SEEKING SOME ELECTRONIC COMPANIONSHIP.

THE KRUSE MURDERS WERE THE LEAD ON THE NEWS. PAUL, SUZANNE, AND LOURDES ESCOBAR, AGE TWENTY-TWO. THE MAID. BACKGROUND ON THE VICTIMS.

A MENTION OF KRUSE'S PARK AVENUE CHILDHOOD. MORE SOURCE MATERIAL FOR SHARON? TRAPP TOOK THE SCREEN, READING A PREPARED STATEMENT. I HOPED MILO HAD STEERED CLEAR OF THE BASTARD AT THE SCENE.

I LIE IN BED FOR WHAT SEEMED LIKE HOURS, TRYING TO FILL MY HEAD WITH PLEASANT VISIONS. NONE STUCK.

I WOKE UP WITH TOO MANY QUESTIONS SWIMMING AROUND IN MY HEAD...DRESSED AND HEADED OUT IN SEARCH OF ANSWERS.

SHARON HAD LIVED LIKE A RICH GIRL...THE CLOTHES, THE CAR, THE HOUSE. PERHAPS LINDA LANIER HAD MARRIED MONEY?

PASSING ALONG TO HER DAUGHTER A CHOICE PIECE OF REAL ESTATE ONCE OWNED BY A DEAD BILLIONAIRE. STILL DEEDED TO THAT BILLIONAIRE'S CORPORATION AND PUT UP ON THE MARKET THE DAY AFTER SHARON DIED.

TWO BOOKS AND DOZENS OF ARTICLES ON LELAND BELDING IN THE RESEARCH LIBRARY, STRETCHING FROM THE THIRTIES TO THE SEVENTIES. NOTHING ON LINDA LANIER.

THE EARLIEST PIECES ON LELAND BELDING WERE WRITTEN WHILE HE WAS STILL IN HIS TWENTIES. BELDING WAS HAILED AS A PRODIGY, A MASTER DESIGNER OF AIRCRAFT WITH SCORES OF PATENTS.

BELDING'S ENORMOUS WEALTH, PRECOCITY, BOYISH GOOD LOOKS, AND SHYNESS MADE HIM A NATURAL MEDIA HERO. ONE ARTICLE DUBBED HIM THE MOST ELIGIBLE BACHELOR OF 1937.

HE'D BEEN BORN TO WEALTH, IN 1910, THE ONLY CHILD OF AN HEIRESS FROM NEWPORT, RHODE ISLAND, AND A TEXAS OIL WILDCATTER TURNED GENTLEMAN RANCHER.

WHEN LELAND WAS NINETEEN BOTH PARENTS PERISHED IN A CAR CRASH AFTER A PARTY NEAR THEIR VILLA ON THE SPANISH ISLAND OF IBIZA. ANOTHER LAYER.

LELAND DROPPED OUT OF COLLEGE AND RETURNED TO HOUSTON TO RUN THE FAMILY OIL BUSINESS.

A YEAR LATER HE TOOK FLYING LESSONS, PROVING TO BE A NATURAL PILOT. HE DEVOTED HIMSELF TO AIRPLANE CONSTRUCTION. WITHIN FIVE YEARS HE FLOODED THE AEROSPACE INDUSTRY WITH TECHNICAL INNOVATIONS.

HE BUCKED THE MOB TO CREATE THE CASBAH...THE LARGEST CASINO IN LAS VEGAS AT THE TIME. BY HIS THIRTIETH BIRTHDAY HE WAS ONE OF THE RICHEST MEN IN AMERICA. HE WAS DEFINITELY ITS MOST SECRETIVE. PRIVACY...THE LAST LUXURY.

AFTER WORLD WAR II THE HONEYMOON WITH THE PRESS STARTED TO SOUR. LEFT-LEANING JOURNALISTS BEGAN TO POINT OUT THAT BELDING HAD USED THE WAR TO BECOME A BILLIONAIRE.

TERMS LIKE ROBBER BARON, PROFITEER, AND EXPLOITER OF THE WORKING MAN BEGAN TO CROP UP IN EDITORIALS. ONE WRITER POINTED OUT THAT HE HADN'T GIVEN A PENNY TO THE WAR BOND DRIVE.

RUMORS OF CORRUPTION SOON FOLLOWED—INTIMATIONS THAT ALL THOSE CONTRACTS HADN'T BEEN WON BY PUTTING IN THE LOW BID. BELDING REFUSED TO SHOW UP AT A SENATE SUBCOMMITTEE HEARING. INSTEAD, HE TURNED HIS TALENTS TO MOVIES.

COMMITTEE INVESTIGATORS CLAIMED BELDING HAD SHIFTED THE ODDS ON CONTRACT BIDS BY THROWING "WILD PARTIES" FOR LEGISLATORS. THAT HE WAS LESS CAPTAIN OF INDUSTRY THAN HIGH-CLASS PIMP.

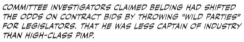

THESE BASHES TOOK PLACE IN SECLUDED HOLLYWOOD HILLS HOUSES PURCHASED BY THE MAGNA CORPORATION EXPRESSLY AS "PARTY PADS," AND FEATURED "STAG MOVIES," "FLOWING BOOZE," AND "YOUNG WOMEN OF LOOSE MORALS."

THESE "PARTY GIRLS" WERE ASPIRING ACTRESSES CHOSEN BY THE HEAD OF BELDING'S STUDIO, WILLIAM HOUCK "BILLY" VIDAL.

THE COMMITTEE ISSUED NOTHING MORE THAN A MILD REPRIMAND. CYNICS SUGGESTED THAT MEMBERS OF CONGRESS MAY HAVE BEEN ON BELDING'S PARTY LIST. PARTY PADS. STAG FILMS. I WANTED TO KNOW A LOT MORE ABOUT BASHFUL BELDING.

COME BACK HOME, ROBIN. WE CAN WORK IT OUT.

AFTER A FEW MORE HOURS SPENT PORING OVER THE DETAILS OF LELAND BELDING'S LIFE, I CALLED ROBIN. WITH THE TRIP TO SEE HER THAT SHE NEVER KNEW ABOUT CANCELED, I STILL CRAVED SOMETHING POSITIVE THERE.

THANK GOD SHE ANSWERED HERSELF. IT WENT AS WELL AS I COULD HAVE HOPED.

A WEEK AGO I WOULD HAVE PUSHED. NOW, WITH GHOSTS TUGGING AT MY HEELS...

I WANT YOU BACK RIGHT NOW, BUT YOU'VE GOT TO DO WHAT'S RIGHT FOR YOURSELF. TAKE YOUR TIME.

YEAH... LOVE YOU TOO.

AH-HUURM.

YEAH... SORRY. SOMEONE'S HERE. MISTER STURGIS.

I'LL TELL HIM. BE WELL, ROBIN.

HELLO, SERGEANT.

MAJOR LEAGUE OOPS. SORRY, BUT THE GODDAMNED DOOR WAS OPEN. HOW MANY TIMES HAVE I TOLD YOU ABOUT THAT?

NO SECRET. TEMPORARY SEPARATION. SHE'S UP IN SAN LUIS OBISPO. WE'LL WORK IT OUT. ANYWAY, YOU PROBABLY FIGURED IT OUT, RIGHT?

I HAD MY SUSPICIONS. YOU'VE BEEN LOOKING STEPPED-ON. AND YOU HAVEN'T BEEN TALKING ABOUT HER THE WAY YOU USUALLY DO.

HOPE YOU GUYS WORK IT OUT. THE TWO OF YOU WERE GOOD.

TRY TO AVOID THE PAST TENSE.

WE SETTLED IN TO TALK ABOUT SOMETHING MORE PLEASANT THAN MY RELATIONSHIP: MURDER.

I FILLED HIM IN ON EVERYTHING, RIGHT UP TO SHARON'S FANTASY CHILDHOOD AND MY RESEARCH. THE EAST COAST SOCIETY BACKGROUND THAT RESEMBLED KRUSE'S, THE ORPHANHOOD THAT ECHOED LELAND BELDING'S.

IT'S AS IF SHE'S COLLECTING FRAGMENTS OF OTHER PEOPLE'S HISTORIES IN ORDER TO BUILD ONE OF HER OWN, MILO.

OKAY, OTHER THAN HER BEING A STONE LIAR, WHAT DOES THAT MEAN?

SERIOUS IDENTITY PROBLEM. WISH FULFILLMENT. MAYBE HER OWN CHILDHOOD WAS FILLED WITH ABUSE OR NEGLECT.

AND THE BELDING CONNECTION IS MORE THAN COINCIDENCE. SHARON'S MOTHER WAS ONE OF BELDING'S PARTY GIRLS. SHARON ENDS UP LIVING IN A HOUSE THAT COULD HAVE BEEN ONE OF HIS PARTY PADS.

SO WHAT ARE YOU SAYING? OLD BASKET CASE WAS HER DADDY?

IT WOULD SURE EXPLAIN THE HIGH-LEVEL COVER-UP, BUT WHO KNOWS?

THE WAY SHE TWISTED THE TRUTH HAS ME DOUBTING **EVERYTHING.**

COP-THINKING.

I CHECKED OUT A COUPLE OF BOOKS ON BELDING. EVEN GOT A COPY OF *THE BASKET-CASE BILLIONAIRE.* MAYBE SOMETHING IN THERE WILL BE USEFUL.

THAT BOOK WAS A SCAM, ALEX. HOW'D YOU FIND IT, ANYWAY? I THOUGHT THE DAMN THING WAS RECALLED.

LARGE LIBRARIES GET ADVANCE COPIES; THE RECALL ORDER ONLY APPLIED TO BOOKSTORES AND COMMERCIAL DISTRIBUTORS. IT'S BEEN BURIED THERE SINCE '73, VERY FEW CHECKOUTS.

AND, SOMETIMES SCAMS ARE LACED WITH A BIT OF TRUTH.

MAYBE.

ANYWAY, MY CORONER SOURCE SAYS THE KRUSE VICTIMS WERE BEATEN AND SHOT. HANDS TIED. SINGLE BULLET IN THE HEAD... EXECUTION-STYLE.

HARD TO PIN DOWN TIME OF DEATH, BUT THEY'D BEEN THERE A WHILE.

THEY WERE AT THAT PARTY LAST SATURDAY...

MEANING THEY COULD HAVE BEEN KILLED EITHER AFTER SHARON DIED, OR BEFORE.

AND IF IT WAS BEFORE, A CERTAIN SCENARIO REARS ITS UGLY HEAD ABOUT RASMUSSEN AND RANSOM.

D.J. PROBABLY HAD HALF HER IQ. SHE WAS PLAYING WITH HIS HEAD. IF SHE HAD A MAJOR BEEF WITH KRUSE AND EVEN HINTED TO RASMUSSEN ABOUT IT...

YOU SAID SHE KNEW HYPNOSIS, RIGHT?

SO SHE COULD HAVE USED IT TO SOFTEN RASMUSSEN UP. ANGLING FOR SOME WHITE-KNIGHT PUSSY, HE WENT AND PLAYED LORD HIGH EXECUTIONER.

KILLING HIS FATHER ALL OVER AGAIN.

AH, YOU SHRINKS. THE MAID AND THE WIFE DIED BECAUSE THEY WERE IN THE WRONG PLACE AT THE WRONG TIME.

I JUST CAN'T SEE HER AS A KILLER, MILO. IT DOESN'T SIT RIGHT.

FORGET IT, THEN. THEORETICAL. THERE'S TOO LITTLE EVIDENCE. CAN'T EVEN LOOK AT THE FILE, 'CAUSE THERE AIN'T NO GODDAMN FILE. COURTESY, TRAPP AND WHO-EVER ELSE IS TRYING TO BURY THIS.

AND THEN THERE'S BELDING, LINDA LANIER, THE BLACKMAILED DOCTOR, AND SHIRLEE, THE MISSING TWIN.

THEY WERE LIKE TWO HALVES OF A WHOLE. TWINS CAN DEVELOP IDENTITY PROBLEMS. SHARON WROTE ABOUT IT IN HER DISSERTATION. TEN TO ONE IT WAS ABOUT HER.

I KNOW A GUY WHO WAS AROUND THIRTY-FIVE YEARS AGO. TRICKY. HE'S UNPREDICTABLE, AND WE'RE NOT EXACTLY GOOD BUDDIES. WHAT THE HELL. WE'LL GO SEE HIM TOMORROW.

YOU KEEP READING. UNCLE MILO WILL BE GIVING YOU A POP QUIZ WHEN YOU LEAST EXPECT IT.

I SPENT THE REST OF THE NIGHT GETTING A MASTER'S DEGREE IN LELAND BELDING.

AFTER THE SENATE REPRIMAND, HE SPENT FIVE YEARS PLAYING IN THE MOVIE BUSINESS. BY 1950 HE HAD GONE INTO DEEPER SECLUSION. IN '52, HE EMERGED AS A NEW MAN.

THE NEW, *PUBLIC* LELAND BELDING GAVE TO CHARITIES, ATTENDED PREMIERES AND DATED STARLETS.

HE MOVED FROM HIS "MONASTIC" APARTMENT AT MAGNA HEADQUARTERS TO AN ESTATE IN BEL AIR. HE BOUGHT EVERY KIND OF TREASURE, FROM RENAISSANCE SCULPTURES TO BASEBALL TEAMS.

THEN, IN '55, BELDING DROPPED COMPLETELY FROM SIGHT. IN 1969, LELAND BELDING'S DEATH WAS REPORTED "SOMEWHERE IN CALIFORNIA, FOLLOWING A PROLONGED ILLNESS." WILLIAM HOUCK VIDAL TOOK OVER MAGNA AS CHAIR OF THE BOARD.

THAT WAS IT, UNTIL 1972, WHEN A FORMER REPORTER NAMED SEAMAN CROSS PRODUCED A BOOK CLAIMING TO BE THE UNAUTHORIZED BIOGRAPHY OF LELAND BELDING.

CROSS CLAIMED BELDING HAD FAKED HIS OWN DEATH. NOW, HE'D DECIDED HE STILL HAD SOMETHING TO SAY TO THE WORLD AND HAD CHOSEN CROSS AS HIS MESSENGER.

CROSS CLAIMED BELDING GRANTED HIM HUNDREDS OF HOURS OF INTERVIEWS BEFORE CHANGING HIS MIND AND CALLING OFF THE PROJECT.

BASKET-CASE BILLIONAIRE

SEAMAN CROS

CROSS COMPLETED THE BOOK ANYWAY, TITLING IT THE BASKET-CASE BILLIONAIRE AND OBTAINING A SIX-FIGURE ADVANCE.

CROSS CLAIMED HE INTERVIEWED BELDING AT A HERMETICALLY SEALED GEODESIC DOME, SOMEWHERE OUT IN THE DESERT, WHICH THE BILLIONAIRE NEVER LEFT.

CROSS WAS DRIVEN, ALWAYS BLINDFOLDED, ALWAYS IN THE MIDDLE OF THE NIGHT, TO A HELIPORT LESS THAN AN HOUR OUT OF L.A., THEN FLOWN TO THE DOME FOR ABOUT TWO HOURS AND WHISKED HOME BEFORE DAWN.

THE DOME WAS EQUIPPED WITH COMPUTERS THAT REGULATED AIR AND WATER PURIFICATION, AS WELL AS A NETWORK OF PIPES AND VALVES THAT KEPT THE WHOLE ENVIRONMENT STERILE AT ALL TIMES.

Leland Belding's Reclusive Home?

ONLY BELDING WAS ALLOWED INSIDE. NO PHOTOS WERE PERMITTED. CROSS HAD TO CONDUCT THE INTERVIEWS FROM A BOOTH ON WHEELS, TALKING TO BELDING THROUGH A SPEAKER PANEL.

CROSS'S DESCRIPTION OF BELDING WAS FRIGHTENING: EMACIATED AND FULLY BEARDED, WITH FINGERNAILS POLISHED A GLOSSY BLACK, SHARPENED INTO POINTS, AND NEARLY TWO INCHES LONG.

CROSS CLAIMED BELDING CONSUMED NOTHING BUT FRESH VEGETABLES AND STERILIZED WATER, URINATING AND DEFECATING IN A BRASS POT HE KEPT ON AN ALTAR.

THE BASKET-CASE BILLIONAIRE CAUGHT MAGNA BY SURPRISE, GARNERING HUGE ATTENTION AND SHOOTING TO THE TOP OF THE NONFICTION BEST-SELLER LIST.

MAGNA QUICKLY SUED CROSS AND HIS PUBLISHERS, CLAIMING THE BOOK WAS A LIBELOUS HOAX. REPORTERS WERE TAKEN TO A GRAVESITE AT COMPANY HEADQUARTERS. BELDING'S BODY WAS EXHUMED AND IDENTIFIED.

CROSS HELD A DEFIANT NEWS CONFERENCE IN FRONT OF A STORAGE UNIT IN LONG BEACH, READY TO REVEAL BOXES OF NOTES SIGNED AND DATED BY LELAND BELDING. THE UNIT HELD NOTHING ABOUT BELDING. CROSS'S CREDIBILITY VANISHED. THE BOOK WAS PULLED.

CROSS WAS ARRESTED FOR FRAUD AND SENT TO RIKER'S ISLAND FOR FIVE DAYS. DURING THAT TIME HE CLAIMED TO HAVE BEEN BEATEN AND RAPED. OUT ON BAIL, HE WAS FOUND DEAD A WEEK LATER. A NOTE ADMITTED THE BOOK HAD BEEN A SCAM.

A MAGAZINE RAN A PHOTO OF WILLIAM HOUCK VIDAL, THE CHAIRMAN OF MAGNA, AT A COURTHOUSE AFTER THE VICTORY OVER CROSS. I KNEW THAT FACE. BIG, SQUARE, AND DEEPLY TANNED. A COUNTRY CLUB FACE.

THE FACE, FIFTEEN YEARS YOUNGER, OF THE MAN I'D SEEN WITH SHARON AT THE PARTY. THE OLD SHEIK SHE'D BEEN TRYING TO CONVINCE OF SOMETHING.

MILO CALLED SUNDAY...SAID HE HAD A HISTORY LESSON LINED UP FOR US.

WHERE'RE WE GOING?

JUST KEEP DRIVING. HEY...I SHOULD TELL YOU...I DROPPED IN ON RASMUSSEN'S OLD LADY YESTERDAY... CARMEN.

HOW'D YOU FIND HER? I NEVER—

RELAX. GOT HER INFO FROM THE POLICE REPORT FOR D.J.'S ACCIDENT.

I RODE HER A LITTLE ABOUT THE MONEY D.J. LEFT. SHE FINALLY 'FESSED THAT THERE WAS MORE.

PARK UP THERE.

SHE FOUND FIVE GRAND. SAID HE'D BEEN THROWING MONEY AROUND FOR A FEW WEEKS.

RUE DE Oscar Wilde

KRANG

HE HAD THE CASH **BEFORE** EVERYONE STARTED DYING. IF IT WAS CASH FOR KILL, YOU KNOW WHAT THAT MEANS. PREMEDITATION.

SOMEONE'D BEEN PLANNING THAT CONTRACT. SETTING IT UP.

DON'T SAY I NEVER TOOK YOU ANYWHERE INTERESTING.

WHO THE HELL IS IT? WHAT DO YOU FRIGGING **WANT**?

MILO! OPENING THE DOOR WOULD BE A NICE START.

SO? WHAT DO YOU WANT **ME** TO DO? BREAK OPEN THE FRIGGING MOUTON ROTHSCHILD?

AFTERNOON, ELLSTON. NICE TO SEE YOU'RE IN YOUR USUAL GOOD CHEER.

PHH-HHTT

NOT BAD, BUT RICK WAS CUTER.

THIS IS DR. ALEX DELAWARE. HE'S A FRIEND.

ANOTHER DOCTOR? WHAT THE HELL YOU UPSCALE MEDICO STUDS SEE IN AN UGLY, UNCOUTH LUMP LIKE HIM?

FRIEND. AS IN FRIEND. HE'S STRAIGHT, ELLSTON.

SURE HE IS, DARLING.

WHAT KIND OF DOCTOR ARE YOU, DR. ALEX?

PSYCHOLOGIST.

OOH. I DON'T LIKE YOUR TYPE, ALWAYS ANALYZING, ALWAYS JUDGING.

ALL RIGHT, ELLSTON, YOU GAVE ME ENOUGH SHIT OVER THE PHONE. I HAVE NO MORE APPETITE FOR IT. C'MON, ALEX.

TOO BAD, ELLSTON. I WAS OFFERING A HUNDRED BUCKS FOR JUST A LITTLE TIME AND EFFORT.

BULLSHIT! LEAST YOU COULD HAVE FRIGGIN' DONE WAS TO BE CIVIL! NOT EVEN A PROPER, CIVIL INTRODUCTION!

AN INTRODUCTION WILL MAKE YOU HAPPY?

DR. ALEX DELAWARE, MEET ELLSTON CROTTY. DETECTIVE ELLSTON CROTTY.

DETECTIVE FIRST GRADE ELLSTON J. CROTTY, JUNIOR. LOS ANGELES POLICE DEPARTMENT, CENTRAL DIVISION, RETIRED.

YOU'RE LOOKING AT THE ACE OF CENTRAL VICE, DR. A PLEASURE TO MAKE YOUR FRIGGING ACQUAINTANCE.

OKAY, LET'S MAKE THIS QUICK. BELDING. LELAND, A. CAPITALIST PIG, TOO MUCH MONEY, NO MORALS, A LATENT FAG.

WHY DO YOU SAY THAT?

BECAUSE I'M A FRIGGING **EXPERT** ON LATENCY IS WHY, DR. PSYCHOLOGY.

YOU MIGHT HAVE THE DIPLOMA, BUT I'VE GOT THE EXPERIENCE. HANDS-ON EXPERIENCE.

LET'S STICK TO BELDING.

LET ME TELL YOU, CURLY, ONE THING I KNOW, IT'S LATENTS. FOR THIRTY YEARS I FRIGGING LIVED THAT TRIP.

YAWWWN.

HE'S FRIGGING BORED! YOU'D THINK SOMEONE IN HIS POSITION WOULD SEEK ME OUT, **BEGGING** FOR A TASTE OF MY ACCUMULATED WISDOM.

BUT NO, HOW DO I MEET THE LUMP? IN THE EMERGENCY ROOM, WITH SWEET RICK BRING-ING ME BACK FROM THE DEAD.

CHECKING HIS WATCH AND WANTING TO KNOW WHEN RICK GETS OFF. THERE I WAS FADING AWAY...

...AND ALL YOU COULD THINK ABOUT WAS YOUR **COCK.**

DON'T MAKE IT SOUND LIFE-THREATENING, ELLSTON. YOU HAD AN UPSET STOMACH. GAS. BELDING, OR GIVE BACK THE BREAD.

BELDING. A CAPITALIST. VICIOUS. **BECAUSE** HE WAS A LATENT. I KNOW WHAT THAT DOES TO A PERSON.

OH, BOY... HERE WE GO.

GLOM THIS.

I WAS **SOME** PIECE OF BEEF BACK THEN!

I WAS AS SWEET AS MARY PICKFORD, TRYING TO CONVINCE MYSELF I WAS FRIGGING GARY COOPER.

WHAT **BETTER** JOB FOR AN OVER-COMPENSATING MACHO BUCK THAN TO WEAR BLUE AND CARRY A BIG STICK?

FOR **TEN** YEARS I WAS AN ACCESSORY TO THE ASSAULT AND MURDER OF GAY MEN, GOING HOME EACH NIGHT...

...PUKING MY OWN GUTS OUT AND DRINKING GIN UNTIL I COULD FEEL MY LIVER **SIZZLING.**

BELDING. THAT'S WHAT WE'RE HERE TO TALK ABOUT.

AH...

MR. CROTTY, WHY DO YOU THINK BELDING WAS LATENT?

AHH, WHO THE HELL KNOWS? MAYBE I'M FULL OF SHIT. HE WAS NO **STUD**, THOUGH, DESPITE WHAT THE GOSSIP RAGE SAID.

I DID MEET HIM. HE USED TO HIRE OFF-DUTY COPS FOR SECURITY. SOMETIMES NOT SO OFF-DUTY. THE DEPARTMENT KISSED HIS RICH ASS 'TIL IT SPARKLED.

STUD BELDING JUST WATCHED EVERY-ONE ELSE. THAT'S WHAT HE WAS... A WATCHER.

I REMEMBER THINKING WHAT A COLD BASTARD HE WAS...REPRESS-ING. LATENT.

HOW ABOUT HIS SIDEKICK, VIDAL?

BILLY THE **PIMP**? HE WAS AT THAT PARTY TOO. VERY SUAVE. GOOD TEETH. EXCELLENT-LOOKING TEETH.

WHAT ABOUT THE WAR BOARD PARTIES? THE ONES BELDING GOT INVESTI-GATED FOR. DID THE DEPART-MENT DO GUARD DUTY ON THOSE?

SURE. LIKE I SAID, THE DEPARTMENT WAS INTO HIM. TWO I KNOW WERE IN HIS POCKET WERE A COUPLE OF SHITS NAMED HUMMEL AND DEGRANZFELD.

HEAD CRACKERS. HUMMEL WAS A RACIST PIG. USED TO BEAT COLORED HOOKERS TO A PULP. BOTH OF 'EM QUIT THE FORCE TO WORK FOR BELDING.

WHAT ABOUT THE HOUSES BELDING OWNED...THE PARTY PADS. KNOW WHERE ANY OF THEM WERE LOCATED?

PARTY PADS? WHERE'D YOU COME UP WITH THAT, LUMP? **PARTY** PADS. THEY WERE **FUCK** PADS. EVERYONE CALLED 'EM THAT.

BELDING BROUGHT BIGWIGS THERE, HAD A STABLE OF BIMBOS ALL SET TO CLEAN THEIR PIPES UNTIL THEY WERE READY TO SIGN ON THE DOTTED LINE.

AND NO, I DON'T KNOW ANY LOCATIONS. NEVER GOT INVITED TO **THOSE** SOIREES.

SORRY YOU HAD TO HEAR HIS LIFE STORY.

IT'S OKAY. IT WAS INTER- ESTING.

NOT AFTER THE THOUSANDTH TIME.

VITAMINS. I'M GETTING TIRED. GET THE HELL OUT OF HERE AND LET ME GET SOME REST.

TAB'S NOT RUN YET, ELLSTON.

GOT A COUPLE MORE NAMES FOR YOU. ACTRESS NAMED LINDA LANIER, RUMORED TO BE ONE OF BELDING'S BIMBOS. AND, SOME DOCTOR SHE SCREWED ON A STAG FILM.

JESUS... WHY'RE YOU POKING AROUND IN THE DEAD-LETTER PILE, LUMP?

SHE WAS **BEAUTIFUL**, WASN'T SHE?

I AGREED THAT SHE WAS. I TOLD ELLSTON I'D SEEN THE TAPE...DESCRIBED IT, ALONG WITH THE DOCTOR.

HE KNEW WHO THE DOCTOR HAD TO BE RIGHT AWAY...SAID HE KNEW THIS DOCTOR AND LANIER HAD A THING GOING ON. DONALD NEURATH, M.D. OBSTETRICIAN.

YOU DON'T HAVE TO PROVE A GODDAM THING. JUST TELL ME WHAT YOU KNOW.

"OKAY, OKAY. ONE OF MY ASSIGNMENTS, WHEN I WASN'T SNARING FAGGOTS, WAS WORKING THE SCRAPER CLUBS... ILLEGAL ABORTIONS. IT WAS STILL ILLEGAL, SO DOCS HAD TO PAY OFF THE DEPARTMENT. I PLAYED BAGMAN, PICKING UP MOOLAH FROM NEURATH. HE WAS AN OBSTETRICIAN. NICE LITTLE IRONY, HUH? NEURATH GIVETH, NEURATH TAKETH AWAY."

I FIBBED, LUMP. WHEN YOU ASKED ABOUT BELDING BEING A KILLER I FUDGED WITH THAT POLITICAL SHIT, 'CAUSE I DIDN'T KNOW WHICH ALLEY CAT YOU WERE CHASING.

I MEANT HE WAS A KILLER, LITERALLY. DIDN'T WANT TO GET INTO IT...NOTHING I COULD EVER PROVE.

"I SPOTTED HIM AT A CHINESE JOINT WITH A BLONDE. NOT HIS WIFE. I RECOGNIZED HER FROM BELDING'S PARTY. SHE'D STUCK IN MY MIND BECAUSE SHE WAS GORGEOUS, BUT ELEGANT. CLASSY. ABOUT A YEAR LATER, HER FACE IS ALL OVER THE PAPERS. THE MORE I LEARNED, THE MORE CURIOUS I GOT."

"THERE WAS THIS DOPE BUST. SHE GOT KILLED, ALONG WITH SOME GUY WHO TURNED OUT TO BE HER BROTHER. PAPER MADE THEM OUT AS BIG-TIME PUSHERS. THEY HAD THIS RITZY PAD ON FOUNTAIN. THEY WERE LIVIN' HIGH. PAPERS SAID THEY'D COME A LONG WAY FOR A COUPLE OF TEXAS CRACKERS."

"HER REAL NAME WAS EULALEE JOHNSON. THE BROTHER WAS A NASTY LITTLE PUNK NAMED CABLE, USED TO STRONG-ARM SMALL-TIME BOOKIES, LEAN ON STREETWALKERS, BUT NEVER GOT TOO FAR...SMALL-TIME ALL THE WAY."

"THE WHOLE THING SMELLED BAD. AND HUMMEL AND DEGRANZFELD DID THE SHOOTING."

THEY SUP-POSEDLY GOT A TIP ABOUT A HUGE STASH. BANG BANG BANG.

BOTH JOHNSONS DEAD. BELDING'S TOY COPS TALLYING UP THIS GIANT DOPE STASH. CUTE, HUH?

WHAT YEAR WAS THIS, ELLSTON?

'53.

JUST BEFORE LELAND BELDING HAD TURNED INTO A PLAYBOY. THE YEAR OF SHARON AND SHIRLEE'S BIRTH.

DID LINDA LANIER LEAVE ANY CHILDREN?

NO. I'D REMEMBER THAT. WHY? YOU GOT FAMILY MEMBERS OUT FOR REVENGE?

REVENGE AGAINST WHO?

OFFENDED HOW?

BELDING. THAT PHONY BUST HAD HIS NAME WRITTEN ALL OVER IT. HUMMEL AND DEGRANZFELD WERE HIS BOYS; LANIER WAS HIS PARTY GIRL.

I FIGURE THEY HAD SOMETHING OR OTHER GOING, SHE OFFENDED BELDING IN SOME SERIOUS WAY, AND HE HAD TO GET RID OF HER.

WHO KNOWS? MAYBE SHE GOT PUSHY ABOUT SOMETHING. MAYBE HER STUPID BROTHER PUT THE ARM ON THE WRONG GUY.

NEURATH WAS AN OBSTETRICIAN. MAYBE LINDA LANIER WAS SEEING HIM PROFES-SIONALLY.

PREGNANT? PUTTING THE PATERNAL SQUEEZE ON BELDING? SURE, WHY NOT?

HOW SOON AFTER THE SHOOT-ING DID HUMMEL AND DEWHATSISNAME QUIT?

NOT LONG AFTER, AND THIS WITH BOTH OF THEM COMMENDED AND PROMOTED.

DEGRANZFELD DIED A FEW YEARS AFTER. AFFAIR WITH A MARRIED WOMAN, HUSBAND HAD A TEMPER.

FAR AS I KNOW, HUMMEL'S STILL IN VEGAS. ONE THING FOR **SURE**, HE'S STILL GOT **PULL** IN THE DEPARTMENT, OR AT LEAST HE DID A COUPLE OF YEARS AGO.

HOW SO?

HE HAD THIS NEPHEW, REAL **FASCIST** FUCKUP, LIKED THE BOOZE, LIKED CHASING YOUNG TAIL TOO.

BULLYING **SON OF A BITCH**— FRIGGING CHIP OFF THE OLD BLOCK.

SHITTY COP BY ALL ACCOUNTS, THEN ALL OF A SUDDEN, GUY'S A BORN-AGAIN CHRISTIAN, PROMOTED TO **CAPTAIN**, WEST L.A.—

SO... WHAT THE **HELL** IS THIS REALLY ABOUT?

WHAT?

LUMP, YOU **CRAFTY** BADGER. GONNA **GET** THAT SCUM, AREN'T YOU?

FINALLY DO A GOOD DEED, AFTER ALL.

FEISTY OLD GUY.

BLUSTER. HE'S BEEN POUR-ING IT ON SINCE HE TESTED **POSITIVE**.

THOSE PILLS WEREN'T **VITAMINS**. SOME KIND OF IMMUNE-STRENGTHENING REGIMEN. HE BEAT HEPATITIS A FEW YEARS BACK, THINKS IF HE'S **MEAN** ENOUGH HE'LL BEAT THIS TOO. **THAT'S** WHY I HUMOR HIM.

TRAPP. PAYING OFF OLD DEBTS TO UNCLE ROYAL HUMMEL. GOT TO FIND OUT WHAT THE BASTARD IS FIXING.

MAYBE A MURDER MADE TO LOOK LIKE SUICIDE?

YOU KEEP COMING BACK TO THAT AND WOULDN'T IT BE NICE. BUT WHERE'S THE EVIDENCE?

BELDING AND MAGNA WERE OLD HANDS AT CAMOUFLAGING MURDER. BELDING MAY BE DEAD, BUT MAGNA LIVES ON.

THE KRUSE KILLINGS WEREN'T MADE TO LOOK LIKE ANYTHING BUT MURDER.

HARD TO COVER UP THREE BODIES. AND MAYBE KILLING KRUSE WASN'T PART OF THE PLAN...IF RASMUSSEN DID IT, THE WAY WE THEORIZED.

WHAT ABOUT LANIER AND HER BROTHER? THE LOOP SEEMED TO BE SETTING NEURATH UP. WHERE'D THOSE PORN FREAKS SAY THEY GOT THE LOOP?

THEY DIDN'T. JUST SAID IT WAS EXPENSIVE.

I'LL BET. LET'S TAKE A SIDE TRIP...

"...SEE IF WE CAN GET THEM TO BE A LITTLE MORE FORTHCOMING."

GONE. VANISHED, ALONG WITH ALL THEIR FANCY CARS. THEIR PRECIOUS LOOP TOO, NO DOUBT.

THEY SAW THE KRUSE MURDERS ON THE NEWS... KNEW ENOUGH TO BE SCARED.

VIDAL'S STILL ALIVE. LOOKING DAMNED ROBUST, IN FACT.

FUCKING CASE. TOO MANY DEAD PEOPLE, TOO LONG AGO.

VIDAL. WHAT DID CROTTY CALL HIM...BILLY THE PIMP? FROM THAT TO CHAIRMAN OF THE BOARD. STEEP CLIMB.

SHARP SPIKES WOULD LEND TRACTION... ALONG WITH A FEW HEADS TO STEP ON.

OH... ALEX! GOOD MORNING.

MONDAY MORNING I WOKE TOO EARLY, FOUND MYSELF WONDERING ABOUT CARMEN SEEBER.

I'D REFERRED CARMEN TO MY OLD THERAPIST, ADA SMALL. I BEAT RUSH HOUR TRAFFIC TO HER OFFICE.

WHAT BRINGS YOU BY SO BRIGHT AND EARLY?

I WANTED TO CHECK UP ON CARMEN SEEBER. COULD HAVE CALLED, BUT IT'S BEEN AWHILE...

GLAD YOU CAME. NICE TO SEE YOU IN THE FLESH. WISH I COULD OFFER YOU BETTER NEWS ON CARMEN, THOUGH.

SHE CAME FOR TWO SESSIONS, THEN DISAPPEARED. I MANAGED TO REACH HER AT HOME. SHE INSISTED SHE WAS FINE, DIDN'T NEED ANY MORE THERAPY.

I'LL TRY CALLING HER NEXT WEEK, BUT I'M NOT OPTIMISTIC. YOU AND I BOTH KNOW ABOUT THE POWER OF RESISTANCE.

I THOUGHT OF DENISE BURKHALTER. AND DARREN.

ALL WE CAN DO IS TRY.

TRUE.

AS I SAID, IT'S NICE TO SEE YOU, BUT IT DOES BEG THE QUESTION...HOW ARE YOU DOING, ALEX?

FORGIVE ME IF I'M OUT OF LINE, BUT WHEN WE'VE SPOKEN LATELY YOU'VE SOUNDED... TIGHT.

NO...JUST A LITTLE TIRED, ADA. I'M FINE. THANKS FOR ASKING.

I'M GLAD TO HEAR THAT. IF YOU EVER DO NEED TO TOSS THINGS AROUND, YOU KNOW I'M HERE FOR YOU.

I DO, ADA. THANKS AND TAKE CARE.

YOU TOO, ALEX. TAKE GOOD CARE OF YOURSELF.

ON CAMPUS, I STOPPED BY THE ED-PSYCH LIBRARY TO REQUEST A DOCUMENT. WAS TOLD TO COME BACK LATER...THEY'D HAVE TO MAKE A COPY.

BREAKFAST WAS A BLACK CUP OF COFFEE IN A PAPER CUP AT THE RESEARCH LIBRARY.

I STARTED DIGGING THROUGH THE ARCHIVES FOR WILLIAM HOUCK VIDAL...CROTTY'S "BILLY THE PIMP."

I FOUND A PIECE ON THE SENATE HEARINGS I'D MISSED WHILE CULLING BELDING MATERIAL.

THERE WAS THE YOUNG VERSION OF THE SHEIK FROM THE BLALOCK PARTY, COMPLETE WITH THE GOOD TEETH CROTTY REMEMBERED.

A SOCIALITE WHO'D PARLAYED SHREWDNESS, CONNECTIONS, AND CHARM INTO A LUCRATIVE MOTION PICTURE CONSULTING POSITION ALONGSIDE LELAND BELDING.

VIDAL AND BELDING HAD BOTH ATTENDED STANFORD. BELONGED TO THE SAME MEN'S CLUB.

IN '41, VIDAL HELPED FACILITATE A DEAL BETWEEN BELDING AND BLALOCK INDUSTRIES, WHICH SUPPLIED WARTIME STEEL TO THE MAGNA CORPORATION AT A DISCOUNT RATE.

CONVENIENTLY, BLALOCK WAS VIDAL'S BROTHER-IN-LAW, MARRIED TO BILLY'S OLDER SISTER, HOPE.

BILLY AND HOPE, BROTHER AND SISTER. IT EXPLAINED VIDAL'S PRESENCE AT THE PARTY, BUT NOT HIS RELATIONSHIP TO SHARON. NOT WHAT THEY'D BEEN TALKING ABOUT...

HENRY BLALOCK DIED IN '53, ONLY 59 YEARS OLD. A STROKE WHILE ON SAFARI IN KENYA. NO MENTION OF CHILDREN. SIX MONTHS AFTER HENRY'S DEATH MAGNA BOUGHT WHAT WAS LEFT OF THE BLALOCK CORPORATION.

FROM THE LOOKS OF HOPE BLALOCK'S LODGINGS, SHE HAD DONE ALL RIGHT IN THE DEAL. BROTHER BILLY PROTECTING HER INTERESTS?

L.A. DAILY

August 9th, 1955

POLICE BUST HEROIN TRAFFICKERS

Dope Dealers Slain in Lightning Operation Shootout

MY THOUGHTS SLID DOWN TO THE LOWER RUNGS OF THE SOCIAL LADDER, ANOTHER BROTHER-SISTER STORY. THE LINDA LANIER DOPE BUST.

I DIDN'T HAVE TO STUDY THE PICTURE OF LINDA LANIER/EULALEE JOHNSON TO RECOGNIZE THE BLOND BOMBSHELL I'D WATCHED SEDUCE DR. DONALD NEURATH.

IN THE MICROFICHE SECTION, I TRACKED DOWN THE STORY. PURPLE PROSE, LURID PHOTOS, AND HEROIC PROFILES OF THE BRAVE COPS WHO MADE THE BUST.

THE PHOTO WAS HIGH-QUALITY, A PROFESSIONAL STUDIO JOB.

CABLE JOHNSON'S CRIMINAL RECORD INCLUDED ARRESTS FOR EXTORTION, PUBLIC DRUNKENNESS, DISORDERLY CONDUCT, LARCENY, AND THEFT. SMALL-TIME.

ANONYMOUS SOURCES PAIRED THE JOHNSONS WITH "MEXICAN MOB ELEMENTS." THEY'D COME FROM TEXAS INTENDING TO PUSH HEROIN TO THE SCHOOLCHILDREN OF BRENTWOOD AND BEVERLY HILLS.

DOPE AND BOLSHEVISM, PRIME DEMONS OF THE FIFTIES.

NOTHING TO SUPPORT THE PAPER'S DESCRIPTION OF A "RUTHLESS DOPE PUSHER."

BOTH WERE KNOWN AS HANGERS-ON AT "LEFT-LEANING FILM INDUSTRY PARTIES ALSO ATTENDED BY KNOWN COMMUNISTS."

ENOUGH TO MAKE SHOOTING A BEAUTIFUL YOUNG WOMAN TO DEATH PALATABLE.

ADMIRABLE, EVEN.

NOTHING LINKING LANIER TO BELDING. NOTHING ABOUT PARTY PADS. NOTHING ABOUT CHILDREN. SINGLY OR IN PAIRS.

OLD STORIES, OLD CONNECTIONS, BUT I WAS NO CLOSER TO UNDERSTANDING SHARON...HOW SHE'D LIVED AND WHY SHE, AND SO MANY OTHERS, HAD DIED.

ANOTHER STOP AT THE ED-PSYCH LIBRARY. THE LIBRARIAN HAD MY DOCUMENT WAITING, AS PROMISED.

SHE NOTED HOW UNUSUAL IT WAS...GETTING *TWO* REQUESTS FOR THE SAME DISSERTATION IN A MONTH.

FIVE HOURS LATER...

THE SILENT PARTNER: IDENTITY CRISIS AND EGO DYSFUNCTION IN A CASE OF MULTIPLE PERSONALITY MASQUERADING AS PSEUDO-TWINSHIP. CLINICAL AND RESEARCH RAMIFICATIONS.

by

Sharon Jean Ransom

A Dissertation Presented to the
FACULTY OF THE GRADUATE SCHOOL
In Partial Fulfillment of the
Requirements for the Degree
DOCTOR OF PHILOSOPHY
(Psychology)
June 1981

...I WAS STILL JUST STARING AT THE DAMNED THING.

TO SHIRLEE AND JASPER, WHO HAVE MEANT MORE TO ME THAN THEY COULD EVER IMAGINE, AND TO PAUL, WHO HAS GUIDED ME, ADROITLY, FROM DARKNESS TO LIGHT.

JASPER? FRIEND? LOVER? ANOTHER VICTIM?

"AND DEEP THANKS TO ALEX, WHO EVEN IN HIS ABSENCE, CONTINUES TO INSPIRE ME."

I TURNED THE PAGE SO HARD IT NEARLY TORE.

SHARON'S DISSERTATION WAS A CASE STUDY OF ONE OF HER PATIENTS...A YOUNG WOMAN FROM AN UPPER-CLASS BACKGROUND. SHARON CALLED HER J.

J. CAME TO SHARON COMPLAINING OF "LOST HOURS". SHE WOULD AWAKEN IN STRANGE SETTINGS WITH NO MEMORY OF HOW SHE GOT THERE:

CHEAP HOTEL ROOMS, STRANGERS' CARS, THE STREETS OF A FOREIGN CITY.

SUCH FUGUE STATES ARE NOT UNCOMMON IN DISSOCIATIVE PATIENTS. ABUSED CHILDREN LEARN EARLY TO CUT THEMSELVES OFF FROM HORROR, AND OFTEN SELF-EJECT FROM STRESS AS ADULTS.

UNDER KRUSE'S GUIDANCE, SHARON USED HYPNOSIS TO TREAT J., DISCOVERING THAT SHE WAS SUFFERING FROM **MULTIPLE PERSONALITY SYNDROME**...THE ULTIMATE DISSOCIATION.

J.'S ALTER EGO JANA WAS AS BLATANT AS J. WAS RETICENT. JANA FAVORED TINTED WIGS, REVEALING CLOTHING.

SHE TOOK DRUGS, ATTENDED ORGIES, FUCKED LIKE A PORN STAR ON FILM IN SEEDY HOTEL ROOMS, AND DRANK...**STRAWBERRY DAIQUIRIS**.

SHARON'S TREATMENT OF J. AND HER "SILENT PARTNER" PERSONALITY, JANA, RESULTED IN NO REAL IMPROVEMENT. EVENTUALLY, J. DISAPPEARED.

CASE OVER, EXCEPT...THERE HAD NEVER REALLY BEEN A CASE. I KNEW J. I'D MADE LOVE TO HER.

I KNEW JANA, TOO, HAD WATCHED HER THROW STRAWBERRY DAIQUIRIS AGAINST A FIREPLACE, WIGGLE OUT OF A FLAME-COLORED DRESS, AND DO WITH ME WHAT SHE WANTED.

AUTOBIOGRAPHY. FOUR HUNDRED-PLUS PAGES OF SOUL-DREDGING, PSEUDO-SCHOLARSHIP. LIES.

I COULDN'T EVEN SUMMON A MODICUM OF SHOCK.

I GAVE OLIVIA BRICKERMAN THE NAMES THE NEXT MORNING: SHIRLEE AND JASPER RANSOM. TWO HOURS LATER, I HAD DATES OF BIRTHS: 1920 AND '22, ALONG WITH AN ADDRESS. WILLOW GLEN, CA.

THE VILLAGE WAS NOTHING MORE THAN A TINY RUSTED SHOPPING MALL AND AN EMPTY PARKING LOT. I DROVE BY THE ABANDONED APPLE PRESS, SKIDDED DOWN A PATH JUST WIDE ENOUGH FOR THE SEVILLE, TO AN INHOSPITABLE PATCH IN THE WILLOWS.

I TRIED TO PLACE SHARON IN THIS SETTING. HAD SHE *ESCAPED* THIS PLACE, FOR GOOD REASON? HAD SHE CONSTRUCTED FANTASIES OF A PERFECT CHILDHOOD TO BLOCK OUT A REALITY TOO TERRIBLE TO CONFRONT?

HELLO.

I HEARD A TRICKLE OF WATER FROM A HOSE, UNDER A SOFT, TUNELESS HUMMING.

HELLO.

HULLO.

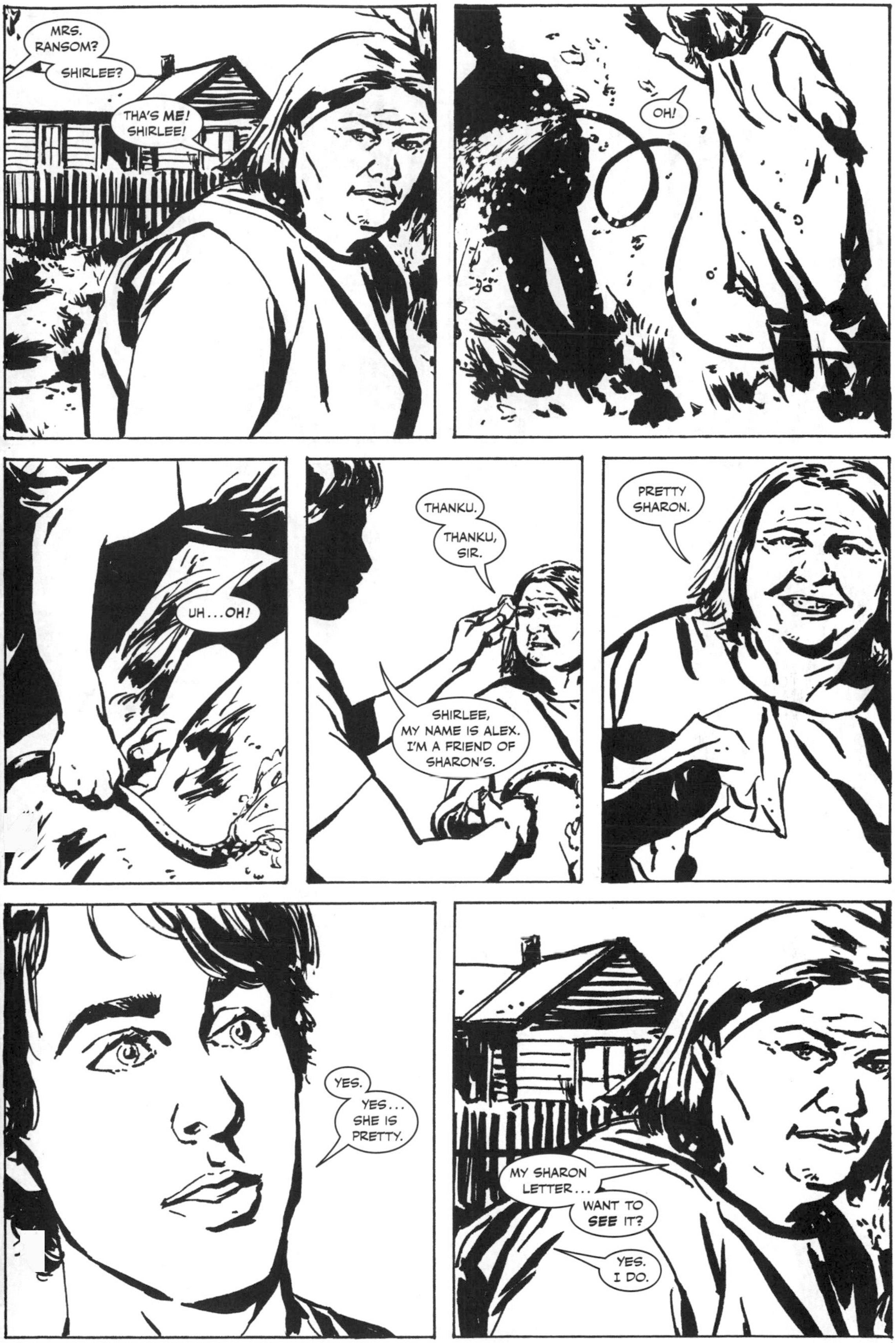
MRS. RANSOM?
SHIRLEE?
THA'S ME! SHIRLEE!
OH!
UH...OH!
THANKU.
THANKU, SIR.
SHIRLEE, MY NAME IS ALEX. I'M A FRIEND OF SHARON'S.
PRETTY SHARON.
YES.
YES... SHE IS PRETTY.
MY SHARON LETTER...
WANT TO SEE IT?
YES. I DO.

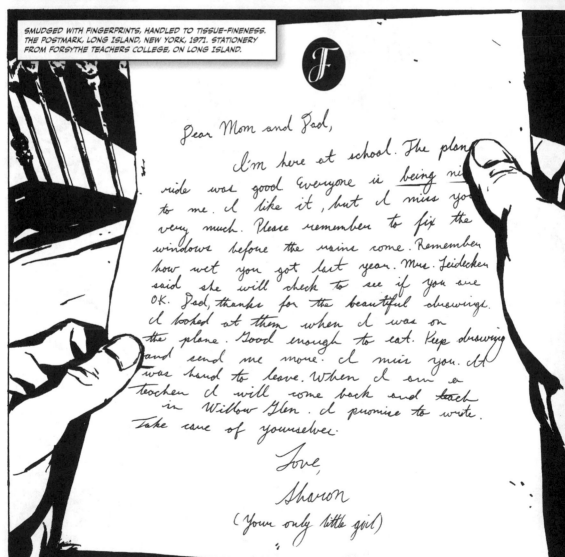

SMUDGED WITH FINGERPRINTS, HANDLED TO TISSUE-FINENESS. THE POSTMARK, LONG ISLAND, NEW YORK, 1971. STATIONERY FROM FORSYTHE TEACHERS COLLEGE, ON LONG ISLAND.

IT'S A NICE LETTER, SHIRLEE. A BEAUTIFUL LETTER.

YES.

DO YOU HAVE MORE?

WE HAD. LOTS. BIG RAINS CAME IN, AND WHOOSH.

RAIN COMES IN. MIZZ LEIDERK SAYS GLASS, SHIRLEE. GLASS IS GOOD. JASP SAY NO, NO. JASP LIKES THE AIR.

MRS. LEIDECKER SOUNDS LIKE A GOOD FRIEND. IS JASP—

MRS. LEIDERK TEACHER. REA SMART.

YES. SHARON WANTED TO BE A TEACHER TOO.

SHIRLEE, WHEN WAS THE LAST TIME YOU HEARD FROM SHARON?

CHRISMUS.

LAST CHRISTMAS?

UH... YES.

SHIRLEE, WAS IT A CHRISTMAS A LONG TIME AGO?

YES.

SOMETHING CAUGHT MY EYE. A BLUE SAVINGS ACCOUNT PASSBOOK.

SHIRLEE DIDN'T SEEM TO MIND MY INTRUSION.

MONEY.

YEARS OF TRANSACTIONS. $500 CASH DEPOSITS ON THE FIRST OF EACH MONTH. OCCASIONAL WITHDRAWALS. BALANCE OF $78,000. A TRUSTEESHIP. THE TRUSTEE, HELEN A. LEIDECKER.

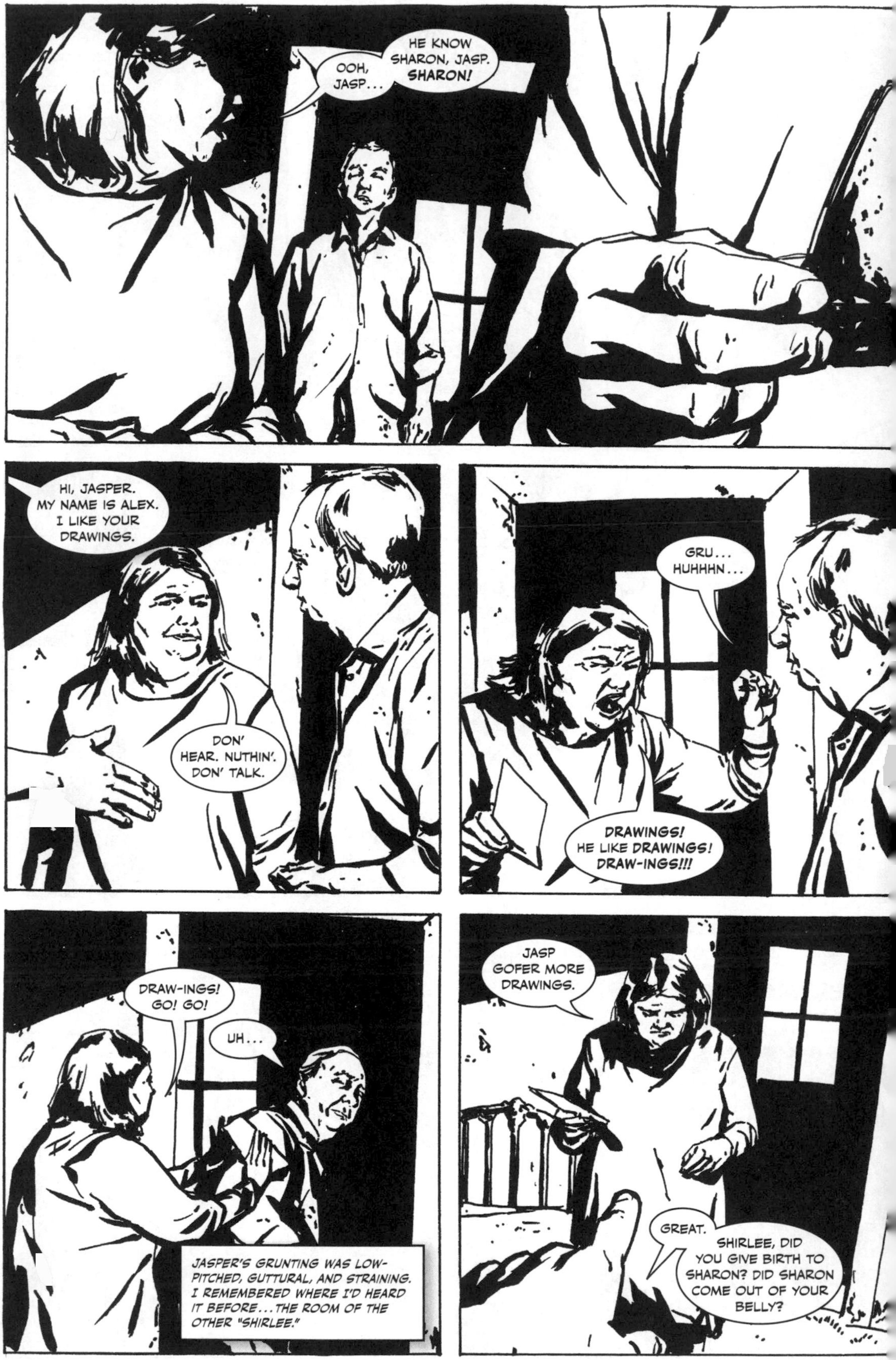
OOH, JASP...
HE KNOW SHARON, JASP. SHARON!
HI, JASPER. MY NAME IS ALEX. I LIKE YOUR DRAWINGS.
DON' HEAR. NUTHIN'. DON' TALK.
GRU... HUHHHN...
DRAWINGS! HE LIKE DRAWINGS! DRAW-INGS!!!
DRAW-INGS! GO! GO!
UH...
JASPER'S GRUNTING WAS LOW-PITCHED, GUTTURAL, AND STRAINING. I REMEMBERED WHERE I'D HEARD IT BEFORE...THE ROOM OF THE OTHER "SHIRLEE."
JASP GOFER MORE DRAWINGS.
GREAT.
SHIRLEE, DID YOU GIVE BIRTH TO SHARON? DID SHARON COME OUT OF YOUR BELLY?

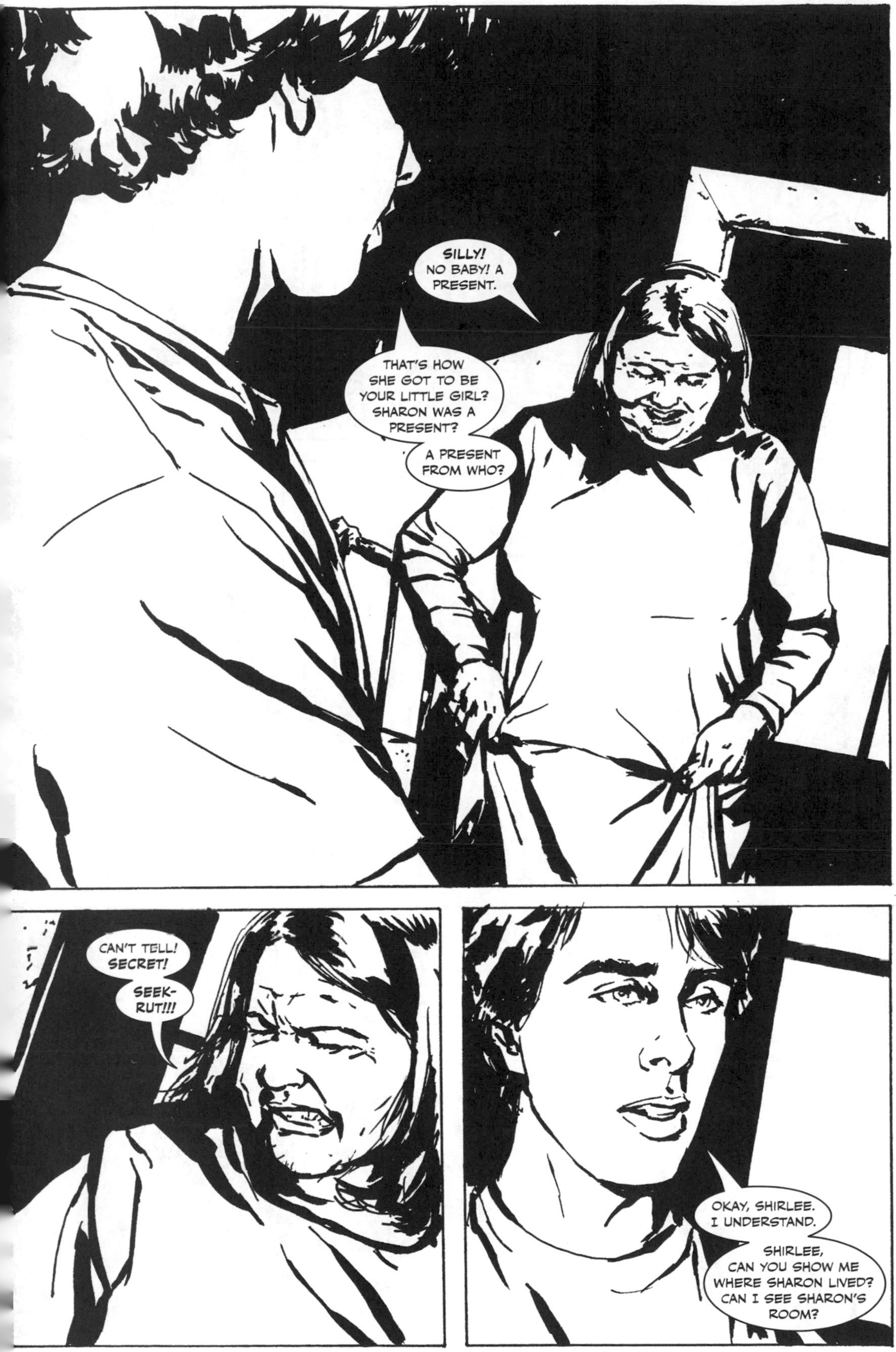
SILLY! NO BABY! A PRESENT.
THAT'S HOW SHE GOT TO BE YOUR LITTLE GIRL? SHARON WAS A PRESENT?
A PRESENT FROM WHO?
CAN'T TELL! SECRET!
SEEK-RUT!!!
OKAY, SHIRLEE. I UNDERSTAND.
SHIRLEE, CAN YOU SHOW ME WHERE SHARON LIVED? CAN I SEE SHARON'S ROOM?

...JUST THE WAY SHE LEFT IT.

HER ROOM...

I TRIED TO PICTURE SHARON LIVING HERE. LIVING WITH SHIRLEE AND JASPER. BEING RAISED BY THEM.

"THEY WERE WONDERFUL PEOPLE, ALEX. VERY GLAMOROUS."

GUH-UH...

TEN MINUTES LATER, I HAD MANAGED TO GATHER SOME DIRECTIONS FROM SHIRLEE ON HOW TO FIND HELEN LEIDECKER. POINTED FINGERS TOWARD A HILL WHERE I WOULD FIND THE SCHOOLHOUSE.

THANK YOU, JASPER.

THANK YOU BOTH.

I TURNED TO LOOK AT THESE PEOPLE WHO SHARON CONSIDERED HER PARENTS FOR ONE LAST TIME.

THEY STARED BACK AT ME AS IF I WAS AN EXPLORER...A CONQUISTADOR SETTING OUT FOR SOME BRAVE NEW WORLD THAT THEY COULD NEVER HOPE TO SEE.

SHIRLEE'S POINTED DIRECTIONS WERE ENOUGH IN SPARSELY-POPULATED WILLOW GLEN.

I FOUND THE SCHOOLHOUSE, ALONG WITH THE WOMAN WHO OVERSAW THE FORTUNES OF THE RANSOMS.

HELLO. WHAT CAN I DO FOR YOU, SIR?

I WANTED TO TALK ABOUT SHARON RANSOM.

I'M ALEX DELAWARE.

OH. I'M HELEN LEIDECKER.

FORGIVE MY COLD GREETING. WE ALMOST NEVER SEE OUTSIDERS IN WILLOW GLEN.

I LOST MR. LEIDECKER LAST SPRING. IT'S JUST ME HERE AFTER THE CHILDREN LEAVE EACH DAY.

PLEASE FORGIVE THE SMALL DESKS, DR. DELAWARE.

DR. DELAWARE. I HADN'T GIVEN HER MY TITLE.

I TOLD HELEN HER SCHOOL WASN'T UNLIKE THE ONE I'D ATTENDED IN MISSOURI.

AH...A MID-WESTERNER. YOU'VE COME A LONG WAY. I NEVER IMAGINED I'D END UP IN A SLEEPY LITTLE HAMLET LIKE WILLOW GLEN.

I'M ORIGINALLY FROM NEW YORK. LONG ISLAND. THE HAMPTONS... NOT THE WEALTHY PART.

MY PEOPLE SERVICED THE IDLE RICH.

THE HAMPTONS. ANOTHER SQUARE IN THE SHARON QUILT OF LIES?

DID YOU MEET SHIRLEE AND JASPER? OH, GOSH...

THEY DON'T READ THE PAPERS... CAN BARELY READ A PRIMER. HOW AM I GOING TO TELL THEM? SHE WAS ALL THEY HAD.

AND ME. I'VE BECOME THEIR MOTHER. I KNOW I'M GOING TO HAVE TO DEAL WITH IT.

PLEASE EXCUSE ME. I'M AS SHAKY AS THE DAY I READ ABOUT IT... THAT WAS A HORROR.

I JUST CAN'T BELIEVE IT. SHE WAS SO BEAUTIFUL, SO ALIVE.

AND NOW SHE'S GONE, AS IF SHE NEVER EXISTED IN THE FIRST PLACE.

SUCH A DAMNED, UGLY WASTE. IT MAKES ME ANGRY AT HER. WHICH IS UNFAIR. IT WAS HER LIFE. SHE NEVER ASKED FOR WHAT I GAVE HER, NEVER...

ALL THOSE YEARS. I FELT I UNDERSTOOD HER. NOW I REALIZE I WAS DELUDING MYSELF. I BARELY KNEW HER.

NO ONE KNOWS WHY. THAT'S WHY I'M HERE, MRS. LEIDECKER.

HELEN.

ALEX DELAWARE. IN A WAY I FEEL I KNOW YOU. SHE TOLD ME ALL ABOUT YOU... HOW MUCH SHE LOVED YOU...

...EVEN THOUGH SHE KNEW IT COULD NEVER WORK OUT BECAUSE OF YOUR SISTER, JOAN... HER CONDITION. HOW'S SHE DOING?

I TRIED NOT TO LET THE CONFUSION SHOW ON MY FACE. I SAID JOAN WAS...ABOUT THE SAME.

POOR THING. SHARON ADMIRED YOU FOR YOUR COMMITMENT TO JOAN. IF ANYTHING, I'D SAY IT INTENSIFIED HER LOVE FOR YOU.

GOD, I'VE BEEN COOPED UP IN HERE ALL AFTERNOON GRADING PAPERS...

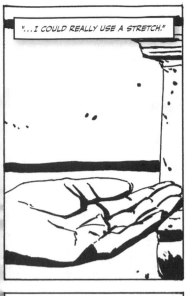

"...I COULD REALLY USE A STRETCH."

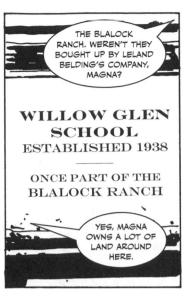

THE BLALOCK RANCH. WEREN'T THEY BOUGHT UP BY LELAND BELDING'S COMPANY, MAGNA?

WILLOW GLEN SCHOOL
ESTABLISHED 1938

ONCE PART OF THE BLALOCK RANCH

YES, MAGNA OWNS A LOT OF LAND AROUND HERE.

WHAT ABOUT THE LAND JASPER AND SHIRLEE LIVE ON?

YES, THAT'S MAGNA LAND.

AND IS IT MAGNA THAT PAYS THEM $500 A MONTH. SORRY...I SAW THEIR BANKBOOK. SITTING ON TOP OF THE DRESSER.

ON THE DRESSER? I'VE TOLD THEM SO MANY TIMES TO KEEP IT HIDDEN. NOT THAT ANYONE FROM AROUND HERE WOULD HURT THEM, BUT...

IT ARRIVES, LIKE CLOCKWORK, THE FIRST OF EVERY MONTH. NO RETURN ADDRESS.

HELEN, IS THERE **ANY** POSSIBILITY THAT SHARON WAS THEIR BIOLOGICAL CHILD?

UNLIKELY. THE DOCTOR EXAMINED ALL OF THEM AND SAID SHIRLEE WAS ALMOST CERTAINLY STERILE. SO WHERE DID SHE COME FROM, RIGHT?

FOR A WHILE I LIVED WITH THE NIGHTMARE THAT SHE WAS SOMEONE'S KIDNAPPED BABY. I CHECKED, BUT NEVER FOUND A CASE THAT MATCHED THE TIMING

WHEN YOU ASK SHIRLEE ABOUT IT, SHE JUST GIGGLES AND SAYS SHARON WAS A PRESENT. NO, ALEX, I HAVE NO IDEA

SHARON MUST HAVE BEEN CURIOUS ABOUT HER ROOTS.

YOU'D EXPECT HER TO BE, BUT I NEVER SAW IT. SHE KNEW SHE WAS DIFFERENT FROM SHIRLEE AND JASPER BUT SHE LOVED THEM, ACCEPTED THINGS THE WAY THEY WERE.

LEAVING FOR COLLEGE...THAT WAS REALLY HARD FOR HER. SHE WAS EXCITED AND FRIGHTENED AND GUILTY ABOUT ABANDONING THEM. SHE KNEW THINGS WOULD NEVER BE THE SAME.

WHEN'S THE LAST TIME SHARON VISITED HERE?

A LONG TIME AGO. ONCE SHE BROKE AWAY, SHE FOUND IT VERY PAINFUL TO RETURN. THE GUILT WAS NEARLY OVERWHELMING.

I TOLD HER SHE WAS DOING THE RIGHT THING. WHAT WAS THE **ALTERNATIVE**? BEING STUCK FOREVER AS A CARETAKER?

OH. I'M SO SORRY. THAT WAS THOUGHTLESS.

FOR A MOMENT I WAS PUZZLED BY HER EMBARRASSMENT.

JOAN.

I THINK YOUR DEVOTION IS WONDERFUL.

I MET SHARON FOR LUNCH ONCE WHEN SHE WAS IN GRAD SCHOOL. SHE WAS SAD. SAID SHE'D MET THE MAN OF HER DREAMS, SPENT A LOT OF TIME DESCRIBING YOUR VIRTUES...

...BEFORE EXPLAINING ABOUT JOAN. HOW YOUR RELATIONSHIP COULD NEVER WORK BECAUSE OF HER.

SHE TOLD YOU ABOUT JOAN'S CONDITION?

THE DROWNING? OH, YES. HOW TERRIBLE, AND YOU A LITTLE BOY, WATCHING. SHE UNDERSTOOD, ALEX. SHE WASN'T BITTER OR ANGRY.

THANK YOU, HELEN. HOW DID YOU FIRST MEET SHARON?

RIGHT AFTER WE ARRIVED HERE, BACK IN '57, I BEGAN HEARING MY PUPILS TALK ABOUT A FAMILY OF "RETARDS" LIVING OUTSIDE THE VILLAGE.

TWO GROWN-UPS AND A LITTLE GIRL WHO RAN AROUND NAKED AND CHATTERED LIKE A MONKEY. OF COURSE, I WENT OUT THERE LOOKING FOR THEM.

"SHE STARED DOWN AT ME WITH THOSE HUGE BLUE EYES..."

"...CLINGING TO A NEARLY-EMPTY JAR OF MAYONNAISE SHE'D BEEN EATING BY THE HANDFUL."

"SHIRLEE CALLED TO HER BY NAME. SHARON IGNORED HER. THERE WAS NO PARENTAL AUTHORITY. SHE ONLY CAME DOWN WHEN I ACTED UNINTERESTED."

"I TOLD HER...'THIS IS EATEN WITH TUNA OR HAM. NOT BY ITSELF.'"

"CLEAR AS DAY, SHE REPLIED, 'I LIKE IT BY ITSELF.'"

"I WAS SHOCKED. I HAD ASSUMED SHE WAS RETARDED, TOO. I LOOKED AGAIN AND THERE WAS SOMETHING THERE... A QUICKNESS IN THE EYES."

"THE RANSOMS DIDN'T HESITATE WHEN I ASKED IF I COULD TAKE HER FOR A FEW HOURS."

"THEY WERE CLEARLY DELIGHTED WITH HER, BUT THERE WAS NO PARENT-CHILD BOND. TO THEM SHE WAS SOMETHING LIKE A TOY."

HOW DID SHARON REACT TO BEING TAKEN AWAY?

SHE WASN'T HAPPY, BUT SHE DIDN'T FIGHT IT. SHE ESPECIALLY DIDN'T LIKE IT WHEN I TRIED TO COVER HER WITH A BLANKET.

FUNNY THING IS, ONCE SHE GOT USED TO CLOTHES, SHE NEVER LIKED TO TAKE THEM OFF...AS IF BEING NAKED REMINDED HER OF THE WAY SHE'D BEEN.

MY MIND FLASHED ON CLOTHED, BACKSEAT LOVEMAKING.

"IT WAS CLEAR THERE HAD BEEN NO LIMIT-SETTING OF ANY KIND."

"WHEN I MADE HER MIND... WHEN SHE KNEW I CARED, THAT WAS THE BEGINNING. SHE WAS CRAVING DISCIPLINE."

"SHE NEVER SPENT THE NIGHT WITH YOU?"

"I SENT HER HOME EACH NIGHT. IT WAS BEST."

YEARS LATER, WITH ME, SHE'D SENT HERSELF HOME. "I HAVE TROUBLE SLEEPING ANYWHERE BUT MY OWN BED." EARLY PATTERNS...EARLY TRAUMA...

BUT SHE DID TALK FLUENTLY?

"IT WAS STRANGE, UNEVEN. SOMETIMES WHOLE PHRASES WOULD POUR OUT, THEN SHE'D BE AT A LOSS TO DESCRIBE SOMETHING SIMPLE."

WHEN SHE GOT FRUSTRATED SHE'D START TO GRUNT AND POINT LIKE JASPER.

FROM THAT TO A PH.D..

I TOLD YOU IT WAS A MIRACLE. SHE LEARNED SO QUICKLY. FOUR MONTHS TO GET HER TALKING PROPERLY, ANOTHER THREE TO TEACH HER TO READ.

SHE WAS READY FOR IT, AN EMPTY GLASS WAITING TO BE FILLED.

THE MORE TIME I SPENT WITH HER, THE CLEARER IT BECAME THAT NOT ONLY WASN'T SHE RETARDED, SHE WAS GIFTED. HIGHLY GIFTED.

SHE WAS A BRILLIANT GIRL, ALEX.

SHE THRIVED. IF I'D CALLED THE AUTHORITIES, THEY WOULD HAVE THROWN SHIRLEE AND JASPER IN AN INSTITUTION AND FARMED SHARON OUT TO A FOSTER HOME.

MY WAY WAS BEST. SHE DID SO WELL. SHE DID SO MUCH. ALL FOR NOTHING.

ALL THOSE YEARS, ALEX. I FELT I UNDERSTOOD HER. NOW I REALIZE I WAS DELUDING MYSELF.

I BARELY KNEW HER.

I GOT DROWSY ON THE LONG DRIVE HOME. PULLED OFF NEAR FONTANA.

STARED AT MY TRUCK STOP COFFEE AND TRIED TO PROCESS THE NEW BOMBSHELLS.

SHARON, QUEEN OF DECEPTION. SHE'D RISEN, LITERALLY, FROM THE MUCK. HELEN HAD WROUGHT A REMARKABLE TRANSFORMATION: A WILD CHILD TAMED.

BUT HELEN HAD NO IDEA WHAT HAD TAKEN PLACE BEFORE. THE FORMATIVE YEARS, WHEN THE MORTAR OF IDENTITY IS BLENDED, THE FOUNDATION OF CHARACTER SET AND HARDENED.

A TWO-YEAR-OLD BOY'S TANTRUM KEPT COMING TO MIND.

EARLY TRAUMA. BLOCKING OUT THE HORROR. WHAT HORROR FOR SHARON?

SHARON HAD GROWN UP ON MAGNA LAND, IN A MAGNA HOUSE. HER MOTHER HAD MADE LOVE TO LELAND BELDING. SHARON AS HIS HEIR? WHY WOULD HE HAVE ABANDONED HER? PALMED HER OFF ON THE RANSOMS?

AND BEFORE THAT...WHAT ABOUT THOSE FIRST THREE-PLUS YEARS OF SHARON'S LIFE?

SHE FABRICATED AN IDENTITY OUT OF FRAGMENTS OF OTHER PEOPLE'S LIVES: KRUSE, HELEN, BELDING...

SHE'D ROTATED THE STORY OF THE DROWNED TWIN ONE WAY FOR HELEN, ANOTHER FOR ME, LYING—TO THOSE SHE OSTENSIBLY LOVED— WITH THE EASE OF BRUSHING HER HAIR. WHY? WHAT TRAUMA FED HER DISSOCIATION?

"ALL THOSE YEARS," HELEN HAD SAID, "I FELT I UNDERSTOOD HER. NOW I REALIZE I WAS DELUDING MYSELF. I BARELY KNEW HER."

WELCOME TO THE CLUB, TEACH.

I AWOKE AT SEVEN THE NEXT MORNING, SHUFFLED TO THE TERRACE TO GET THE PAPER.

MORNING, BIG FELLA. HOW 'BOUT THEM DODGERS?

TRAPP HAS ME BACK ON NIGHTS. STUPID PRICK DOESN'T REALIZE HE'S GIVEN ME MORE TIME TO DIG. FOUND A NEW SOFT SPOT.

ON TOP OF HIS OTHER VIRTUES, THE CAPTAIN HAS A FONDNESS FOR UNDERAGE GIRLS. TEENAGE JAILBAIT. FOUND A FORMER VICTIM. IF I CAN GET CORROBORATION...

ANYWAY, THOUGHT I'D COME BY FOR SOME SHOW-AND-TELL.

FED THE FISH. PRETTY SURE THE BLACK AND GOLD ONE IS GROWING TEETH.

I'VE BEEN TRAINING HIM ON SHARK CHUM.

IT'S WORKING.

SO, BURGLARY CALL CAME IN LAST NIGHT. NORTH CRESCENT DRIVE. THE FONTAINES. PLACE LOOKS LIKE POMPEII AFTER THE BIG LAVA PARTY.

NEAT. SOMEONE'S TYING UP LOOSE ENDS.

I FILLED MILO IN ON WHAT I'D LEARNED IN WILLOW GLEN. HE LISTENED...

...THEN DEMANDED A BEER.

SO, LET'S SAY SHARON AND HER TWIN SPRUNG FROM AN AFFAIR BETWEEN BELDING AND LINDA LANIER. LINDA KEPT THE PREGNANCY SECRET. THOUGHT BELDING MIGHT FORCE HER TO TERMINATE.

CROTTY SAW LANIER WITH NEURATH. WHAT IF HE WAS HER DOCTOR AND HER LOVER?

AS HER GYNECOLOGIST, NEURATH WOULD BE THE FIRST TO KNOW SHE WAS PREGNANT. MAYBE HE GOT ANGRY. JEALOUS.

HE THREATENS TO TELL BELDING. LINDA'S BROTHER COMES UP WITH A PLOT: SEDUCE THE DOC ON FILM.

LINDA LEAVES TOWN, GIVES BIRTH, TO **TWINS**. NOW SHE FIGURES IT'S SAFE TO TELL BELDING: ABORTING A FETUS IS ONE THING; REJECTING TWO ADORABLE GIRL BABIES IS ANOTHER.

WITH BROTHER CABLE'S ENCOURAGEMENT, LINDA PAYS BELDING A VISIT, SHOWS HIM THE GIRLS, DEMANDS THAT HE PAY UP.

SOUNDS JUST LIKE THE KIND OF STUPID SCAM STONE LOSERS ALWAYS TRY TO PULL.

THE DUMB STORY YOU PIECE TOGETHER AFTER THEY'VE ENDED UP ON A SLAB.

THEY WEREN'T EQUIPPED FOR BELDING'S RESOURCES. HIS **ENTIRE** FORTUNE WAS AT STAKE. BUT THAT "DRUG BUST" ONLY TOOK CARE OF **HALF** THE PROBLEM. BELDING STILL HAD TWO BABIES TO GET RID OF.

SET UP HIS OWN KID'S MOTHER, AND THEN SELL AWAY THE BABIES? COLD. **ULTRA-COLD.**

WHY THE RANSOMS, THOUGH? AND YOU SAID YOU SAW BOTH GIRLS IN THE OLD PHOTO. SO WHAT THE **HELL** HAPPENED TO THE SISTER?

THERE'S SOMEONE WHO COULD CLEAR IT UP FOR US. **VIDAL**... ALIVE AND WELL IN EL SEGUNDO.

RIGHT. LET'S JUST WALTZ INTO HIS OFFICE AND TELL HIS SECRETARY'S ASSISTANT'S GOFER WE WANT AN AUDIENCE WITH THE BIG BOSS.

JUST A FRIENDLY CHAT ABOUT CHILD ABANDONMENT, BLACKMAIL, INHERITANCE CLAIMS, MULTIPLE MURDERS.

I NEED SOME SHUTEYE. ALL WE CAN DO IS KEEP DIGGING. AND, **DELAWARE**... WATCH YOUR REAR.

YOU TOO, STURGIS. YOURS AIN'T SCORCH-PROOF.

THE CAMPUS LIBRARY SYSTEM HAD THREE LISTINGS FOR NEURATH, DONALD. A BOOK AND TWO ARTICLES ON FERTILITY, HOUSED IN THE BIOMEDICAL LIBRARY, ALONG WITH THE L.A. COUNTY MEDICAL ASSOCIATION DIRECTORY.

HIS OFFICE WAS ON WILSHIRE, JUST WHERE CROTTY HAD PUT IT. A MEMBER OF THE AMA, FIRST-RATE EDUCATION, AND AN ACADEMIC APPOINTMENT AT THE SCHOOL THAT LOOSELY EMPLOYED ME.

HIS RESEARCH INVOLVED THE TREATMENT OF INFERTILITY WITH INJECTIONS OF SEX HORMONES TO STIMULATE OVULATION. REVOLUTIONARY STUFF AT THE TIME.

NEURATH HAD INJECTED HALF A DOZEN BARREN WOMEN WITH HORMONES OBTAINED FROM THE OVARIES OF FEMALE CADAVERS. AFTER SEVERAL MONTHS OF REPEATED TREATMENTS, THREE OF THE WOMEN BECAME PREGNANT.

TWO SUFFERED MISCARRIAGES, BUT ONE CARRIED A HEALTHY BABY TO TERM. FERTILITY AND ABORTION. NEURATH GIVETH; NEURATH TAKETH AWAY.

ANOTHER HOUR'S DIGGING YIELDED ONE MORE PERTINENT MENTION OF DR. NEURATH. AN OBITUARY. DEAD AT FORTY-FIVE, OF UNSPECIFIED CAUSES, WHILE VACATIONING IN MEXICO. AUGUST, 1953.

THE SAME MONTH AS LINDA LANIER AND BROTHER CABLE.

PIECES BEGAN TO FALL INTO PLACE. I THOUGHT OF SOMETHING ELSE, ANOTHER PART OF THE PUZZLE CRYING OUT FOR A SOLUTION. LEFT BIOMED AND HEADED FOR THE RESEARCH LIBRARY.

RUNNING, FEELING LIGHT-FOOTED, FOR THE FIRST TIME IN A LONG TIME.

IN THE RESEARCH LIBRARY'S SPECIAL COLLECTIONS ROOM I REQUESTED VOLUMES FROM THE L.A. SOCIAL REGISTRY. LISTINGS OF COUNTRY CLUBS, CHARITY GALAS, GENEALOGICAL SOCIETIES...A ROSTER OF THE RIGHT PEOPLE.

SELF-CONGRATULATION FOR THOSE WHOSE FASCINATION WITH THE US-THEM GAME HADN'T ENDED IN HIGH SCHOOL.

I FOUND WHAT I WANTED, COPIED DOWN NAMES, CONNECTED THE DOTS UNTIL THE TRUTH, OR SOMETHING DAMNED CLOSE TO IT, BEGAN TO TAKE SHAPE.

I KNEW WHERE TO FIND THE REST: HOLMBY HILLS. SKYLARK. HOME TO HOPE BLALOCK.

MY OLD FRIEND RAMEY ANSWERED THE CALL PHONE. SAID MRS. BLALOCK COULD NOT BE BOTHERED.

I MENTIONED HOW MUCH THE PRESS LOVES A HUMAN INTEREST STORY, ESPECIALLY ONE WITH HEAVY IRONY.

MADAM.

SUDDENLY, HOPE BLALOCK WAS AVAILABLE.

SHE OFFERED ME A DRINK OUT OF HABITUAL COURTESY. LOOKED PUT OUT WHEN I ACCEPTED.

NICE SUN-ROOM. YOU HAVE THEM IN ALL YOUR HOMES?

JUST WHAT KIND OF DOCTOR ARE YOU?

PSYCHOLOGIST.

I MIGHT AS WELL HAVE SAID WITCH DOCTOR.

I JUST GOT BACK FROM WILLOW GLEN. I RAN INTO SHIRLEE AND JASPER RANSOM.

PSYCHOLOGISTS. KEEPERS OF SECRETS. HOW MUCH DO YOU WANT? DOCTOR.

KLK KLIING

I'M NOT INTERESTED IN YOUR MONEY.

HEH-HAHA... OH, EVERYONE'S INTERESTED IN MY MONEY.

I'M LIKE SOME BAG OF BLOOD CRUSTED WITH LEECHES. THE ONLY QUESTION IS HOW MUCH BLOOD EACH OF THEM GETS.

HARD TO THINK OF SHIRLEE AND JASPER AS LEECHES. ACTUALLY, THE TWO OF THEM HAVE DONE QUITE WELL FOR THEMSELVES.

BETTER THAN YOU EVER EXPECTED. HOW LONG DID YOU FIGURE THEY'D LAST, LIVING OUT THERE IN THE DIRT?

CASH IN AN ENVELOPE FOR PEOPLE WHO DIDN'T KNOW HOW TO MAKE CHANGE. VERY GENEROUS. AS WAS YOUR OTHER GIFT.

I GUESS YOU DIDN'T REALLY VIEW IT AS A GIFT. MORE OF A THROWAWAY. LIKE OLD CLOTHES TO YOUR FAVORITE CHARITY.

WHO THE HELL **ARE** YOU! AND **WHAT** DO YOU WANT!

I'M AN OLD, CLOSE FRIEND OF SHARON RANSOM'S. ALSO KNOWN AS JEWEL RAE JOHNSON. SHARON JEAN BLALOCK. TAKE YOUR PICK.

AND ALL I WANT... IS THE **TRUTH**, FROM THE BEGINNING.

OH, GOD. NO. I...IT'S IMPOSSIBLE... WRONG OF YOU TO DO THIS.

I'LL START. YOU FILL IN THE BLANKS.

PLEASE. IT'S **OVER**. DONE WITH. YOU OBVIOUSLY KNOW ENOUGH TO UNDERSTAND HOW I'VE SUFFERED.

YOU HAVEN'T A PATENT ON SUFFERING. EVEN KRUSE SUF- FERED—

OH, **SPARE ME!** SOME PEOPLE **REAP** WHAT THEY SOW!

"LOURDES ESCOBAR WAS THE KRUSES' MAID. AN INNOCENT YOUNG WOMAN WHO ENDED UP LOOKING LIKE DOG FOOD."

"WHAT DID **SHE** SOW, MRS. BLALOCK?"

"THAT'S **DISGUSTING!** I HAD **NOTHING** TO DO WITH ANYONE'S DEATH."

YOU SET WHEELS IN MOTION. TRYING TO SOLVE YOUR LITTLE PROBLEM. NOW, IT'S FINALLY SOLVED.

THIRTY YEARS TOO LATE.

"LET ME TELL YOU A FAIRY TALE."

"ONCE UPON A TIME THERE WAS A YOUNG WOMAN, BEAUTIFUL AND RICH...A VERITABLE PRINCESS. AND LIKE A PRINCESS IN A FAIRY TALE SHE HAD EVERYTHING..."

"...EXCEPT THE THING SHE WANTED MOST."

"AND THEN, ONE DAY, HER PRAYERS WERE ANSWERED, JUST LIKE MAGIC. BUT IT ALL TURNED SOUR. SHE HAD TO FIX THINGS...MAKE ARRANGEMENTS."

HE TOLD YOU *EVERYTHING!* THE MONSTER...HE PROMISED ME! DAMN HIM TO *HELL!*

KRUSE DIDN'T TELL ME ANY- THING.

IT'S ALL THERE FOR THE LOOKING.

YOUR HUS- BAND'S OBITUARY IN 1953 SHOWS NO CHILDREN.

SAME WITH YOUR BLUE BOOK ENTRIES...

...UNTIL THE FOLLOWING YEAR. TWO NEW DAUGHTERS: SHARON JEAN. SHERRY MARIE.

OH MY GOD.

HENRY WANTED HEIRS SO BADLY. A REAL *MAN'S MAN,* BUT HIS SEED WAS ALL WATER! WOULDN'T HEAR OF ADOPTING. HAD TO BE HIS OWN BLOOD!

"BUT HE DIED, AND BROTHER BILLY SHOWED UP MONTHS AFTER THE FUNERAL, AS IF TO ANSWER YOUR PRAYERS."

"THE TIMING WAS PERFECT. LET EVERYONE THINK HENRY HAD FINALLY COME THROUGH...IN SPADES. *TWO BEAUTIFUL LITTLE GIRLS.*"

"THEY *WERE* BEAUTIFUL. SO TINY, BUT ALREADY BEAUTIFUL. MY OWN LITTLE GIRLS."

"I GAVE THEM NEW NAMES... FOR THEIR NEW LIVES."

WHERE DID YOUR BROTHER SAY HE GOT THEM?

HE DIDN'T. JUST THAT THEIR MOTHER HAD FALLEN ON HARD TIMES, AND COULDN'T CARE FOR THEM.

BILLY SAID THE LESS ANY OF US KNEW, THE BETTER.

135

HOW LONG UNTIL THINGS STARTED TO GO BAD BETWEEN THEM?

EARLY. I DON'T KNOW. SEVEN OR EIGHT MONTHS.

THEY'D JUST STARTED CRAWLING AND GETTING INTO EVERYTHING...HOW OLD WOULD THAT BE?

THEY WERE SO IDENTICAL, BUT SO DIFFERENT. CONFLICT WAS INEVITABLE.

SHERRY WAS ACTIVE, DOMINANT, STRONG. SHE KNEW WHAT SHE WANTED AND WENT RIGHT FOR IT. WOULDN'T TAKE NO FOR AN ANSWER.

WHAT WAS SHARON LIKE?

A WILTED FLOWER... EPHEMERAL, DISTANT. NEVER DEMANDED A THING.

THE TWO OF THEM ESTABLISHED THEIR ROLES AND PLAYED THEM TO THE HILT...LEADER AND FOLLOWER.

IF THERE WAS A BIT OF CANDY OR A TOY THAT THEY BOTH WANTED, SHERRY WOULD JUST MOVE RIGHT IN AND TAKE IT.

SHARON LEARNED THAT, ONE WAY OR THE OTHER, SHERRY WAS GOING TO TRIUMPH.

I'D SEEN THAT SMILE BEFORE...

...ON THE FACES OF INEFFECTUAL PARENTS SADDLED WITH EXTREMELY DISTURBED, AGGRESSIVE YOUNGSTERS.

POOR SHARON REALLY DID GET KNOCKED AROUND.

"OH, I SUPPOSE THEY LOVED EACH OTHER. WHEN THEY WEREN'T FIGHTING, THERE WERE THE USUAL HUGS AND KISSES."

"THEY WERE INSEPARABLE... BUT ALWAYS, THE FIGHTING."

SHERRY ALWAYS WON. IF SHARON EVER DARED NOT DO AS SHE SAID, SHERRY LASHED OUT. SLAPPING, KICKING, BITING.

I TRIED TO SEPARATE THEM. SHERRY THREW TANTRUMS. SHARON JUST HUDDLED IN THE CORNER. THEY WEREN'T COMPLETE WITHOUT EACH OTHER.

SILENT PARTNERS.

HOW SERIOUS WERE HER INJURIES?

IT WASN'T CHILD ABUSE, IF THAT'S WHAT YOU'RE GETTING AT.

CLUMPS OF HAIR PULLED OUT, BITES, SCRATCHES. NOTHING SERIOUS.

UNTIL THE DROWNING.

BOTTOMS UP.

HERE'S TO GLORIOUS, GLORIOUS TRUTH.

MY HOUSE IN SOUTHAMPTON. THE LAST DAY OF HOLIDAY. THEIR NANNY WAS A SLAB-FACED ENGLISH PUDDING! SLUT.

THE GIRLS GOT AWAY FROM HER, RAN TO THE LATTICED POOL HOUSE. WE WENT LOOKING... HEARD LAUGHTER FROM THE POOL HOUSE...

SHERRY WAS JUST STANDING BY THE POOL, LAUGHING.

THE PUDDING DOVE INTO THE FILTHY WATER... DRAGGED SHARON OUT.

SHARON WASN'T SERIOUSLY HURT, BUT SHE SWALLOWED SOME WATER. SHE VOMITED IT ALL UP...

AND SHERRY KEPT LAUGHING.

KRRESH

SHERRY MARCHED UP TO US, THUMPING HER LITTLE CHEST, SAYING "I PUSH HER."

JUST LIKE THAT... "I PUSH HER." I KNEW THEY HAD TO BE SEPARATED... FOREVER.

ENTER BROTHER BILLY.

BILLY ALWAYS TOOK GOOD CARE OF ME.

THE RANSOMS WORKED FOR HIM. HE KNEW THEY COULDN'T HAVE CHILDREN. IT SEEMED LIKE A GOOD SOLUTION FOR EVERYONE.

MY GUESSES TURNED TO FACT, THE PIECES FINALLY FITTING.

IT SICKENED ME, LIKE A BAD-NEWS DIAGNOSIS. MY JAW TIGHTENED.

THE VODKA HAD WORN DOWN HOPE'S DEFENSES. MAYBE PART OF HER ACTUALLY RELISHED THE OPPORTUNITY TO GET IT ALL OUT THERE...TO SOMEONE.

HOPE TOLD HER FRIENDS THAT SHARON HAD DIED. PNEUMONIA. AT SOME LEVEL, DID YOUNG SHERRY WONDER IF IT WAS CAUSED BY THE DROWNING INCIDENT?

HOPE WANTED PEACE FOR EVERYONE...STABILITY. SHE DIDN'T GET IT. SHERRY SUFFERED FROM HORRIBLE SEPARATION ANXIETY.

UNCONTROLLABLE ACTING OUT. TANTRUMS. ONE ENDED WITH SHERRY DIGGING MANICURE SCISSORS INTO HOPE'S ARM. THEN, AT THE AGE OF TEN, THE CAVALRY WAS CALLED IN. KRUSE.

KRUSE LIVED NEARBY. HAD A BEAUTIFUL OFFICE WITH A PRIVATE ENTRANCE. HOPE THOUGHT HE'D BE DISCREET. SHE LAUGHED AS SHE SAID IT. A DRUNKEN, STRIDENT LAUGH.

OF COURSE, HOPE GOT UPDATES FROM BROTHER BILLY. SHARON WAS DOING GREAT OUT THERE IN WILLOW GLEN. THRIVING. YEAH, I THOUGHT...UNTIL LAST WEEK.

A DECADE OF THERAPY WITH SVENGALI KRUSE. NO IMPROVEMENT. OLDER SHERRY WOULD DISAPPEAR FOR WEEKS. EVEN DROVE HOPE'S BENTLEY IN THE OCEAN AND JUST... WALKED AWAY.

EVENTUALLY, KRUSE DISCOVERED SHERRY'S ORIGINS. DISCOVERED SHARON, SEEMINGLY IDENTICAL TO HIS FORMER PATIENT, AT A COLLEGE CAREER DAY.

"HE BLED ME DRY FOR YEARS, THE MONSTER."

"I HOPE HE'S WRITHING IN ETERNAL HELLFIRE."

EXTORTION. I HAD TO GIVE HOPE ONE THING: SHE CAME BY HER DISTRUST OF PSYCHOLOGISTS HONESTLY.

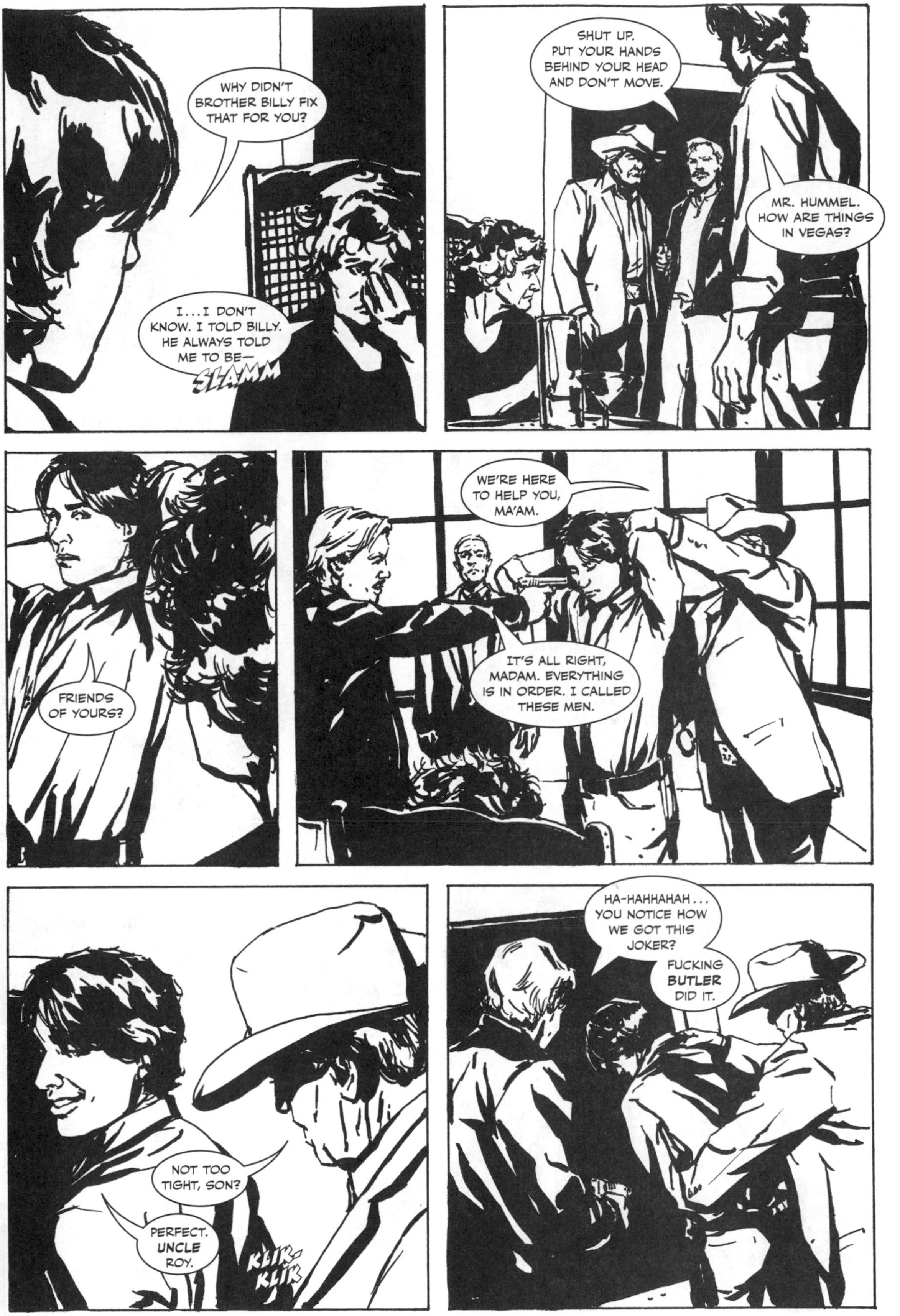
WHY DIDN'T BROTHER BILLY FIX THAT FOR YOU?
I...I DON'T KNOW. I TOLD BILLY. HE ALWAYS TOLD ME TO BE—
SLAMM
SHUT UP. PUT YOUR HANDS BEHIND YOUR HEAD AND DON'T MOVE.
MR. HUMMEL. HOW ARE THINGS IN VEGAS?
FRIENDS OF YOURS?
WE'RE HERE TO HELP YOU, MA'AM.
IT'S ALL RIGHT, MADAM. EVERYTHING IS IN ORDER. I CALLED THESE MEN.
NOT TOO TIGHT, SON?
PERFECT. **UNCLE** ROY.
KLIK-KLIK
HA-HAHHAHAH... YOU NOTICE HOW WE GOT THIS JOKER?
FUCKING **BUTLER** DID IT.

BLINDFOLDED, SEARCHED, STRIPPED OF MY WATCH, KEYS AND WALLET, AND EASED INTO A CAR THAT SMELLED BRAND NEW.

ROBBED OF MY SENSES, THE ONLY MENTAL SIGNPOST I HAD LEFT WAS TIME. I BEGAN COUNTING.

FORTY-FIVE MINUTES IN THE CAR. TWO HOURS IN A HELICOPTER, AND THEN HUMMEL ESCORTED ME...

...HERE.

NINETEEN MINUTES NOW. DONALD NEURATH'S OBITUARY CAME TO MIND...UNSPECIFIED CAUSES WHILE VACATIONING IN MEXICO.

I TOOK A TENTATIVE STEP. ANOTHER. SWUNG MY FOOT OUT IN A SLOW ARC, TESTING.

NO TRIPWIRES...WAS INCHING FORWARD... WHEN AN ELECTRIC WHINE SOUNDED FROM SOMEWHERE BEHIND ME.

CUTE LITTLE DANCE, SON.

WE COULD USE THE RAIN.

STAY LOOSE AND NO ONE'LL HURT YOU.

THROUGH SEVERAL DOORS. AIR CONDITIONING.

CUFFS OFF. FINGERS FILLED MY MOUTH, PRIED UNDER MY TONGUE.

STRIPPED. HANDS RAN A MARATHON OVER MY BODY, PROBING.

DRESSED AGAIN, IN MY OWN SWEAT-STAINED CLOTHES. ALL OVER IN A MATTER OF MINUTES.

BY THE TIME I WAS ALLOWED TO REMOVE MY BLINDFOLD...

...I WAS IN BILLY VIDAL'S OFFICE.

DR. DELAWARE, THANK YOU FOR COMING.

HIS VOICE DIDN'T FIT WITH THE REST OF HIM...A HOARSE, WISPY CROAK, CRACKING BETWEEN WORDS.

SORRY... THAT WAS AN ICEBREAKER THAT FELL FLAT.

PLEASE FORGIVE ANY INCONVENIENCE YOU'VE BEEN CAUSED. THERE DIDN'T SEEM TO BE ANY OTHER WAY.

I WASN'T SURE IT WAS WISE FOR US TO MEET. TODAY, WHEN YOU VISITED MY SISTER, YOU MADE THE DECISION FOR ME.

KOFF KOFF THINGS HAD TO BE DONE QUICKLY AND CAREFULLY.

SO ONCE AGAIN, I'LL APOLOGIZE FOR THE **WAY** YOU WERE BROUGHT HERE.

I HOPE WE CAN PUT THAT TO REST AND MOVE ON.

I COULD STILL FEEL THE CHAFE OF THE CUFFS AROUND MY WRISTS, THOUGHT OF THE COPTER RIDE.

MAINLINING FEAR WHILE WAITING FOR HUMMEL AND HIS GOLF CART, FINGERS UP MY ASS. "CUTE LITTLE DANCE, SON."

I KNEW MY RAGE WOULD WEAKEN ME IF I LET IT TAKE OVER.

MOVE ON TO **WHAT**?

PLEASE, DOCTOR... KOFF...

...DON'T WASTE PRECIOUS TIME BEING COY.

SHORT ON TIME, ARE YOU?

VERY MUCH SO.

AN UNFORTUNATE SIDE EFFECT OF WITNESSING AN ATOMIC TEST CONDUCTED BY MAGNA AND THE U.S. ARMY, SOME THIRTY YEARS AGO.

A WONDERFUL EVENT, UNTIL A SUDDEN SHIFT IN THE WINDS: ALL OF US WERE EXPOSED TO RADIOACTIVE DUST.

NO ONE THOUGHT MUCH ABOUT IT UNTIL FIF-TEEN YEARS AGO, WHEN THE CANCERS BEGAN APPEARING. IT'S ONLY A MATTER OF TIME FOR ME.

YOU LOOK HEALTHIER THAN I DO.

DEBATABLE.

NEVERTHELESS, DO I SOUND HEALTHY?

WHAT ABOUT BELDING? WAS HE EXPOSED?

LELAND WAS **PROTECTED.**

AS ALWAYS.

DOCTOR, I'M WILLING TO SATISFY YOUR CURIOSITY ON CONDITION THAT YOU STOP TURNING OVER ROCKS.

I KNOW YOUR INTENTIONS ARE HONORABLE BUT YOU DON'T REALIZE HOW **DESTRUCTIVE** YOU COULD BE.

KUSSH

I DON'T SEE HOW I COULD ADD TO THE DESTRUCTION THAT'S ALREADY TAKEN PLACE.

I WANT TO LEAVE THIS EARTH KNOWING EVERYTHING'S BEEN DONE TO CUSHION CERTAIN INDIVIDUALS.

YOU'VE SEEN ONLY PART OF THE PICTURE. IF YOU WILL GIVE ME YOUR WORD THAT YOU'LL STOP PROBING, I'LL SHOW YOU THE REST.

YOU BELIEVE I'VE DESTROYED ALL THOSE PEOPLE?

WHY PRETEND THAT I HAVE A CHOICE?

YOU CAN ALWAYS JUST SQUASH ME. LIKE SEAMAN CROSS, EULALEE AND CABLE JOHNSON, DONALD NEURATH, THE KRUSES.

HA-HEHEH... DOCTOR, EVEN IF I WANTED TO **SQUASH** YOU...I WOULDN'T. YOU'VE ACQUIRED A CERTAIN...AURA OF GRACE.

SOMEONE CARED DEEPLY ABOUT YOU. SOMEONE LOVELY AND KIND...DEAR TO US **BOTH.**

IF MY OFFER DOESN'T APPEAL TO YOU, I'LL HAVE YOU FLOWN BACK HOME IMMEDIATELY.

WHAT ARE MY CHANCES OF ARRIVING THERE ALIVE?

ONE HUNDRED PERCENT. BARRING ACTS OF GOD.

OR GOD PRETENDING TO BE THE MAGNA CORPORATION.

HAH! I'LL TRY TO REMEMBER THAT ONE.

WHAT IS IT THEN, DOCTOR? STAY FOR DINNER?

MY EYES SETTLED ON A SPOT IN THE LAWN, SEEKING OUT A WOODEN BENCH. NOTHING, BUT MY MEMORY PLACED ONE THERE ANYWAY.

A POSING SPOT...TWO GIRLS IN COWGIRL SUITS, EATING ICE CREAM.

AND NOW, HERE I WAS...WITH THE FORMER BILLY THE PIMP, OFFERING ME A LOVELY MEAL...AND ANSWERS.

TEN MINUTES LATER, I WAS WATCHING VIDAL ENJOY HIS MEAL DESPITE A SLIGHT WINCE EVERY TIME HE SWALLOWED.

WHY DID SHARON KILL HERSELF?

HURMM...THAT'S AN END POINT. LET'S PROCEED CHRONO-LOGICALLY.

OKAY. HOW ABOUT STARTING WITH EULALEE AND CABLE JOHNSON. PARTY GIRL AND PETTY CROOK.

"I ALWAYS KNEW HER AS LINDA...AN *EXQUISITE* CREATURE. SHE HAD A VERY...*EASYGOING* NATURE. I FELT SHE WAS THE RIGHT WOMAN TO *HELP* LELAND. HE DIDN'T UNDERSTAND WOMEN...FROZE UP WHEN HE WAS AROUND THEM, COULDN'T...*PERFORM*."

"HE WAS TOO INTELLIGENT TO MISS THE IRONY: RICH, POWERFUL, THE COUNTRY'S MOST ELIGIBLE BACHELOR, AND A VIRGIN AT FORTY. EVERY KETTLE HAS ITS BOILING POINT. THE FRUSTRATION WAS INTERFERING WITH HIS WORK. I HAD TO FIND A...*GUIDE* FOR HIM."

SEXUAL FAVORS FOR A *FEE*. SOUNDS LIKE SOMETHING ELSE. YOU DIDN'T JUST PICK HER FOR HER *PERSONALITY*.

YOU THOUGHT SHE WAS UNABLE TO BEAR CHILDREN.

YOU'RE A VERY BRIGHT YOUNG FELLOW.

DID THEY DEVELOP FEELINGS FOR EACH OTHER?

LELAND BELDING DIDN'T **FEEL**, DOCTOR. HE WAS AS CLOSE TO MECHANICAL AS A HUMAN BEING COULD BE

MY GUESS IS THAT HE SAW HER AS ANOTHER OF HIS MACHINES. WHICH ISN'T TO SAY HE DISPARAGED HER. **MACHINES** WERE WHAT HE ADMIRED MOST.

I'D IMAGINE LINDA VIEWED LELAND WITH A MIXTURE OF AWE AND PITY... THE WAY A DOCTOR MIGHT REGARD A PATIENT WITH A RARE DISEASE.

*I KNEW THEN THAT LINDA LANIER HAD BECOME **MORE** TO VIDAL THAN A HAREM GIRL ON ASSIGNMENT. KNEW I COULDN'T TOUCH THAT.*

AND THEN BROTHER CABLE STEPPED IN.

CABLE JOHNSON WAS **DESPICABLE**. WHEN HE AND LINDA WERE TEENS HE SOLD HER TO THE LOCAL BOYS FOR MONEY. HE WAS PURE **FILTH**.

I KNEW HE WAS RISKY...THOUGHT IT HAD BEEN DEALT WITH, BUT HE WAS A COMPULSIVE CRIMINAL, COULDN'T STOP CONNIVING.

ENTER DONALD NEURATH, M.D. FERTILITY EXPERT AND MEAL TICKET. A **TRADE**. THE PORN LOOP IN EXCHANGE FOR HORMONAL TREATMENT FOR LINDA.

MY, MY...YOU **ARE** A THOROUGH RESEARCHER, DOCTOR

CACTUS ICE CREAM. VERY SOOTHING.

AFTER A MATTER OF MONTHS, LINDA CAME TO ME WITH A NOTE ON NEURATH'S STATIONARY THAT SAID SHE HAD CONTRACTED SOME SORT OF VAGINAL INFECTION.

I GAVE HER TEN THOUSAND DOLLARS' SEVERANCE PAY AND WISHED HER WELL.

"OF COURSE, WE WEREN'T RID OF CABLE JOHNSON. NEARLY A YEAR LATER, HE INFORMED ME I'D BETTER MEET WITH HIM IF I KNEW WHAT WAS GOOD FOR LELAND. 'THE *SQUEEZE*' WAS ON."

"OH, HE THOUGHT HE WAS A SMART ONE. KEPT SAYING THE JOHNSONS AND THE BELDINGS WERE GOING TO BE *KINFOLK*."

"HE BROUGHT LINDA IN WITH HER 'LITTLE GIFTS'. ALL THREE OF THEM. JEWEL RAE, JANA SUE, AND POOR JOAN DIXIE, BORN BLIND, DEAF, AND PARALYZED. SHE WAS SO TINY. LINDA COOED AT HER, MASSAGING HER LIMBS. PRETENDING HER TWITCHES WERE VOLUNTARY."

"PRETENDING SHE WAS *NORMAL*. OF COURSE, JOAN'S DEFORMITIES WERE AN INSULT TO LELAND...THE IMPLICATION THAT HE'D TAKEN PART IN CREATING SOMETHING DEFECTIVE."

"I KNEW HOW HE'D REACT. I WANTED TO KEEP ALL OF IT FROM HIM, WORK THINGS OUT IN MY OWN WAY. BUT CABLE WANTED IT *ALL*, RIGHT NOW."

"SHE WENT TO HIS OFFICE WITH THE BABIES LATE ONE NIGHT. THE POOR, *STUPID* GIRL, BELIEVING THE SIGHT OF THEM WOULD IGNITE HIS PATERNAL PRIDE."

THE MOMENT SHE WAS GONE HE PHONED...ORDERED ME OVER FOR A 'PROBLEM-SOLVING SESSION.'

HE'D COME TO A DECISION: ALL OF THEM WOULD HAVE TO BE ELIMINATED. **PERMANENTLY.**

I WAS TO BE THE ANGEL OF DEATH.

I **SAVED** THOSE BABIES. ONLY I COULD HAVE. ONLY I HAD ENOUGH OF LELAND'S TRUST TO DISAGREE WITH HIM AND GET AWAY WITH IT.

I USED THE ONLY LOGIC HE WOULD UNDERSTAND...TOLD HIM THAT IF IT EVER CAME OUT HE'D BE **RUINED.** MAGNA WOULD BE RUINED.

I TOLD HIM I'D QUIT BEFORE CARRYING OUT **THIS** ORDER. AND IF THOSE BABIES DIED, I COULDN'T GUARANTEE MY SILENCE.

WAS HE PREPARED TO ELIMI-NATE ME, AS WELL? EVENTUALLY, HE AGREED.

NEW NAMES, NEW LIVES...EXCEPT FOR THE JOHNSONS.

WAS IT YOU OR BELDING WHO THOUGHT OF THE DOPE DEALER ANGLE?

THAT...IT WASN'T SUPPOSED TO HAPPEN THE WAY IT DID. LINDA WASN'T SUPPOSED TO BE THERE.

CABLE GRABBED HER, THE FILTH, USED HER AS A *SHIELD.* SHE WAS SHOT BY ACCIDENT. WITH HER BROTHER GONE, WE COULD HAVE HANDLED—

NO WAY. SHE WOULDN'T HAVE LET HER CHILDREN BE TAKEN FROM HER WITHOUT A FUSS.

"SHE HAD TO DIE. YOU EITHER KNEW THAT FROM THE BEGINNING OR CHOSE NOT TO SEE IT WHEN YOU SET UP THE BUST."

"IF I GIVE YOU THE BENEFIT OF THE DOUBT, THEN BELDING TOOK CARE OF IT BEHIND YOUR BACK."

"HUMMEL AND DEGRANZFELD WERE HIS BOYS. HE WAS PLEASED WITH THE JOB THEY'D DONE...REWARDED THEM WITH CUSHY JOBS IN LAS VEGAS. SET FOR LIFE."

ARE YOU THE FATHER?

I... I DON'T KNOW.

LELAND AND I HAD THE SAME BLOOD TYPE. I NEVER DID A MORE THOROUGH INVESTIGATION. DIDN'T SEE THE *VALUE.*

WHEN THE TIME CAME, WHY BANISH **SHARON**? FROM THE MANSION TO A DIRT PATCH. TWO RETARDED PEOPLE AS CARETAKERS. HER IDENTITY STRIPPED AWAY—

FOR **HER** SAKE!

I'D HAVE **NEVER** DONE ANYTHING TO HARM HER!

HUK, HKECCH... HURRRK. EXCUSE ME. SHE...SHE HAD HER MOTHER'S FACE. SHERRY HAD THE FEATURES, BUT **ONLY** SHARON HAD THE FACE.

I'D ARRIVED HATING HIM, PREPARED TO STOKE MY HATE. NOW I FELT LIKE PUTTING MY ARM AROUND HIM.

I DID EVERYTHING I COULD TO FIND THE BEST SOLUTIONS... FOR **EVERYONE** INVOLVED.

ALL RIGHT, YOU'RE MOTHER TERESA. SO HOW COME PEOPLE KEEP DYING?

SOME PEOPLE **DESERVE** TO DIE.

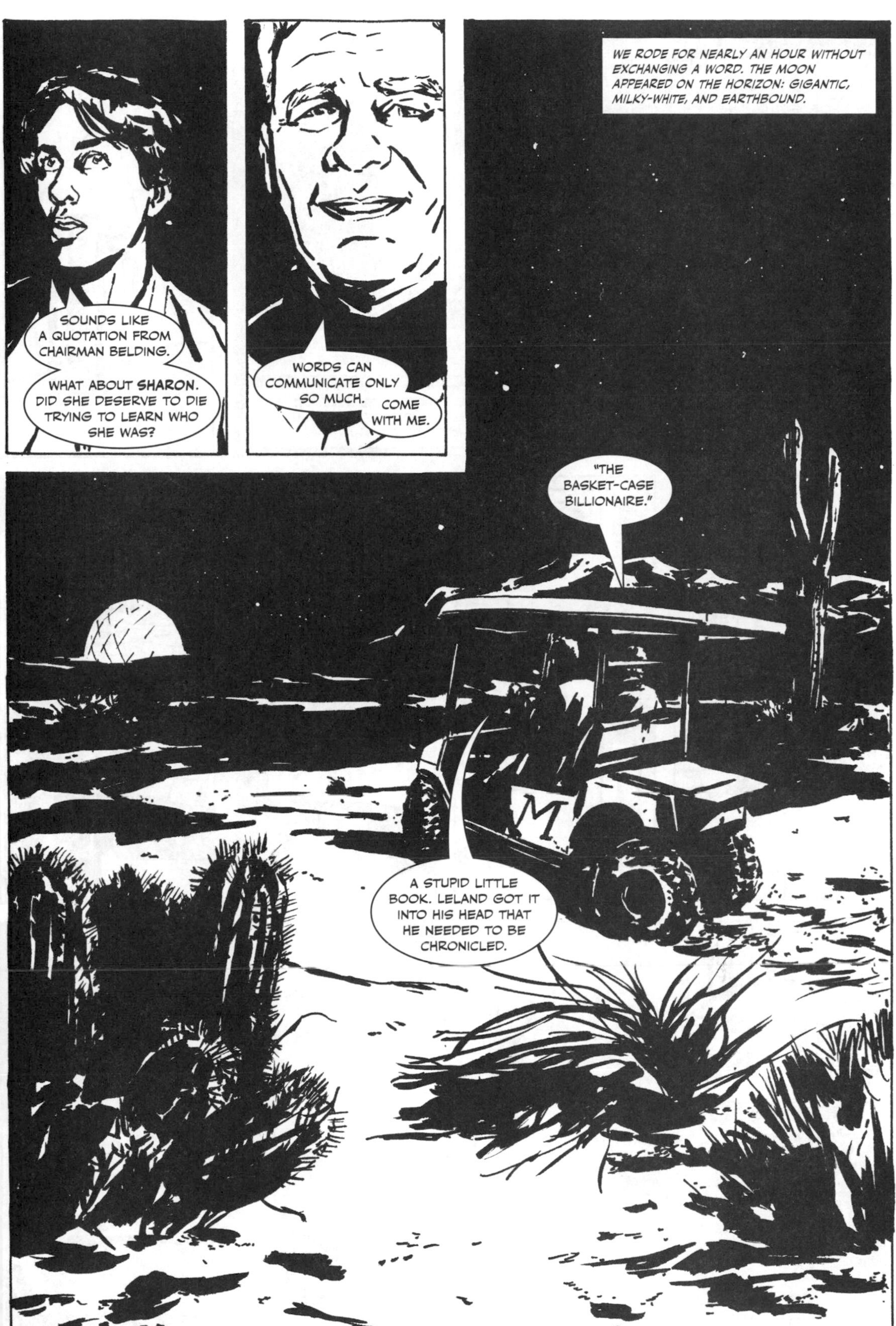
SOUNDS LIKE A QUOTATION FROM CHAIRMAN BELDING.
WHAT ABOUT **SHARON**. DID SHE DESERVE TO DIE TRYING TO LEARN WHO SHE WAS?
WORDS CAN COMMUNICATE ONLY SO MUCH.
COME WITH ME.
WE RODE FOR NEARLY AN HOUR WITHOUT EXCHANGING A WORD. THE MOON APPEARED ON THE HORIZON: GIGANTIC, MILKY-WHITE, AND EARTHBOUND.
"THE BASKET-CASE BILLIONAIRE."
A STUPID LITTLE BOOK. LELAND GOT IT INTO HIS HEAD THAT HE NEEDED TO BE CHRONICLED.

AND, BEFORE YOU ACCUSE ME OF **"SQUASHING"** THE AUTHOR, SEAMAN CROSS WAS NO THREAT.

NO ONE BELIEVED HIM.

BILLY FROZE AT THE DOOR, FOR JUST A SECOND, TO LET THE MESSAGE SINK IN:

CROSS HAD POISONED THE WELL FOR LELAND BELDING STORIES. NO ONE WOULD BELIEVE ME ABOUT THIS DAY.

HELLO, ALEX.

RISEN LIKE LAZARUS.

NEVER GONE.

COME.

SOMEONE IS GONE. THE RED DRESS? STRAWBERRY DAIQUIRIS?

YES. HER.

SLEEPING WITH YOUR PATIENTS? KRUSE'S PORN LOOP RECREATION? ALL HER...ALL SHERRY?

ALL OF IT. THE LOOP...I KNOW HOW IT LOOKS, BUT PAUL THOUGHT IT WOULD BE CURATIVE.

I NEVER THOUGHT SHE'D CARRY THINGS THAT FAR. I KNEW SHE RESENTED ME, BUT I DIDN'T THINK...

IS THAT WHAT YOU AND UNCLE BILLY WERE TALKING ABOUT AT THE PARTY? HER?

SHE WAS FORCING HERSELF ON ME AGAIN...SCREAMING AND CURSING, CRAWLING INTO BED WITH ME AND MAULING ME, TRYING TO SUCK MY BREASTS.

I HOPED YOU'D ATTEND. YOU WERE ALWAYS MY ROCK. I THOUGHT HISTORY MIGHT REPEAT ITSELF.

WHEN OUR EYES MET I COULDN'T BELIEVE IT. DESTINY.

AND NOW YOU'RE HERE. HELLO, STRANGER.

HELLO.

BEFORE YOU KNEW ABOUT SHERRY...DID YOU EVER FANTASIZE ABOUT HAVING A TWIN?

ALL THE TIME, WHEN I WAS A CHILD.

BUT I NEVER GAVE MUCH CREDENCE TO THAT. I WAS THE TYPE OF KID WHO FANTASIZED ABOUT **EVERYTHING**.

AND THAT AUTUMN KRUSE INTRODUCED YOU TO YOUR REAL SILENT PARTNERS.

AT FIRST, HEARING ABOUT MY TWINS WAS **WONDERFUL**. A WAVE OF HAPPINESS WASHED OVER ME.

THEN, **SUDDENLY**, EVERYTHING GOT COLD AND DARK AND THE WALLS STARTED CLOSING IN.

I WAS SURE I WAS ABOUT TO DIE. I TRIED TO SCREAM, BUT NO SOUND CAME OUT. THEN SOMETHING CAME OUT, FROM DEEP INSIDE OF ME...A **TERRIBLE** SCREAM.

"PAUL HELD ME UNTIL I WAS CALM, THEN HE GAVE ME THE SNAPSHOT. ME AND ANOTHER ME. HE'D WRITTEN SOMETHING ON THE BACK..."

"...'S AND S, SILENT PARTNERS.' FOR THREE DAYS I DIDN'T DRESS OR EAT OR GET OUT OF BED. JUST SAT STARING AT THAT SNAPSHOT."

THE THIRD DAY WAS WHEN YOU FOUND ME. WHEN I SAW YOU I WENT CRAZY. I'M **SORRY**, ALEX. I LOST CONTROL.

DON'T WORRY. LONG FORGOTTEN.

WHERE DID YOU GET THE HOUSE? THE CAR?

PAUL.

THE HOUSE WAS A RENTAL NO ONE WAS USING. A CAR HE BOUGHT FOR HIS WIFE, BUT SHE HATED DRIVING A STICK.

HE SAID I **DESERVED** IT... AFTER **EVERY-THING.**

KRUSE DOLING OUT GIFTS...FROM HIS EXTORTION OF HOPE BLALOCK? FROM UNCLE BILLY?

HOW DID UNCLE BILLY CHANCE TO FIND YOU?

"PAUL HAD TRACED MY ROOTS AND FOUND HIM. HE JUST SHOWED UP ONE DAY, EXPLAINING THAT HE WAS THE BROTHER OF THE WOMAN WHO'D GIVEN ME UP."

"HE APOLOGIZED FOR THE WAY I'D BEEN TREATED. SAID HE'D ALWAYS LOOK AFTER ME... AS AN UNCLE AND AN EMISSARY OF MY FATHER."

WE DRANK WINE, TALKED ABOUT SHERRY. I COULD TELL HE WASN'T FOND OF HER. WE TALKED ABOUT MY ROOTS.

WE WERE THE CHILDREN OF MR. BELDING AND AN ACTRESS WHOM HE LOVED BUT COULDN'T MARRY. SHE DIED OF CHILDBIRTH COMPLICATIONS.

UNCLE BILLY'S PROTECTION. HE HAD SPUN A COMFORTABLE COCOON OF LIES FOR SHARON.

I INSISTED ON GOING TO VISIT JOAN IN CONNECTICUT. UNCLE BILLY AGREED TO MOVE HER TO CALIFORNIA.

I CAME TO REALLY LOVE HER.

SHIRLEE. A NEW NAME TO SYMBOLIZE A NEW LIFE.

SHE GOES ON FOREVER. SHE'S BEEN A CONSTANT IN MY LIFE. A **REAL** COMFORT.

UNLIKE YOUR OTHER PARTNER.

YES, UNLIKE *HER.* WELL, ALEX, I'M POOPED. WE'VE COVERED A LOT OF GROUND.

THERE ARE A FEW OTHER THINGS, IF YOU DON'T MIND?

NO. OF COURSE NOT.

I'D LIKE TO HEAR ABOUT HOW THINGS WENT SO BAD WITH SHERRY.

"WHEN I FIRST SAW HER A JOLT OF ELECTRICITY SHOT UP MY SPINE. I COULDN'T MOVE. SHE LOOKED *EXACTLY* LIKE ME."

"WE THREW OUT OUR ARMS AND RAN TOWARD EACH OTHER...IT WAS LIKE RUNNING INTO A MIRROR."

"IT WAS ALL SO *GOOD* AT FIRST."

"IT DIDN'T LAST LONG. SHE QUICKLY BECAME ERRATIC. SHE'D VANISH WITHOUT A WORD."

SHE WENT ON WILD BINGES... SEX PARTIES, DRUGS. FUGUE STATES—

LIKE JANA. YOUR DISSERTATION.

I READ IT. I WAS INTERESTED IN YOU.

OH...I... PAUL THOUGHT I SHOULD DOCUMENT THE EXPERIENCE.

HE THOUGHT IT WOULD BE FINE TO USE IT...THAT SHE *OWED* ME THAT MUCH.

PAUL HAD WORKED WITH HER FOR SO LONG...YEARS. SHE JUST KEPT DETERIORATING.

SHE WAS PARANOID...NEAR PSYCHOTIC.

SHE WAS CONVINCED I WAS OUT TO GET HER. SHE SLEPT WITH MY PATIENTS, DESTROYED MY PRACTICE.

SHE'D ALREADY TRIED TO DESTROY US.

THE PARTY... WHERE I SAW YOU AGAIN... IT PUSHED HER OVER THE EDGE. PAUL HAD REFUSED TO LET HER ATTEND. IT WAS A BIG NIGHT FOR HIM.

HE TOLD HER HE COULDN'T RISK HER ACTING OUT...RUINING IT. AFTER, SHE...

MUST WE GO FURTHER, ALEX? IT'S SO UGLY. SHE'S GONE NOW, OUT OF MY LIFE... OUT OF OUR LIVES.

HARD TO BEGIN WITH- OUT ENDING.

CLOSURE. FOR BOTH OF US.

FOR YOU...ONLY FOR YOU. BECAUSE YOU MEAN SO MUCH TO ME.

SHE CAME TO MY HOUSE...AFTER. TOLD ME WHAT SHE'D DONE. LAUGHING.

THE HORROR OF IT AND SHE WAS LAUGHING!

SHE DIDN'T DO IT BY HERSELF. WHO HELPED HER? D.J. RASMUSSEN?

YOU KNEW D.J.?

I MET HIM. AT YOUR HOUSE. WE BOTH THOUGHT YOU WERE DEAD.

OH, GOD, POOR, POOR D.J. SHE TOLD ME HE'D BEEN ONE OF HER CONQUESTS...ONE OF HER VICTIMS.

YES, IT WAS D.J. SHE LAUGHED WHEN SHE TOLD ME HOW SHE'D GOTTEN HIM TO DO IT...USING DOPE, BOOZE. HER BODY.

LAUGHING, ABOUT HOW SHE'D TIED THEM, WATCHED AS D.J. DID THEM...WITH A BASEBALL BAT AND A GUN.

HIM THINKING ALL THE TIME THAT IT WAS ME HE WAS DOING IT FOR...ME WHO'D USED HIM.

SHE SAID THAT MADE ME A MURDERER TOO. THAT WHEN YOU REALLY GOT DOWN TO IT, WE WERE ONE AND THE SAME!

GO ON. GET IT OUT.

HER... HER LAUGHTER GOT CRAZY...WEIRD, HYSTERICAL.

IT HIT HER ALL AT ONCE: BY DESTROYING PAUL, SHE'D DESTROYED HERSELF. SHE NEEDED HIM.

NOW HE WAS GONE AND IT WAS HER FAULT.

"HE WAS *EVERYTHING* TO HER, THE CLOSEST SHE'D EVER COME TO A FATHER."

"I COULD HAVE CALMED HER DOWN. THE WAY I'D DONE SO MANY TIMES BEFORE. INSTEAD, I TOLD HER PAUL WAS NEVER COMING BACK, THAT IT WAS *HER FAULT*."

"SHE TORE OFF HER CLOTHES. THREW PILLS DOWN HER THROAT LIKE CANDY...AND I JUST KEPT TELLING HER THAT PAUL WAS *DEAD*."

"I SAID THE WORD OVER AND OVER. DEAD. DEAD. DEAD."

SHE TOOK A GUN OUT OF HER PURSE. SHE POINTED IT AT ME.

I SAID, "GO *AHEAD*, SPILL SOME MORE INNOCENT BLOOD. GET *FILTHIER*, YOU WORTHLESS PIECE OF SCUM."

SHE SAID, "I'M SORRY, *PARTNER*," PUT THE GUN TO HER TEMPLE, AND PULLED THE TRIGGER.

I JUST SAT THERE LOOKING AT HER FOR A WHILE. WATCHING HER BLEED, HER SOUL PASS OUT OF HER. WONDERING WHERE IT WAS HEADED.

THEN I CALLED UNCLE BILLY. HE TOOK CARE OF THE REST.

AND THAT'S ALL THERE IS, MY DARLING. AN *ENDING*. AND A *BEGINNING*. FOR US.

I'M CLEANSED NOW. *FREE*. READY TO GIVE YOU *EVERYTHING*, TO GIVE MYSELF IN A WAY I'VE *NEVER* GIVEN TO *ANYONE*.

THIS IS A **LOT** TO HANDLE.

I KNOW IT IS, DARLING, BUT WE'VE GOT **TIME**. ALL THE TIME IN THE WORLD. I'M FINALLY **FREE**.

I'M **HERE**, WITH **YOU**. IN THIS WONDERFUL PLACE, WHERE NO ONE CAN **FIND** US OR **SOIL** US.

YOU AND ME AND SHIRLEE. WE'LL MAKE A **FAMILY**, BE TOGETHER FOR-EVER.

IT'S NOT THAT **SIMPLE**, SHARON.

I...I DON'T UNDERSTAND.

OH, ALEX, **PLEASE** DON'T DO THIS TO ME. I WANT TO **TOUCH** YOU, WANT YOU TO **HOLD** ME!

SHERRY KILLING KRUSE. IT WASN'T ALL ABOUT THE PARTY. SHE'D BEEN PRIMING HIM FOR **WEEKS**, PAYING HIM **THOUSANDS**.

EVER SINCE **YOU** SENT HER A COPY OF YOUR DISSERTATION AND **CONFIRMED** HER WORST ANXIETIES.

WHAT DO YOU MEAN?

WHAT I MEAN IS THAT **YOU** SET IT UP. PLANTED THE SEEDS.

GO TO **HELL!**

YOU KNOW IT'S TRUE, SHARON. SHE WAS BORDERLINE FROM THE BEGINNING, BUT YOU *PUSHED* HER OVER THE BORDER.

THE SAD THING IS, YOU'D GOTTEN OVER THERE YOUR-SELF, FIRST.

LET GO OF ME, YOU *BASTARD!*

YOU'RE *HURTING* ME! FUCK *YOU,* LET GO!

WHAT MADE YOU *BREAK? FINDING* THE TWO OF THEM?

UP IN HER ROOM, DOING WHAT THEY'D PROBABLY BEEN DOING FOR *YEARS?*

INCEST BETWEEN DOCTOR AND PATIENT. THE *WORST* KIND. DADDY FUCKING *HER.* HE WAS YOUR DADDY TOO.

NO! NO, NO, NO, NO! YOU SLIME-BASTARD, YOU LYING *FUCKING BASTARD! NO!* SHUT UP!

GET *OUT,* YOU *FUCK,* YOU PIECE OF *SHIT!*

TWO BIRDS WITH *ONE* STONE, SHARON. TURN SHERRY ON KRUSE, THEN WAIT FOR HER TO COME FOR YOU.

SHE STEPPED RIGHT INTO YOUR TRAP AND YOU WERE *READY.*

FUCKING... BASTARD...FUCKDICK SLIMEBASTARD...

FIRST YOU *SHOT* HER, THEN YOU *POURED* DOPE AND BOOZE DOWN HER THROAT.

THERE WOULD NEVER BE A FORENSIC ANALYSIS TO PROVE IT BECAUSE UNCLE BILLY TOOK *CARE* OF IT... ALONG WITH *EVERY-THING* ELSE.

LIES, ALL LIES, YOU *FUCK!*

I DON'T THINK SO, SHARON. AND NOW YOU'VE GOT *EVERYTHING.* ENJOY IT.

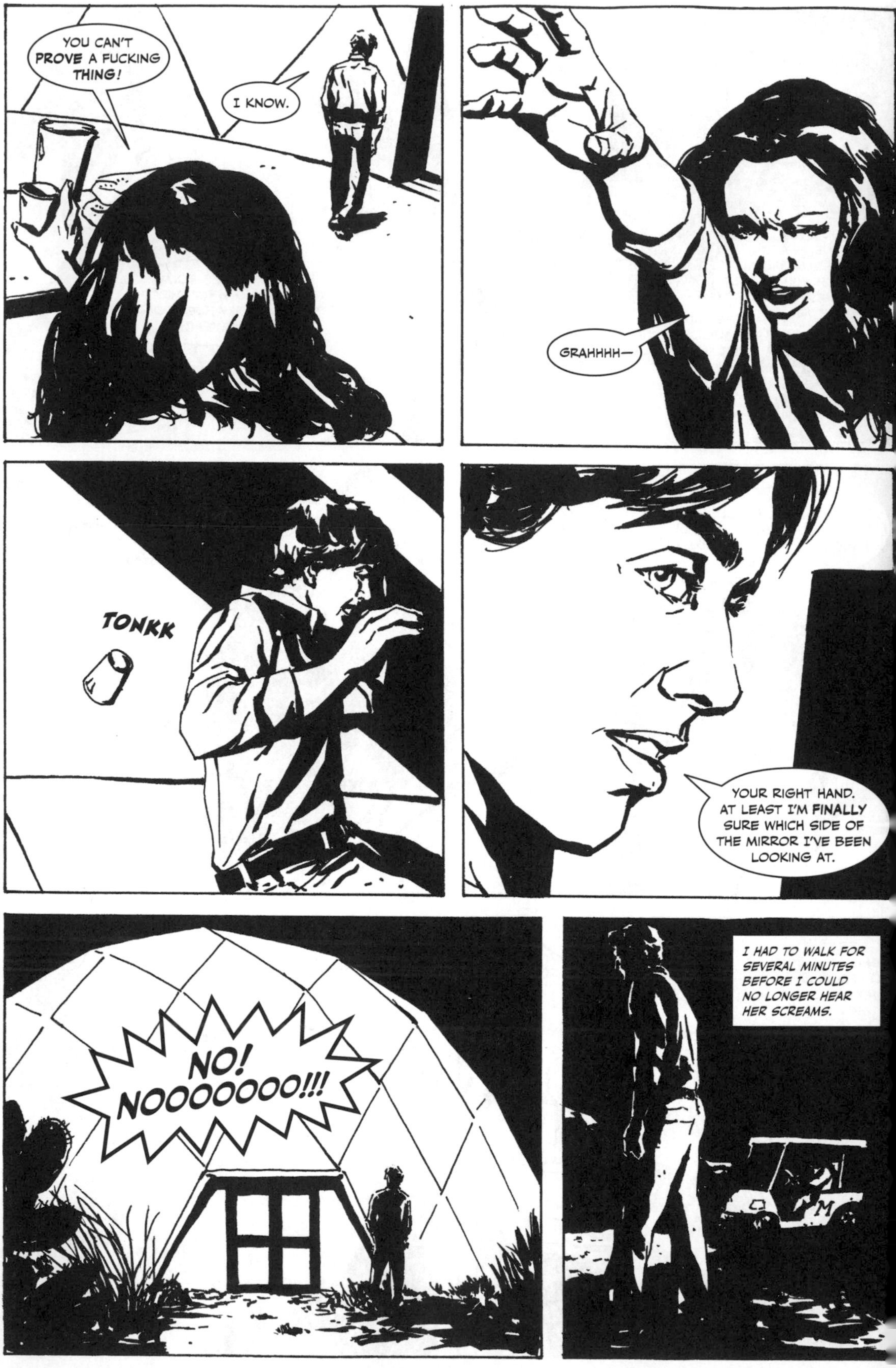
YOU CAN'T PROVE A FUCKING THING!
I KNOW.
GRAHHHH—
TONKK
YOUR RIGHT HAND. AT LEAST I'M FINALLY SURE WHICH SIDE OF THE MIRROR I'VE BEEN LOOKING AT.
NO! NOOOOOOO!!!
I HAD TO WALK FOR SEVERAL MINUTES BEFORE I COULD NO LONGER HEAR HER SCREAMS.

YOU HEARD **EVERYTHING?**

CONSTANT MONITORING IS NECESSARY.

SHE NEEDS **CARE, WATCHING.** YOU SAW THAT FOR YOURSELF.

CONVENIENT OF BELDING TO DIE WHEN HE DID. IT SPARED HIM... AND **YOU**... CONFRONTING SHARON AND SHERRY.

NOW HE CAN REMAIN A **BENEVOLENT** FIGURE FOR HER. SHE'LL NEVER KNOW HE WANTED TO KILL HER.

DO YOU THINK THAT KNOWLEDGE WOULD BE GOOD FOR HER... **THERAPEUTIC?**

MY ROLE IN LIFE IS TO **SOLVE** PROBLEMS, NOT **CREATE** THEM. IN THAT SENSE, I'M A **HEALER.** JUST LIKE **YOURSELF.**

TAKING CARE OF OTHERS REALLY HAS BEEN YOUR THING, HASN'T IT? BELDING, YOUR SISTER, SHERRY, SHARON, WILLOW GLEN, THE CORPORATION.

DOESN'T IT WEIGH ON YOU ONCE IN A WHILE?

NO REPLY.

HAVE YOU REACHED A **DECISION,** DOCTOR? ABOUT PROBING FURTHER?

WILL YOU **CONTINUE** TO STIR THINGS UP AND RUIN WHAT'S **LEFT** OF A VERY ILL YOUNG WOMAN'S LIFE?

NOT **MUCH** OF A LIFE.

BETTER THAN ANY **ALTERNATIVE.** SHE'LL BE WELL TAKEN CARE OF.

PROTECTED. AND THE **WORLD** WILL BE PROTECTED FROM **HER.** EVEN AFTER I'M GONE... **EVERYTHING'S** BEEN WORKED OUT.

I WON'T STIR ANYTHING UP. WHAT WOULD BE THE POINT?

GOOD. WHAT ABOUT YOUR DETECTIVE FRIEND?

HE'S A REALIST.

GOOD FOR HIM.

ARE YOU GOING TO KILL ME ANYWAY? HAVE ROYAL HUMMEL DO HIS THING?

HAH-HAHA... OF COURSE NOT. HOW AMUSING THAT YOU STILL SEE ME AS ATTILA THE HUN.

NO, DOCTOR, YOU'RE IN NO DANGER. WHAT WOULD BE THE POINT?

WHY? WHY'D YOU LET KRUSE GO ON FOR SO LONG?

UNTIL RECENTLY, I BELIEVED HE WAS HELPING SHARON... HELPING BOTH OF THEM.

HE WAS A CHARISMATIC MAN, VERY ARTICULATE.

BY THE WAY, DOCTOR, ROYAL HUMMEL WILL NO LONGER BE FUNCTIONING IN A SECURITY CAPACITY.

YOUR COMMENTS ON LINDA'S DEATH GAVE ME QUITE A BIT OF PAUSE... AMAZING WHAT A FRESH PERSPECTIVE WILL DO.

ROYAL AND VICTOR WERE PROFESSIONALS. ACCIDENTS NEEDN'T HAPPEN WITH PROFESSIONALS. AT BEST, THEY WERE SLOPPY. AT WORST...

WELL, ROYAL HAS A NEW JOB. SOMETHING ABOUT CHICKEN COOPS AND A SHOVEL.

YOU BROUGHT ME INSIGHT LATE IN LIFE, DOCTOR. FOR THAT I OWE YOU A LARGE DEBT.

IS THERE ANYTHING I CAN DO FOR YOU?

ACTUALLY, THERE IS A SMALL FAVOR...

I COULDN'T GO HOME. AFTER THEY DROPPED ME ON CAMPUS I DROVE. ENDED UP AT A MOTEL NEAR THE SANTA MONICA PIER.

FOR THREE DAYS I WENT THROUGH IT ALL: RAGE, TEARS, TENSION SO VISCERAL MY TEETH CHATTERED. A LONELINESS I COULD HAVE GLADLY ANESTHETIZED WITH PAIN.

ON THE FOURTH DAY I VENTURED OUT FOR A NEWSPAPER. A HEADLINE TOLD ME VIDAL HAD HONORED HIS WORD. TRAPP HAD BEEN NAILED FOR SCREWING UNDERAGE POLICE SCOUTS WHILE ON DUTY. TERMINATED IMMEDIATELY.

WITHIN HOURS OF ME GETTING BACK HOME, DETECTIVE STURGIS CAME KNOCKING.

WHERE THE HELL HAVE YOU BEEN?

OUT. I DON'T WANT TO GET INTO IT.

GET INTO IT **ANYWAY**.

JESUS! YOU WERE SUPPOSED TO BE MAKING SOME CALLS, DOING THE **SAFE** STUFF. INSTEAD, YOU **DISAPPEAR**?!

I NEEDED TO GET AWAY. I'M **FINE**. I WAS NEVER IN DANGER.

HOW, ALEX? HOW THE **FUCK**?! BYE-BYE, CYRIL...LIKE I'VE GOT A GODDAMN GENIE. **HOW**?

L.A.P.D. Captain Charged With Sexual Misconduct Resigns

TRAPP'S A **SMALL** PART OF IT, MILO.

I JUST DON'T WANT TO PAINT THE WHOLE PICTURE RIGHT NOW.

TEMPORARY REPRIEVE, PAL. SOME DAY...**SOON**...WE'RE GONNA HAVE OURSELVES A LITTLE SIT-DOWN.

SERIOUSLY, ALEX. HOW'RE YOU DOING?

GOOD...FINE. MILO, I APPRECIATE THAT YOU CARE. I APPRECIATE EVERYTHING YOU'VE DONE FOR ME.

RIGHT NOW I COULD REALLY USE BEING ALONE.

YEAH...ALL RIGHT. I'LL BE **AROUND**, DELAWARE. TAKE SOME KIND OF CARE OF YOURSELF.

I MANAGED TO SLEEP PAST SEVEN THE NEXT MORNING.

ROBIN HAD COME HOME, WEARING A DRESS I'D NEVER SEEN BEFORE AND THE LOOK OF A FIRST-GRADER ABOUT TO RECITE IN FRONT OF THE CLASS.

HELLO, ALEX. YOU'RE NOT HAPPY TO SEE ME.

I AM. YOU TOOK ME BY SURPRISE.

I WANTED TO TALK TO YOU A FEW DAYS AGO. YOUR SERVICE KEPT GIVING ME THE SAME MESSAGE.

I GOT WORRIED.

CHARITY TIME.

I'M SORRY, BUT RIGHT AT THIS MOMENT, I'M NOT GOING TO BE THE MAN YOU WANT.

WE TALKED. SHE TOLD ME THERE HAD BEEN ANOTHER MAN. AN OLD FLAME FROM COLLEGE. "NOTHING SERIOUS." SHE NIPPED IT IN THE BUD.

I SAID THERE HAD BEEN ANOTHER WOMAN TOO. ONE WHO CAPTURED MY **HEAD**, NOT MY COCK. NOW THAT WOMAN WAS GONE FOREVER, AND I WAS **CHANGED**.

WE MADE **LOVE**...MADE **SEX**. COMPETENT, SEAMLESS UNION BORN OF PRACTICE AND RITUAL. SO SEAMLESS IT VERGED ON INCEST.

ROBIN ASKED WHAT WAS GOING TO BECOME OF US. I SAID IT WASN'T GOING TO BE EASY. WHAT IS THAT'S WORTHWHILE? WE STAYED TOGETHER, CHEEK TO CHEEK, BEFORE THE RESTLESSNESS SET IN, THEN WENT OUR SEPARATE WAYS.

ALONE AGAIN, I PULLED MY PHYSICAL APPEARANCE INTO LINE. THE **REST** WOULDN'T BE SO EASY.

MY MIND TURNED TO UNFINISHED BUSINESS.

MRS. BURKHALTER? DENISE? THIS IS DR. DELAWARE.

OH. HI.

NO, **NO**... IT'S NOT A BAD TIME. IT'S FUNNY. I WAS JUST THINKING OF YOU. DARREN'S STILL... UH...CRYING...

...LOTS. SINCE THE LAST TIME HE SAW YOU. AND NOT SLEEP-ING OR EATING RIGHT.

IT'S BEEN TOUGH. MR. WORTHY SAYS IT COULD TAKE MONTHS FOR THE MONEY TO COME IN.

MEANWHILE, WE'RE STILL GETTING BANK LETTERS AND...I'M SORRY. WHY AM I GOING ON LIKE THIS?

I'M **REAL** SORRY. ABOUT THE WAY I RAN MY MOUTH AT YOU.

THAT'S OKAY. YOU'VE BEEN THROUGH **PLENTY.** I WISH I COULD TAKE AWAY YOUR PAIN.

IF YOU'D LIKE TO BRING HIM IN, I'D BE **HAPPY** TO SEE HIM. I CAN SEE YOU **TOMORROW,** FIRST THING.

"THANK YOU, DR. DELAWARE. YOU'RE A **NICE MAN.**"

"YOU REALLY KNOW HOW TO **HELP A PERSON.**"

DENISE'S WORDS SHORED ME UP FOR MY NEXT CALL... TO DR. ADA SMALL.

ALEX. NO... JUST FINISHING SOME PAPER-WORK.

I TRIED TO REACH CARMEN SEEBER, BUT HER LINE'S BEEN DISCONNECTED AND THERE'S NO—

THIS ISN'T ABOUT HER.

IT'S ABOUT ME.

A LOT'S BEEN PILING UP.

I THOUGHT... IF YOU THOUGHT IT WOULD BE APPROPRIATE FOR ME TO COME IN...

IT...IT'S HARD SLIPPING OUT OF THE COLLEAGUE ROLE, ADMITTING HELPLESSNESS.

"YOU'RE FAR FROM HELPLESS, ALEX. JUST INSIGHTFUL ENOUGH TO KNOW YOU'RE NOT INVULNERABLE."

INSIGHTFUL. HEH...FAR FROM IT.

"YOU CALLED, DIDN'T YOU?"

"ALEX, I UNDERSTAND WHAT YOU'RE SAYING. SHIFTING ROLES MUST SEEM LIKE A STEP BACKWARD. I DON'T SEE IT THAT WAY."

"LET ME CHECK MY BOOK...HOW ABOUT TOMORROW AT SIX? THE OFFICE WILL BE QUIET THEN."

SIX WOULD BE GREAT, ADA. SEE YOU THEN.

"I'M LOOKING FORWARD TO IT. AND, ALEX..."

"...IT'S A VERY GOOD THING YOU'RE DOING."

—END—

Read on for an excerpt from
Jonathan Kellerman's
exciting new Alex Delaware novel,

VICTIMS

CHAPTER 1

This one was different.

The first hint was Milo's tight-voiced eight a.m. message, stripped of details.

Something I need you to see, Alex. Here's the address.

An hour later, I was showing I.D. to the uniform guarding the tape. He winced. "Up there, Doctor." Pointing to the second story of a sky-blue duplex trimmed in chocolate-brown, he dropped a hand to his Sam Browne belt, as if ready for self-defense.

Nice older building, the classic Cal-Spanish architecture, but the color was wrong. So was the silence of the street, sawhorsed at both ends. Three squad cars and a liver-colored LTD were parked haphazardly across the asphalt. No crime lab vans or coroner's vehicles had arrived yet.

I said, "Bad?"

The uniform said, "There's probably a better word for it but that works."

Milo stood on the landing outside the door doing nothing.

No cigar-smoking or jotting in his pad or grumbling orders. Feet planted, arms at his sides, he stared at some faraway galaxy.

His blue nylon windbreaker bounced sunlight at strange angles. His black hair was limp, his pitted face the color and texture of cottage cheese past its prime. A white shirt had wrinkled to crepe. Wheat-colored cords had slipped beneath his paunch. His tie was a sad shred of poly.

He looked as if he'd dressed wearing a blindfold.

As I climbed the stairs, he didn't acknowledge me.

When I was six steps away, he said, "You made good time."

"Easy traffic."

"Sorry," he said.

"For what?"

"Including you." He handed me gloves and paper booties.

I held the door for him. He stayed outside.

The woman was at the rear of the apartment's front room, flat on her back. The kitchen behind her was empty, counters bare, an old avocado-colored fridge free of photos or magnets or mementos.

Two doors to the left were shut and yellow-taped. I took that as a *Keep Out.* Drapes were drawn over every window. Fluorescent lighting in the kitchen supplied a nasty pseudo-dawn.

The woman's head was twisted sharply to the right. A swollen tongue hung between slack, bloated lips.

Limp neck. A grotesque position some coroner might label "incompatible with life."

Big woman, broad at the shoulders and the hips. Late fifties to early sixties, with an aggressive chin and short, coarse gray hair. Brown sweatpants covered her below the waist. Her feet were bare. Unpolished toenails were clipped short. Grubby soles said bare feet at home was the default.

Above the waistband of the sweats was what remained of a bare torso. Her abdomen had been sliced horizontally below the navel in a crude approximation of a C-section. A vertical slit crossed the lateral incision at the center, creating a star-shaped wound.

The damage brought to mind one of those hard-rubber change purses that relies on surface tension to protect the goodies. Squeeze to create a stellate opening, then reach in and scoop.

The yield from this receptacle was a necklace of intestines placed below the woman's neckline and arranged like a fashionista's puffy scarf. One end terminated at her right clavicle. Bilious streaks ran down her right breast and onto her rib cage. The rest of her viscera had been pulled down into a heap and left near her left hip.

The pile rested atop a once-white towel folded double. Below that was a larger maroon towel spread neatly. Four other expanses of terry cloth formed a makeshift tarp that shielded beige wall-to-wall carpeting from biochemical insult. The towels had been arranged precisely, edges overlapping evenly for about an inch. Near the woman's right hip was a pale blue T-shirt, also folded. Spotless.

Doubling the white towel had succeeded in soaking up a good deal of body fluid, but some had leaked into the maroon under-layer. The smell would've been bad enough without the initial stages of decomp.

One of the towels beneath the body bore lettering. Silver bath sheet embroidered *Vita* in white.

Latin or Italian for "life." Some monster's notion of irony?

The intestines were green-brown splotched pink in spots, black in others. Matte finish to the casing, some puckering that said they'd been drying for a while. The apartment was cool, a good ten degrees below the pleasant spring weather outside. The rattle of a wheezy A.C. unit in one of the living room windows was inescapable once I noticed it. Noisy apparatus, rusty at the bolts, but efficient enough to leach moisture from the air and slow down the rot.

But rot is inevitable and the woman's color wasn't anything you'd see outside a morgue.

Incompatible with life.

I bent to inspect the wounds. Both slashes were confident swoops unmarred by obvious hesitation marks, shearing smoothly through layers of skin, subcutaneous fat, diaphragmatic muscle.

No abrasions around the genital area and surprisingly little blood for so much brutality. No spatter or spurt or castoff or evidence of a struggle. All those towels; horribly compulsive.

Guesses filled my head with bad pictures.

Extremely sharp blade, probably not serrated. The neck-twist had killed her quickly and she'd been dead during the surgery, the ultimate anesthesia. The killer had stalked her with enough thoroughness to know he'd have her to himself for a while. Once attaining total control, he'd gone about choreographing: laying out the towels, tucking and aligning, achieving a pleasing symmetry. Then he'd laid her down, removed her T-shirt, careful to keep it clean.

Standing back, he'd inspected his prep work. Time for the blade.

Then the real fun: anatomical exploration.

Despite the butchery and the hideous set of her neck, she looked peaceful. For some reason, that made what had been done to her worse.

I scanned the rest of the room. No damage to the front door or any other sign of forced entry. Bare beige walls backed cheap upholstered furniture covered in a puckered ocher fabric that aped brocade but fell short. White ceramic beehive lamps looked as if they'd shatter under a finger-snap.

The dining area was set up with a card table and two folding chairs. A brown cardboard take-out pizza box sat on the table. Someone—probably Milo—had placed a yellow plastic evidence marker nearby. That made me take a closer look.

No brand name on the box, just *PIZZA!* in exuberant red cursive above the caricature of a portly mustachioed chef. Curls of smaller lettering swarmed around the chef's fleshy grin.

Fresh pizza!
Lotta taste!
Ooh la la!
Yum yum!
Bon appétit!

The box was pristine, not a speck of grease or finger-smudge. I bent down to sniff, picked up no pizza aroma. But the decomp had filled my nose; it would be a while before I'd be smelling anything but death.

If this was another type of crime scene, some detective might be making ghoulish jokes about free lunch.

The detective in charge of this scene was a lieutenant who'd seen hundreds of murders, maybe thousands, yet chose to stay outside for a while.

I let loose more mental pictures. Some fiend in a geeky delivery hat ringing the doorbell then managing to talk himself inside.

Watching as the prey went for her purse? Waiting for precisely the right moment before coming up behind her and clamping both his hands on the sides of her head.

Quick blitz of rotation. The spinal cord would separate and that would be it.

Doing it correctly required strength and confidence.

That and the lack of obvious transfer evidence—not even a shoe impression—screamed experience. If there'd been a similar murder in L.A., I hadn't heard about it.

Despite all that meticulousness, the hair around the woman's temples might be a good place to look for transfer DNA. Psychopaths don't sweat much, but you never know.

I examined the room again.

Speaking of purses, hers was nowhere in sight.

Robbery as an afterthought? More likely souvenir-taking was part of the plan.

Edging away from the body, I wondered if the woman's last thoughts had been of crusty dough, mozzarella, a comfy barefoot dinner.

The doorbell ring the last music she'd ever hear.

I stayed in the apartment awhile longer, straining for insight.

The terrible competence of the neck-twist made me wonder about someone with martial arts training.

The embroidered towel bothered me.

Vita. Life.

Had he brought that one but taken the rest from her linen closet?

Yum. Bon appétit. To life.

The decomp reek intensified and my eyes watered and blurred and the necklace of guts morphed into a snake.

Drab constrictor, fat and languid after a big meal.

I could stand around and pretend that this was anything comprehensible, or hurry outside and try to suppress the tide of nausea rising in my own guts.

Not a tough choice.

CHAPTER 2

Milo hadn't moved from his position on the landing. His eyes were back on Planet Earth, watching the street below. Five uniforms were moving from door to door. From the quick pace of the canvass, plenty of no-one-home. The street was in a working-class neighborhood in the southeastern corner of West L.A. Division. Three blocks east would've made it someone else's problem. Mixed zoning allowed single-family dwellings and duplexes like the one where the woman had been degraded. Psychopaths are stodgy creatures of routine and I wondered if the killer's comfort zone was so narrow that he lived within the sawhorses. I caught my breath and worked at settling my stomach while Milo pretended not to notice. "Yeah, I know," he finally said. He was apologizing for the second time when a coroner's van drove up and a dark-haired woman in comfortable clothes got out and hurried up the stairs. "Morning, Milo."

"Morning, Gloria. All yours."

"Oh, boy," she said. "We talking freaky-bad?"

"I could say I've seen worse, kid, but I'd be lying."

"Coming from you that gives me the creeps, Milo."

"Because I'm old?"

"Tsk." She patted his shoulder. "Because you're the voice of experience."

"Some experiences I can do without."

People can get used to just about anything. But if your psyche's in good repair, the fix is often temporary.

Soon after receiving my doctorate, I worked as a psychologist on a pediatric cancer ward. It took a month to stop dreaming about sick kids but I was eventually able to do my job with apparent professionalism. Then I left to go into private practice and found myself, years later, on that same ward. Seeing the children with new eyes mocked all the adaptation I thought I'd accomplished and made me want to cry. I went home and dreamed for a long time.

Homicide detectives get "used" to a regular diet of soul-obliteration. Typically bright and sensitive, they soldier on, but the essence of the job lurks beneath the surface like a land mine. Some D's transfer out. Others stay and find hobbies. Religion works for some, sin for others. Some, like Milo, turn griping into an art form and never pretend it's just another job.

The woman on the towels was different for him and for me. A permanent image bank had lodged in my brain and I knew the same went for him.

Neither of us talked as Gloria worked inside.

Finally, I said, "You marked the pizza box. It bothers you."

"Everything about this bothers me."

"No brand name on the box. Any indies around here deliver?"

He drew out his cell phone, clicked, and produced a page. Phone numbers he'd already downloaded filled the screen and when he scrolled, the listings kept coming.

"Twenty-eight indies in a ten-mile radius and I also checked Domino's and Papa John's and Two Guys. No one dispatched anyone to this address last night and nobody uses that particular box."

"If she didn't actually call out, why would she let him in?"

"Good question."

"Who discovered her?"

"Landlord, responding to a complaint she made a few days ago. Hissing toilet, they had an appointment. When she didn't answer, he got annoyed, started to leave. Then he thought better of it because she liked things fixed, used his key."

"Where is he now?" He pointed across the street. "Recuperating with some firewater down in that little Tudor-ish place."

I found the house. Greenest lawn on the block, beds of flowers. Topiary bushes.

"Anything about him bother you?"

"Not so far. Why?"

"His landscaping says he's a perfectionist."

"That's a negative?"

"This case, maybe."

"Well," he said, "so far he's just the landlord. Want to know about her?"

"Sure."

"Her name's Vita Berlin, she's fifty-six, single, lives on some kind of disability."

"Vita," I said. "The towel was hers."

"*The* towel? This bastard used every damn towel she had in her linen closet."

"*Vita* means 'life' in Latin and Italian. I thought it might be a sick joke."

"Cute. Anyway, I'm waiting for Mr. Belleveaux—the landlord—to calm down so I can question him and find out more about her. What I've learned from prelim snooping in her bedroom and bathroom is if she's got kids she doesn't keep their pictures around and if she had a computer, it was ripped off. Same for a cell phone. My guess is she had neither, the place has a static feel to it. Like she moved in years ago, didn't add any new-fangled stuff."

"I didn't see her purse."

"On her nightstand."

"You taped off the bedroom, didn't want me in there?"

"I sure do, but that'll wait until the techies are through. Can't afford to jeopardize any aspect of this."

"The front room was okay?"

"I knew you'd be careful."

His logic seemed strained. Insufficient sleep and a bad surprise can do that.

I said, "Any indication she was heading to the bedroom before he jumped her?"

"No, it's pristine. Why?"

I gave him the delivery tip scenario.

"Going for her purse," he said. "Well, I don't know how you'd prove that, Alex. Main thing is he confined himself to the front, didn't move her into the bedroom for anything sexual."

I said, "Those towels make me think of a stage. Or a picture frame."

"Meaning?"

"Showing off his work."

"Okay . . . what else to tell you . . . her wardrobe's mostly sweats and sneakers, lots of books in her bedroom. Romances and the kinds of myster-ies where people talk like Noël Coward twits and the cops are bumbling cretins."

I wondered out loud about a killer with martial arts skills and when he didn't respond, went on to describe the kill-scene still bouncing around my brain.

He said, "Sure, why not."

Agreeable but distracted. Neither of us focusing on the big question. *Why would anyone do something like this to another human being?*

Gloria exited the apartment, looking older and paler.

Milo said, "You okay?"

"I'm fine," she said. "No, I'm lying, that was horrible." Her forehead was moist. She dabbed it with a tissue. "My God, it's grotesque."

"Any off-the-cuff impressions?"

"Nothing you probably haven't figured out yourself. Broken neck's my bet for COD, the cutting looks postmortem. The incisions look clean so maybe some training in meat-cutting or a paramedical field but I wouldn't put much stock in that, all kinds of folk can learn to slice. That pizza box mean something to you?"

"Don't know," said Milo. "No one admits delivering here."

"A scam to get himself in?" she said. "Why would she open the door for a fake pizza guy?"

"Good question, Gloria."

She shook her head. "I called for transport. Want me to ask for a priority autopsy?"

"Thanks."

"You might actually get it because Dr. J. seems to like you. Also with something this weird, she's bound to be curious."

A year ago, Milo had solved the murder of a coroner's investigator. Since then Dr. Clarice Jernigan, a senior pathologist, had reciprocated with personalized attention when Milo asked for it.

He said, "Must be my charm and good looks."

Gloria grinned and patted his shoulder again. "Anything else, guys? I'm on half-shift due to budgetary constraints, figure to finish my paperwork by one then go cleanse my head with a couple of martinis. Give or take."

Milo said, "Make it a double for me."

I said, "Was significant blood pooled inside the body cavity?"

Her look said I was being a spoilsport. "A lot of it was coagulated but yes, that's where most of it was. You figured that because the scene was so clean?"

I nodded. "It was either that or he found out a way to take it with him."

Milo said, "Buckets of blood, lovely." To Gloria: "One more question: You recall anything remotely like this in your case files?"

"Nope," she said. "But we just cover the county and they say it's a globalized world, right? You could be looking at a traveler."

Milo glared and trudged down the stairs.

Gloria said, "Whoa, someone's in a mood."

I said, "It's likely to stay that way for a while."

JONATHAN KELLERMAN is one of the world's most popular authors. He has brought his expertise as a clinical psychologist to more than thirty bestselling crime novels, including the Alex Delaware series, *The Butcher's Theater*, *Billy Straight*, *The Conspiracy Club*, *Twisted*, and *True Detectives*. With his wife, the novelist Faye Kellerman, he coauthored the bestsellers *Double Homicide* and *Capital Crimes*. He is the author of numerous essays, short stories, scientific articles, two children's books, and three volumes of psychology, including *Savage Spawn: Reflections on Violent Children*, as well as the lavishly illustrated *With Strings Attached: The Art and Beauty of Vintage Guitars*. He has won the Goldwyn, Edgar, and Anthony awards and has been nominated for a Shamus Award. Jonathan and Faye Kellerman live in California, New Mexico, and New York. Their four children include the novelists Jesse Kellerman and Aliza Kellerman.

After a long career as a comic book artist, **ANDE PARKS** has become a full-time writer in recent years. His writing credits include the graphic novels *Union Station* and *Capote in Kansas*. The latter was named a Notable Book for the state of Kansas in 2006, the first graphic novel to receive such an honor.

Ande currently writes *The Green Hornet* and *The Lone Ranger* monthly comics for Dynamite Press. He is also developing new graphic novel projects. Ande lives in Baldwin City, Kansas, with his lovely wife and two children. He enjoys crime fiction, golf, vintage fedoras, and a nice glass of bourbon.

Illustrator, painter, and printmaker **MICHAEL GAYDOS**'s list of credits includes illustrations, graphic novels, and sequential artwork for Marvel, DC, NBC, Dark Horse, Image, IDW, Top Cow, Fox Atomic, Virgin, Tundra, NBM, Caliber, and White Wolf, among others. He has received two Eisner Award nominations for his work on *Alias* with Brian Michael Bendis for Marvel. Michael's fine artwork has also been the subject of a number of solo exhibitions the past few years and his work is collected worldwide.